BOOK 3 OF THE DARK ILLUSION TRILOGY

THE GIRL IN THE BACKGROUND

MARION HUGHES

Published in Australia by Sid Harta Books & Print Pty Ltd,
ABN: 34632585293
23 Stirling Crescent, Glen Waverley, Victoria 3150 Australia
Telephone: +61 3 9560 9920, Facsimile: +61 3 9545 1742
E-mail: author@sidharta.com.au

First published in Australia 2024
This edition published 2024
Copyright © Marion Hughes 2024
Cover design, typesetting: WorkingType (www.workingtype.com.au)

Hughes, Marion
The Girl in the Background
Book Three, The Dark Illusion Trilogy
ISBN: 978-1-922958-59-4

About the Author

Marion Hughes lives on the Mornington Peninsula, Victoria, Australia.

Also by Marion Hughes:

The Von Mueller Deception

Watch Your Back – Book One, The Dark Illusion Trilogy

I'm Back – Book Two, The Dark Illusion Trilogy

1

She sensed something wasn't right. *It's just the wind,* she reassured herself. Up ahead, trees swayed precariously, and in the distance, waves thundered and crashed over ageless rocks. It was a walk she'd done a hundred times before, although usually in the company of another person. However, the uneasy feeling persisted. *Perhaps I should think of turning back …*

But it was too late. Her assassin closed in silently, and Jennifer Lorenzo didn't stand a chance. One quick blow to a pressure point at the base of her neck rendered her unconscious, and she slid to the ground in the arms of the assassin, who followed up with a lethal injection to her thigh.

He had no idea who the woman was or what she'd done. He could have struck any number of blows – a twisting neck-break lock or knee drop. But he'd promised to ensure the end was as sudden and pain-free as possible. And he kept to his word.

He lifted her off the track, her slight frame like a child in his arms, and carried her to a small, secluded clearing. Once he was convinced there were no signs of life, he was off like a cheetah towards the dirt road where his car was parked.

9

Nic Drakos sat in the shadows of the small cove, waiting. He rechecked his phone. Five-thirty. Two-and-a-half hours until it was fully dark and the boat would arrive to pick him up. He'd heard nothing to indicate things weren't going according to plan. *That had to be a good thing. Didn't it?* But the longer time passed, the more on edge he became.

The arrangement seemed water-tight enough. The small boat with Angelina aboard would anchor around fifty metres from where he sat. Too many submerged rocks to risk coming closer. Once he'd swum out and climbed aboard, there'd be a change of clothes ready. The boat trip back to Queenscliff should take no longer than half an hour, where they'd be met by a driver and taken to Angelina's rented Docklands apartment to collect their luggage. They should reach the airport with plenty of time to spare before their flight to Madrid, departing at 12:30 a.m., armed with new mobile numbers and false passports. But it all hinged around Angelina's contacts keeping their word. *Who in the hell were they, and could they be trusted like she said?*

He pulled out his phone and clicked on the voice message she'd left the previous night while he was in the shower. A message he could only dream she might send. A message he'd lost track of the times he'd replayed since:

Hey Nic, just wanted you to know … it's taken all this time to figure out I love you, and I wish I'd told you last night. I never want us to be apart, and thank God I went ahead with having our baby. I'm sorry for all I've put you through. I'll make up for it, I promise.

Too overcome to return the call, he'd texted a message instead: *Needed to hear that. Call when you get to Queenscliff.*

She'd told him she'd seek help, and this time he believed her. Whatever had gone on in her life, he'd find a way of fixing things. Somehow.

Maybe in time, she'd allow him to call her by her real name, Angelina – a name he considered far more beautiful than Ava.

The piercing wail of a passing siren caused him to jump. *Shit, I've lost track of time!* Nic grabbed his phone to check. Six-thirty. Kai Tanko would have carried out the hit within minutes of Jennifer Lorenzo setting out for her walk at five. He'd be well out of there by now.

Nic had known Kai for several years, having occasionally linked up for jobs that required the expertise of both – Nic's in sniping and Kai's with close-range hits, using his special skills in the martial arts. Kai was one of the few hitmen Nic trusted enough to work alongside, and the feeling was reciprocated. Six years ago in Lebanon, Nic had saved his friend's life. 'I owe you,' Kai had said. Never did Nic think he'd be calling in the debt.

Nic surmised that it would have taken until now for the events relating to Jennifer Lorenzo's death to have played out. When she didn't return from her walk, the family would organise a search, and may well have contacted the police at that point concerning their fears. However, even if Jennifer's body was located relatively quickly, an assessment of probable murder would be required for the Homicide Squad to be called in. By the time they arrived from Melbourne, he and Angelina would be long gone — hopefully well on the way to the airport.

Still, they were cutting things fine. The cove in which he sat was a few minutes as the crow flies from the sandy stretch of beach near where Jennifer's body would be discovered. *How long before the police began scouring the area? And will I make it out in time?*

9

There was no moon. As Nic's eyes slowly adjusted to the dark, he swore he could see a faint light from afar. He ran down to the shoreline for a better look, his heart thumping so loudly he was sure it could be heard above the wind that showed no signs of abating.

It was the light from a vessel of some description. Nic swallowed hard. *Please, God, let it be them and not some passing fishing boat,* he thought desperately, his back a mass of sweat despite the cold, his throat parched. But the distant vessel kept approaching, bobbing and weaving its way through the choppy swell. He ran to get his backpack and hooked it through his arms, then rolling up his jeans he waded ankle-deep into the ice-cold water.

The boat only made it a little further before exploding into a huge ball of orange …

Nic stood, stunned. He tried to cry out, but the words never came. The flames leapt high into an inky sky that camouflaged the thick, black fumes that followed. Hurling his backpack onshore, he dived in and began to swim – long, frantic strokes against the squally waves. The salt stung his eyes and burned his throat as he took in an occasional involuntary gulp of seawater. His brain kept telling him there'd be next to no chance of anyone surviving, yet he clung to the hope that Angelina may have somehow miraculously made it overboard.

The burning wreckage was further out than it appeared, and he found himself gasping for breath and forced to stop every now and then for a moment. All the while the ferocious flames, resembling something from the bowels of hell, showed no signs of letting up. And this would be the case as long as fuel remained on the surface.

Daring to venture no closer than twenty metres, Nic swam around the boat in a wide arc, looking for signs of movement. Nothing. He could feel the scorching heat from this far back. Could smell the unmistakable, sharp stench of acrid smoke.

There was nothing he could do but get the hell out of there …

Nic hardly recalled the swim back to shore. Once he struck shallow waters he stood up, staggering and heaving until he made it onto the sand, stumbling about in search of his backpack in the dark.

Frantically, with fingers numb from the icy waters, he struggled with the zip, reefing out his mobile and tapping on his messages. Nothing.

Flicking on the phone's lamplight, he stripped off his sodden shirt, tossed it in the sand, retrieved a jacket and gloves from his backpack, shoved the shirt back in and made the quick change. And ran.

Five minutes in the opposite direction, the police officer investigating the hit heard the loud boom and ran down the cliff path to determine what had occurred. By the time he got there, the boat was well and truly consumed by flames.

2

The blaze had subsided by the time Nic reached the town, but groups of onlookers remained on the beach with their mobiles, speculating among themselves. Pulling his hoodie over his head and dropping his jog to a brisk walk, he gave them a wide berth, skirting around behind them like a panther at midnight. Once past town, it was only another few minutes' jog to the car with the keys still where he had left them. Hastily brushing the sand from his feet, he reached for his shoes, then tossed his backpack onto the front seat, climbed in and fired up the engine.

He'd witnessed the sudden death of his father, and right now, he felt the same sense of numbness −acknowledging what had happened, yet grappling to take it in. His mind was on autopilot as he turned onto the main road and headed for the city, focused solely on arriving safely without causing undue attention.

He reached Docklands at 10:30 p.m., his mind on one

thing alone. Turning into the underground car park to Angelina's apartment, he tapped in the code, watched the boom gate rise, and parked. With gloves still on, he pulled out the access lift and room cards from his wallet, still in its waterproof cover, thankful Angelina had provided spares.

Heart pummelling and sick with dread, he jumped out of the car and entered the building. He had no idea where the security cameras might be, but by habit he pulled the black hoodie over his head and, against his instincts, slowed his walk to create the impression that nothing was out of the ordinary.

As he inserted the card into Angelina's room, the memory of their final night's sensuous embrace against the wall inches from where he stood flashed through his mind, and he felt a stab of burning pain.

One click, and Nic stepped inside, rushing towards the bedroom where they'd left their luggage. Nothing appeared to have been disturbed. He let out a cry of anguish and dropped to his knees beside the suitcase that she'd left unlocked. He unzipped the main compartment and flipped open the lid with shaking hands.

Angelina's passport, their boarding passes and travel documents were sitting on top of her case, along with a purse containing her driver's licence, two credit cards, and a handful of others. The only thing missing was her phone. He dialled her number. The line was dead and his heart sank.

His thoughts were confused, his mind still reeling from the shock of the explosion. There was nothing to do but wait, in the wild hope that something had gone wrong and she'd walk in the door at any moment. As one hour passed and the next, he knew he'd lost her. How he'd deal with that, only time would tell.

It was now a matter of survival, and this was the last place to be hanging about.

He quickly grabbed any documents that could identify him and stuffed them in his jacket, then zipped her case closed and reached for his luggage. No need to wipe down surfaces. By habit, he'd not removed his gloves. Pulling his hoodie over his head, he wheeled his luggage out of the room and into the passageway, head lowered once more, all the while in a cold sweat that he would run into someone who might remember him, a late reveller returning home perhaps. He was in luck. The building was as deserted as when he'd arrived.

Tossing his gear into the backseat, he jumped in the car and drove out of the car park. Fuelled by adrenaline, he was already thinking ahead, with thoughts of Angelina forced from his mind. He stopped some way along under a street light and reached for his mobile. It was close to 1 a.m., but several city hotels offered 24/7 book-ins. Scrolling through the list, he tapped on one of the lesser-known ones and booked a room online. Confirmation was instantaneous. He sank back in the seat with a sigh of relief and closed his eyes for a few moments. It was a start.

He'd booked three nights but that could easily be extended according to circumstances. It took less than fifteen minutes to get to the hotel, located in a quiet lane in the middle of the CBD. With twenty-nine storeys and over 200 rooms, it was big enough to remain under the radar until he figured out what to do next.

He pulled into the underground car park, grabbed his things and headed inside. The check-in clerk had his room ready and seemed keen to strike up a conversation. It was the last thing Nic needed, but he couldn't afford to draw attention to himself, so he returned the stream of questions with a friendly tone and a lot of bullshit. *Poor bugger is probably bored witless standing here all night,* he thought as he took his key card and made his way to his room on the twenty-first floor.

The hotel had a modern, oriental feel, with his room tastefully decorated in subtle shades of pink, blue and jade — soothing somehow, despite the turmoil of his mind.

Dumping his bags in the bedroom, he turned on the television immediately to the news channel. Jennifer's death was already breaking news, now a confirmed murder investigation, with details to come. Nic's heart all but stopped as an image of Jennifer flashed onto the screen, then another of the burning boat already suspected to be linked to her death. He flicked off the remote, not able to watch anymore. By morning, the whole thing would be splashed all over the media, with Jennifer, a well-known socialite, sure to create headlines in the days to come.

He closed his eyes for a moment, swallowing hard. *What if I'd carried out Jennifer Lorenzo's death as I'd led Angelina to believe? It would be a totally different ball game. I'd be high on adrenaline right now. But where to? And what then?*

He ran his hands down his face, thanking God he'd been spared that fate. Kai would have been clinical in his preparations for Jennifer Lorenzo's demise and well on his way home to Macau. There'd be nothing at the crime scene for the police to trace.

But what of the boat explosion investigation? he found himself asking. Given what Nic knew on the subject, forensics could take days, if not weeks, to release their findings. And until they determined the cause and identified Angelina's remains and whoever was with her, there'd be no closure. Not for the first time he rued his decision not to probe Angelina further about her contacts when he had the chance. He'd placed his life and hers in the hands of people he knew nothing about, something he would never have done in normal circumstances.

But it was what it was. Nic had no choice but to move on. Best to catch up on some badly needed sleep and see what unfolded in the morning. Only now that he'd stopped running, he felt how stiff his body was from the hours of sitting, cramped on the cold sand, followed by the panic-stricken, precarious swim.

Rising and stripping off his clothes, he stepped into the shower, remaining there for some time. As he gave himself a towel down, he glanced at the dirty pool of clothes on the floor, wondering what the laundry staff would think. He shrugged. He'd handed in far worse.

Too tired to think any further, he rummaged for a T-shirt and pair of jocks in his bag and headed to bed. Pulling across the heavy drapes, he climbed into bed and fell into an exhausted sleep.

He awoke later than expected at nine, groggy and disoriented, but was soon reaching for the remote on the bedside table to check for updates. Jennifer's murder was believed to be a contract killing, with the killer still at large and the police following up on a list of suspects. Another reference was made linking the murder and boat explosion, with requests for witnesses of both to come forward. Apart from that, little more was disclosed.

9

Nic rose and made himself a coffee, revived by seven hours of uninterrupted sleep, mind alert. He thought he'd be safe here, for a while at least, unless … a shadow crossed his face.

Angelina had given her contacts his motel address to drop off the stolen car, but had she provided his contact details? *Would they be after me now for extortion money? Were they perhaps waiting for a reward before turning me in, particularly with my track record?*

It all depended on what she had told them. *Shit!* Nic exclaimed, running a hand through his hair. *They have to find me first,* he was quick to remind himself. Now was as good a time as any to stay low until he had some answers. He had some breathing space yet. Besides, he was in no state of mind to make plans.

Meanwhile, something required his immediate attention.

Wasting no time, he left his barely touched coffee on the bench, grabbed his mobile, wallet, gloves, key card and car keys, and made his way to the car park. After settling his parking fee, he pulled out of the car park and headed west out of the city. Fifteen minutes later, he turned off into an industrial estate and parked among a stream of cars in a busy street, leaving the keys on the floor. The area was frequented by gangs and bored young kids on the lookout for an unlocked vehicle for joy riding. The car would most likely be found miles away, torched or abandoned by morning when the fuel ran out.

He climbed out, removed his gloves, and headed towards West Footscray. It was only a ten-minute wait for the express train to the CBD, and he arrived back at the hotel at 11 a.m., taking the lift to the twenty-ninth-floor restaurant offering all-day dining service. He wasn't particularly hungry but had learned from experience that operating on empty did not help his mind at all. Or his body, for that matter.

Forty minutes later and energised by the generous serving of pasta and slabs of thick, crusty bread, he returned to his room where he remained for the day, watching for updates as they flashed across the TV screen, and flicking between Foxtel sports channels.

He didn't recall dozing off, and it was 10 p.m. when he awoke, wishing he could have slept straight through and delayed consideration of his circumstances for a while yet.

It was about to be a long, troublesome night. And he didn't know that he was prepared to handle it.

Heading to the bathroom and splashing cold water over his face, he put on his jacket, grabbed his key card and wallet, and headed for the door.

Out on the street, the still night air was chilly. He pulled on his hoodie, glancing both ways along the laneway before stepping onto the pavement. Few were about, but he wasn't going to venture out for long, having decided to stay indoors as much as possible. Dropping by a Thai restaurant, he ordered takeaway Pad Pak satay and fried rice, then stopped at a nearby bottle shop for a bottle of bourbon and a large bottle of Coke.

Ten minutes later, he returned to his room, appetite recovered, and tucked into his meal before a long shower and change of clothes. Settling on the sofa, he unscrewed the bourbon bottle and poured a double shot, adding Coke and ice.

It was a while since he'd drunk spirits in this fashion. Probably not since he'd returned to his Docklands apartment close to ten months ago after being stood up by Angelina as he was about to leave Bangkok. If only he hadn't let her back into his life a second time. If only…

But it was too late for 'if onlys'. Nic tipped some more ice into his glass, settled back into the sofa with a sigh, and started his second drink. With inhibition soon gone, thoughts drifted about where to head next. He had several contacts in the immediate vicinity where he could seek refuge, but he'd gone to all this trouble to escape the contract killing scene. Sold his apartment, slipped under the radar, and called it a day with his job. And he was determined never to return to that life.

First and foremost on his mind was the baby, and it took every sense of his being not to throw caution to the wind, pick up his mobile and book the next available flight to Spain. But that would be sheer recklessness. There was no way of knowing where Antonio was hiding his child, and even if there was, he'd have the formidable gang boss to deal with before he even considered the guards.

The image of the baby Angelina had shown him came to mind, and he felt an overwhelming sense of frustration and helplessness. There had to be a way to get her, and he was determined to find it. But as he had another drink, then another, doubts entered his mind. *What if Angelina had been lying all along? What if there'd never been a baby?* He shook his head and closed his eyes for a moment, willing himself to believe otherwise. It was all he had to hold on to. All he had left. Angry tears stung his eyelids. He wished he'd never set eyes on Angelina Lorenzo from the very beginning.

¶

At four in the morning, Alex Dimitriades's mobile rang. 'What the fuck?' He fumbled for it on the bedside table until he saw the number. Instantly he was alert.

'Nic?'

There was silence followed by a choked sob.

'Are you okay?'

More silence.

'She's dead, li'le bro,' came the slurred response.

'Who? The chick you told me about?'

'Could'n save her. I tried.'

'You still in Melbourne?'

'Yeah.'

'Out of your apartment by now, right?'

'Yeah.'

'Text me your address. I'll be on the next flight out.'

3

It had been a long and drawn-out investigation into Jennifer Lorenzo's death. Sergeant Sam Walsh had never felt so depleted by a case in his twenty-five years as a police officer. Perhaps it was his failure to protect the woman after she'd desperately turned to him to safeguard her family. Maybe it was a lack of success in capturing her deranged adopted daughter when she was at large.

He had felt the accusation, too, in the eyes of Cara Lorenzo when she first looked up at him, shocked and shivering, arms wrapped tightly around her knees, just metres from where her mother's body lay.

It was like a dagger through his heart.

He ran his hands down his face. Perhaps Cara Lorenzo would never find it in her heart to forgive him. And he'd have to live with that.

Thoughts flooded back once again to the night of the crime. *What was it, close to three months now?* He frowned. Seemed much longer. What had initially appeared to be a straightforward murder investigation turned out to be anything but. He'd received the call at six, just as he was about to end his shift. The voice was shaky, and the words stilted. Still, he immediately recognised it as Cara Lorenzo's.

He had quickly arranged an offsider and rushed to the scene, heart thudding wildly and mouth dry, knowing the chances of finding a heartbeat were remote but refusing to give up hope until he'd seen for himself.

The ambulance arrived not long afterwards. The driver accompanied him to where Jennifer Lorenzo lay, and the remaining paramedic fetched an emergency blanket to wrap around Cara Lorenzo's shoulders while the constable bent down gently to take her witness statement.

A lump formed in his throat when Sam spotted Jennifer Lorenzo's inert body metres from the path. No visible signs from a distance, no stab or bullet wounds, but as they neared, he noticed a tiny bloodstain on the thigh of her pants. She looked at peace, if that was any consolation, as if she was a sleeping child placed gently to rest.

Once the paramedic checked for vital signs and pronounced Jennifer deceased, Sam asked him to cut away the patch of bloodstained clothing with scissors, which revealed slight bruising and a needle mark. Wasting no time, Sam called the local CIB detectives to make their own assessment, then directed the constable to escort Cara back to the house and arrange for a close contact or family member to come.

¶

The CIB took little time determining the death as a homicide and called the coroner's court to register the details and another to the Homicide Squad, who took a few hours to form a team and make the trip from the city.

The CIB had barely left when there was a sudden thundering boom coming from the direction of the beach, startling Sam and the ambulance driver mid-sentence, and sending Sam rushing down the path to investigate. A boat had exploded some way out at sea, and was well alight. He watched the distant flames raging high into the night sky, knowing there was little that could be done.

Sam's mind was already jumping ahead. Given the timing of the explosion and its close proximity to the crime scene, he thought there must be a possibility that the two could be linked. *Had Angelina and a killer accomplice been making their escape by boat?* But he couldn't jump to conclusions at that early stage. If Forensics found no evidence of DNA where Jennifer's body was lying, perhaps there would be signs of it, or fragments of human remains on the boat.

If this became a dual investigation Sam knew it could drag on for days, possibly weeks. His suspicions were revealed to the water police when he reported the explosion. It took them some time to arrive and by then there was little chance anyone could have survived. Even if someone had been hurled overboard on impact, the conditions and lack of light were far from ideal.

Sam sighed as he watched the distant flames, still blazing against the night sky for another five minutes. *Whichever way things went,* he thought, *let's hope I'm right and Angelina Lorenzo is found responsible so that the family can be at peace. But at such a cost?* His chest tightened. He'd dealt with Jennifer Lorenzo several times since her daughter had gone on the run, and found the woman to be nothing but caring and considerate. So young. So vibrant. She didn't deserve to die like this. No one did …

9

Sam took another sip of his barely touched beer in the darkness of his loungeroom and reflected on the many twists and developments in the investigation since that night. Hours liaising with the Homicide Squad's officer in charge, Inspector George Fleming, a veteran of thirty years, had left no stone unturned to find Jennifer's killer. Fleming had become more like a friend than a colleague through the investigation, sensing Sam's feeling of guilt at not being there for the victim when she sought his protection. 'If Angelina Lorenzo was found to be complicit in the crime, she would have come up with some way of carrying out her threats, given what we know already,' he'd said. There was little comfort in the words, though Sam knew them to be true.

The coroner determined the cause of Jennifer's death to be a blow to a pressure point at the back of the neck, rendering her unconscious, followed by the lethal injection to her thigh that ended her life. There would have been no suffering.

The words caused a surge of relief in Sam. He didn't know how he would have fared if things had been otherwise.

Clearly this was the work of a trained killer: clinical and precise, leaving no trace of DNA or other incriminating evidence. His suspicions were confirmed when a set of footprints, size eleven and a half, were found leading to and away from the scene. This was no surprise, given Angelina's earlier clumsy attempt at ending her sister's life, and her lack of skills in martial arts. But he'd bet his life she was behind it all. So much to unravel. So many unanswered questions.

Had she been responsible for the murder of Lee Farrell eleven months ago? Sam thought. Everything pointed to it, but it was yet to be proven that she was one of the black-clad figures on the marina's CCTV footage that night. No incriminating evidence. Another professional job. What bothered him was her brazenness in turning up in the first place. She seemed to have the contacts to carry out her vengeful assignments efficiently and undetected. *Where she found them was anyone's guess. How much was she prepared to pay?* he wondered.

There were others in line waiting to interview Angelina Lorenzo …

Sam had been hoping against hope that traces of her would be found in what was left of the boat. *But what if the timing of the explosion was merely coincidental and had nothing to do with the murder. What if Angelina was still at large and planning her next move?* He believed she wouldn't hesitate to return for another attempt on her sister's life. Even though her survival was remote, Sam couldn't rule it out.

However, he'd got to know a bit about David, Cara's biological father and boyfriend Will, who'd provided a protective shell for Cara. It came as some comfort.

Meanwhile, things were kept as low key as possible with the media, in accordance with the family's wishes. But it hadn't been easy, given their high social status. Sam revealed only what was necessary until the findings were released. However, with Angelina Lorenzo theoretically still at large, it was necessary to announce her as a person of interest, wanted for questioning, with a photo and requests for sightings to be forthcoming.

There were no leads, but that came as no surprise.

He remained restless and barely slept for weeks, moving into the spare bedroom and trying not to take out his frustrations on Diana, his long-suffering wife of thirty years. It was a wonder she hadn't left years ago.

The time spent waiting for forensic evidence from the boat explosion had to be the most frustrating of his life. The cause was determined to be human error. A case of the pilot failing to completely shut off the port bypass fuel feed when he started the starboard engine, causing fuel to drip into the engine room and fuel fumes to build up and ignite. Nothing surprising there. Two people were identified as being on board with DNA found on bits of life jackets positively identifying Angelina Lorenzo and a thirty-five-year-old male, a member of a Middle Eastern gang with prior criminal convictions.

But what should have come as closure turned out to be

anything but. No human remains were found on board, and despite an extensive sea and rescue search of the surrounding area, no trace of the missing two was forthcoming. With Angelina Lorenzo and the prime suspect now presumed dead, there was no option but for the investigation to move on.

Only days later, there was another twist linked to the case. Angelina Lorenzo had been living under the identity of Ava Ferreira, reported as missing hours after the murder by the agent of her Docklands apartment. She'd not handed in her key at the end of her lease and her packed luggage, false passport and credit cards remained untouched. According to her passport, Angelina Lorenzo had spent most of the past year in Brazil and Spain. *No wonder all past leads had turned into dead ends. God knows what she'd been up to,* and Sam didn't care. Twelve weeks had passed, and her bank accounts were still untapped. Everything pointed to her demise, and that was the nearest thing to closure he could hope for. Finally, Cara Lorenzo could get some peace.

But he felt nothing but emptiness …

4

During the days and weeks that followed the boat explosion, Nic Drakos scanned the media daily for updates, but progress was painstakingly slow. And when the findings were finally released, they came as bittersweet.

Angelina had been aboard. She'd been on her way to pick him up as she'd promised. *That should be enough. Shouldn't it?* The explosion was deemed an accident, and nothing more could have been done.

But doubts and uncertainties persisted. No bodies were found on the boat or in the waters surrounding it. *Who's to say she's not still alive? Highly improbable, but not impossible.*

He trusted her before and been made a fool of. *What's to say she hadn't done it again? What if …* Nic was going round in circles. *Just shut the fuck up. Let it rest,* he told himself. If she'd somehow survived and got cold feet on him, her passport and boarding pass were in her apartment, good to go. He'd seen for himself. He reminded himself that there'd been no sightings or trace of her since, and her bank accounts remained untouched. Nic knew that he had to be satisfied with the investigation's findings of 'Missing, presumed dead', if he was to move on.

Easier said than done, he thought grimly.

§

Months later, Nic sat on the wide verandah of his brother Alex's old Queenslander farmhouse in the lush Atherton Tablelands. Alex had gone for the day with his family to visit his wife's mother in Mareeba.

It was rare to be alone like this. The house was usually filled with the raucous squeals of the twins, who were into every conceivable mischief they could find from the moment they awoke. Only yesterday, they'd discovered the drawer where Claire kept her make-up and had scribbled all over each other's faces and the newly painted wall in the ensuite. Nic smiled as he sipped his beer and reached down to stroke the head of his brother's old black and tan kelpie by his side, with its cloudy, trusting eyes.

There was a certain kind of magic in the late-afternoon stillness as he gazed over the serene vista below. The fragrant scent of frangipanis wafted up from the garden, and high in the distant trees came the unmistakable wail of the Spotted Catbird that was often heard at dawn or dusk.

It would be dark in another hour or two, but the nightly temperature would barely drop below twenty-one degrees. Nic was already becoming accustomed to the temperate climate, which sat around the high-twenties to low-thirty degrees. But the wet summer season, with its sticky days and heavy tropical rains, was yet to come. He doubted that a few months of discomfort would worry him too much. Preferable to Melbourne's cold, long winters that could last well beyond spring with, at times, little summer to follow.

His brother's mango farm's remote, rural setting provided the ideal place to bring up a young family, and Nic wished them every happiness. Yet deep down, he felt a raw sense of pain whenever he joined them at dinner, played with or read bedtime stories to his nephews. He knew that his brother, Alex, sensed it too. He'd never hidden from him that he'd wanted a family of his own. He'd often thought back to his ex-wife Kelly, who was similar in many ways to Claire — natural, kind and warm-hearted. She'd have made a perfect mother for their kids. *What if she'd stayed. Would they still be together after eight years? Would they have a family by now?* Nic rubbed the back of his neck. It was no use thinking about the what-ifs now. It had all come down to her or the job, and he chose the latter. Even in hindsight, he doubted that would have changed. Young, invincible, thirsty for adventure — the lure of crisscrossing the world to exotic places while earning megabucks was too much to resist.

He thought he loved Kelly at the time. Thought there'd never be another woman, and then Angelina entered his life. He had never mentioned his desperate hope of a child between them to Alex until everything blew up in his face a month ago.

He and Alex had been in town picking up supplies and stopped for a beer afterwards at the local pub when his phone beeped. He looked down and frowned. 'I need to get this,' he said quickly. 'Do you mind?'

Alex nodded and watched his brother rush outside, fearing bad news. He wasn't wrong.

'Have you heard something?' Nic's voice had a sense of urgency. He'd been expecting word from his long-term contact hours earlier.

There was a pause at the other end.

'Well, what is it?' he demanded.

'You were right. According to my source, Antonio's niece did give birth in Spain, but few knew about it apart from a handful in his gang. You know how tight-lipped Antonio is. She left him in charge while she came to Australia but—'

'But what?' Nic gripped the phone with an impending sense of dread.

'It's not good. The baby was killed during a botched kidnapping attempt by a rival gang two weeks ago in Buenos Aires.'

'I don't believe you!'

'Was it your baby, Nic?'

'What does it matter?' the response was barely audible.

A brief silence. 'Look, I didn't mean to pry or anything. Just thought it might help you to know Antonio went all out to get his revenge. And it wasn't pretty.'

The words came as little comfort.

Things from there on were somewhat of a blur, his

brother's protective arms around him, sitting in a quiet corner getting wiped out on neat scotch over ice as he bared his soul.

'It's shit, but life can be a shit, Nic. There's nothing more you could have done,' Alex consoled. 'Remember when I got to your hotel after the explosion? You said you didn't even know whether there *was* a baby. Whether your girlfriend had made the whole thing up.'

'I know, but – I could have tried finding out earlier.'

'Maybe, but even so, you would have come up with a dead end by the sounds of it. Anyway, your hands were tied until you knew for sure that it was your girlfriend on that boat when it exploded.'

The words came out before he knew it. 'Sorry, I shouldn't have—'

'Nah, you're all good.' Nic paused for a moment. 'Do you mind if we don't bring this up again for a while? I need to work through things in my own time, in my own way.'

'Sure.'

Nic downed the last of his scotch and summoned the drinks waiter.

'Maybe make this the last round, huh?' Alex looked at him in concern.

'We'll see.'

'What will I tell Claire? She expected us home two hours ago.'

'You'll figure out something.' Nic paused momentarily, a dark shadow crossing his face. 'You never told her about the baby, did you?'

'No. I made a promise. Remember?'

'Thanks.'

'You'd do the same.'

Nic remembered little else apart from arriving home in darkness and his brother's powerful fingers digging into his arms as he heaved him up the outside steps and onto the verandah.

After fourteen weeks on his brother's farm, Nic was already at peace with nature, something he hadn't felt in a long time. Not since …

He thought about the morning after he'd hooked up with Angelina Lorenzo. The day he swore he'd give up the role of assassin for good. Start afresh, somewhere like this. The day they'd driven down the long stretch of the Wilson Promontory's unspoiled national park, with Mt Oberon looming majestically as they drew closer. At that time, he hardly knew the beautiful woman sitting beside him. Could only dare to dream she could one day be part of his life.

Nic put his legs up on the verandah rail, hands clasped behind his head and reflected some more. At peace with nature, sure, but far from at peace with himself. He still flinched when an image of Jennifer Lorenzo appeared in the media. After her death there'd been an outpouring of grief and tributes from charities and everyday people she'd reached out to. He had no idea of the woman and what she stood for. Had been blindsided by Angelina's vitriolic, albeit convincing, portrayal. Coerced into agreeing to a hit job on an innocent woman because of a child he didn't know existed, let alone knew was his.

He squeezed his eyes shut, trying to block Jennifer Lorenzo's face from his mind.

The part that cut so deeply was that he'd allowed himself to be victim once more to Angelina's half-truths and lies. He didn't know that he could ever totally trust a woman again. Long days spent working outdoors with this brother had given Nic little time to dwell on it. In retrospect, bringing him here was probably the best thing his brother could have done. In the interim, at least.

In the meantime, Nic could rest easy. He'd not been in the vicinity of the crime scene, and everything pointed to the guy on the boat with Angelina as the assassin. He had the credentials, the links to crime gangs and bikie groups. Not that he'd rated so much as a mention among Nic's connections. He wondered how in the hell she got onto him in the first place.

None of that mattered now. If the guy's mates were hell-bent on hunting him down for some reason, it would have happened by now. They probably had more important things to deal with, like targeted police raids on local gangs and bikie groups.

If only that was all there was to deal with. When Angelina returned from Brazil, he'd already decided to turn his back on contract killing. Not that it was common knowledge. Not something he'd want his contacts to get wind of. He knew the whereabouts and affiliations of too many should he decide to go rogue and wouldn't put it past any of them to set in place his demise rather than face that risk.

But he couldn't afford to dwell on that. He had to believe there was a safe haven out there. Somewhere.

He'd been planning to move from Australia altogether. He'd thought of buying some land and transporting his things, still in storage, but he didn't know he'd ever be safe in Australia and began to consider moving to Greece on his dual passport. To deepen his bond and immerse himself in the history and culture of his forebears.

To this point there'd been little cause for concern. But things could well change. If he chose to stay at all, that is. No one was untraceable, even in this remote part of the world.

The rundown mango farm Alex purchased five years ago called for a substantial overhaul, and his initial outlay and hard work were finally returning dividends. Extra seasonal workers had been signed up, and Alex had just struck a deal with one of the country's largest supermarket chains at the commencement of the upcoming mango season. Less than two weeks away now.

Nic had already been allocated a role overseeing the daily operations of the workers. Most were seasonal workers or backpackers, accommodated at a nearby backpacker hostel where they'd be collected and taken back after their shifts, six days a week. The hours would be lengthy, and the work varied, either outdoors picking the fruit or in the shed grading, packing and stacking.

It wasn't so long back that Alex lost everything in a

business partnership gone wrong, and he and Claire had to start again from scratch. The old Queenslander farmhouse had been derelict for years when they first moved in. The verandah and foundations under the house had all but rotted away, the windows needed replacing, and certain rooms had to be gutted and redone. Alex had offered a local carpenter free rent on the old workers' living quarters in return for help with the renovations.

The floor was stripped back and repolished, and the rusty corrugated roof was replaced. The exterior painting was the last thing to be done, and Nic was happy to lend his brother a hand after he arrived. Alex and Claire chose a traditional Queenslander colour scheme of muted grey contrasted with white on the window sills, canopies and verandah. It wasn't until Nic had stepped back to admire the finished product that he felt a sense of satisfaction. Something he'd not felt in a long time.

At Claire's insistence, he'd stayed in the house with them when he first arrived from Melbourne. It only took a week for Nic to make a tactful suggestion to relocate to the 1920s workers' cottage.

'Too long living on your own, huh?' she'd said.

'Something like that. Besides, you guys need your space.'

Truth was, he felt stifled and confined. The house was smaller than it appeared from the outside, and he felt as if he was stepping on everyone's feet. Claire and Alex had an ensuite, but he had to share a bathroom with the twins, and he never knew what the right time was to use it.

Night-time was the worst. Nic was used to sitting for hours watching sport or a late-night flick. Conscious not to awaken the twins in the adjoining room, he'd lie awake, willing himself to sleep, knowing from experience that never worked.

He cast his gaze around the late-afternoon shadows and finished his beer. They'd be home soon. Best to feed the dog, put it to bed, and then head back to his quarters. He rose and headed inside.

5

Antonio Alvarez sat in the kitchen of his old stone farmhouse, finishing off the last of his *caldo gallego*, a traditional hearty thick soup of potatoes, local vegetables and sausage. He ate most nights in the adjoining cottage with his caretakers, Filipe and Rosa, but when he chose to dine alone, as was the case this night, Rosa sent over a serving of whatever she'd been cooking.

He reached for the last slice of thick, crusty bread as he watched the rain pelting at the window in the dark night, glad that he'd collected sufficient dry wood to last the night. At this time of year, the open fire was going most days.

It was already December and the weather would be bleak, rainy and cold like this for the next few months, perhaps more. Not what most people would expect from Spain. He neither, until he departed Rio de Janeiro a few years back in search of a rundown hamlet, of which there were many in this part of northern Spain. He saw it as an investment and a possible location to extend his clandestine activities.

Antonio always made a point of visiting his hamlet for a week or so before he returned to Australia after his annual four-monthly visits to his gang's headquarters in Rio de Janeiro. Although Brazil's hot, balmy conditions came as a welcome relief from Melbourne's long, cold winters, it was refreshing to spend some time here in the crisp, chilly air. Or feel the Atlantic's cold, salty air biting his face as he strolled around the harbour of the historic fishing village of Viveiro, the closest town.

He'd postponed his trip to Australia this time, and the two members of his gang based there were yet to learn that his next trip home would be the last. They'd worked under him for the past twelve years, and he had complete confidence in them managing operations while he based himself in Rio de Janeiro.

The events of the last fourteen months had a profound effect on his life, and there was no turning back.

Antonio reached for his glass of wine and took a sip thoughtfully, casting his mind back to the day it all began, the day Angelina first contacted him, the niece he hadn't known existed. The image of her pulling off her hoodie to reveal the face identical to that of his sister, the same dark hair that tumbled down over her shoulders, would haunt him forever. The day they'd met on a garden seat in Carlton on that frigid winter's day.

He swore on the memory of his deceased sister that he'd be there for her only child if she so chose. It mattered not that Angelina ran from the police and was as much into crime as he was. *Surely it wasn't too late to turn things around,* he'd naively thought. *Turn her away from the dangerous path she'd chosen to follow?*

If only he'd known then what he'd learned in the months since. The real Angelina. The one who lied, deceived and charmed the unsuspecting into meeting her demands, like a black widow spider. He'd known from the outset that she'd killed before. *Who knows how many times?* But who was he to judge?

Their relationship was bound to be rocky. From the beginning, Angelina proved strong-willed and feisty, as was he. She clearly had no intention of coming clean, so he might as well make the best of things. Her looks and charm were an asset, and she'd quickly proved her worth when he dealt with shady criminals. Unbeknown to her, he had big plans for her future. And then it all turned belly up, and things went from bad to worse. Antonio never thought that it would end in such acrimony, with neither on speaking terms.

By the time Angelina departed Spain for good, he never thought he'd forgive her for walking out on her newborn without a second glance. She told him she had no intention of returning for the baby, and he believed her. Yet, he knew how easily things could change. No matter the circumstances, Angelina would be denied access to Talita from that day on. Talita was family. And under his control.

Gut instinct told him that Angelina was placing herself in grave danger by returning to Australia, and he was rarely wrong. *Not my problem,* he'd thought at the time. *She wants to go it alone, that's her choice.* All thoughts of giving her a leading role in the gang were long gone.

And now she was gone.

When news of her death broke, he felt no grief, no emotion, just a deep, dark void. The sense of a wasted life and squandered opportunities. She'd spoken little of her background, but further investigations led to a prestigious life that most could only dream of. And for reasons he'd never know, she'd blown it all away.

He couldn't bring himself to pity her. She'd chosen to go down the path she did. By the time she came to him, it was all too late. Not for the first time, he regretted reconnecting with her at all. If not for Talita …

The small child, swaddled in her bunny blanket, whom he'd left not so long ago in the caretaker's cottage nursery, had provided him with contentment he'd not felt in a long time. He felt whole again. Younger. Talita would have everything he would have bestowed on his own child. The child he regretted not having all those years ago to Lucia Ramos, the only woman he ever loved. But he'd chosen gang life over family life and paid a steep price.

Antonio ran a finger around the rim of the glass. If anything, Angelina's demise brought a palpable sense of relief. He no longer feared his niece having a change of heart and returning for the child, no matter how remote the possibility. People changed. He'd learned that years ago. Not that he wouldn't have dispensed with Angelina if things had come to that.

Rosa showed no emotion when told of his niece's death,

but Antonio sensed a secret sigh of relief. He could hardly blame her. She'd bent over backwards to be of assistance to Angelina while she stayed at the hamlet, and Angelina, in return, had been cold, indifferent and petulant. She'd treated Rosa with disdain, as though she was a second-rate servant, and that was one thing Antonio would never forgive her for.

Rosa was fiercely protective of Talita, like a lioness of her cubs, and Antonio knew no one would get to her child. Yet deep down, Antonio knew that Rosa had considered Angelina a threat. That she'd change her mind one day and return to claim Talita. She didn't have to worry now.

Little did Rosa know of Antonio's plans for Talita in the years to come, once she was old enough to become part of his life, and he got to say what was best for her. He'd talked to the caretaker couple soothingly as though he was a doctor reassuring his patient. When Antonio first told them they could adopt the baby, they were led to believe the child could be raised in the hamlet. That's the way he'd play things. For now.

But what of Talita's father? The thought had always sat uneasily in his mind. Angelina had claimed no knowledge of his identity, but Antonio very much doubted that. His niece was far too savvy.

It therefore came as a complete shock to learn that Nic Drakos, the freelance assassin he'd crossed paths with several times, appeared to be the biological father of his great-niece. From what Bernado had said of his reaction when told the baby was dead, it had to be. Antonio was surprised the thought hadn't crossed his mind before. After all,

Angelina had accompanied Drakos when he blew up the Lorenzo yacht. Still, it intrigued Antonio that the Greek wasn't aware that the baby existed when he started fishing around for information. He found himself wondering, *What the hell had she told him?*

The fake news of the baby's death couldn't have been timelier. Antonio had thought of spreading the rumour not long after Talita's birth. The fact she was in safe hands in an isolated location of another country was irrelevant. From the outset, he'd been worried about kidnapping attempts by rival gangs the moment word of the birth got around, and he booked an immediate flight to his hamlet in Spain, keeping watch as does a security guard over a priceless painting. But this was unsustainable. He had pressing matters to attend to in Rio. Only the inner circle members of his gang and the child's adoptive parents knew the truth. And now, there'd no longer be the threat of Talita's father returning for the child.

Little did he know how wrong he was …

6

Angelina did not meet Rafiq Khalil until the day she walked along the pontoon at the Queenscliff Marina, where the two small boats were moored side-by-side. Raf stepped off the nearest boat to shake her hand. He was an imposing presence, around six-feet, with a powerful build and muscles straining under the weatherproof jacket. She couldn't see much of his face under his baseball cap apart from his olive complexion, brown eyes and dark beard.

'Theo tells me you can handle a boat,' he said.

She nodded.

'Well, you need to know what you're doing as it looks as if things are going to cut up rough out there.'

Angelina tilted her chin. 'I can hold my own. You needn't worry.'

'Okay then, stay close behind.' He handed her a walkie-talkie. 'And do as I say, okay?'

Angelina nodded once more.

They headed off towards the cove. The waves were already

building, and darkness had set in as they embarked on their thirty-five-minute journey. By the time they arrived, there was a five-metre swell, filling Angelina with a sense of exhilaration. It was like being blindfolded on a rollercoaster ride. As instructed, she turned off her navigation lights. Raf signalled he was ready to stop some way out from the cove, and Angelina drew close alongside. Raf took off his life jacket, signalled her to throw hers over and tossed them under the seat.

He then quickly jumped aboard and grabbed the wheel. 'Let's get out of here!' he yelled.

The boat sped away. 'How long before the explosion?' she shouted.

'I don't know.' His words were barely audible above the swirling wind. 'I cut the fuel line not long back. It won't take long for the engine room to be flooded with fuel. Probably a matter of minutes.'

They'd gone just a hundred and fifty metres when there was a massive boom from behind, causing Angelina to spin around on the spot, transfixed by the orange flames shooting into the night sky. Raf navigated the boat through the darkness, using the distant lighthouse as a beacon and heading towards the lights of Point Lonsdale, then switching on the navigation lights once they were well out of sight of the cove. Sheets of icy water splashed over the side of the boat, soaking Angelina's clothes and numbing her hands and fingers. She pulled her saturated gloves off with her teeth and blew on her fingers, hoping to return some warmth, but it only seemed to make things worse. It reminded her of the day she was caught jogging along the beach in the middle of summer when the skies suddenly turned black, the temperature plummeted like an aircraft falling from the sky, and the heavens opened.

Time seemed suspended until they motored into the safety of Queenscliff Harbour. Theo was already waiting at the marina to tie the boat to its moorings. He held out a hand to pull them ashore, then conversed briefly with Raf to one side, and gestured with a wave of his hand to Angelina to follow them.

'I've got a place organised not far from here to stay for the night,' he said over his shoulder.

She nodded, shivering.

The original weatherboard fisherman's house, two streets away, was in darkness as Theo opened the gate to a picket fence, and they headed towards the porch. She wondered who it belonged to.

'You can leave your coats and shoes outside. I'll see to them later,' Theo told them, as he opened the front door, flicked the light switch and stood aside to let them enter. The heater had already been turned on, and the small living room was warm and cosy. Framed family photos sat on top of the old mantlepiece, and two leather recliners sat before a small table facing a flat-screen TV on the wall.

'The pair of you need to get out of those wet clothes,' Theo said. 'There are two showers in the place. Yours is down the hall, Raf, and Ava's is in her ensuite. We can talk later.'

The back of the house smelled of fresh paint and varnish as Theo led the way to a bedroom where her small case lay on the floor beside the bed. He nodded towards the ensuite door that stood open and said, 'There's fresh towels on the rack. The laundry has a washing machine and dryer for your wet clothes.'

Angelina nodded. 'Thanks.'

'I'll leave you to it, then.'

'Wait,' Angelina said as he turned to go, 'you've made it clear to Raf that I want to be left alone from now on, right?'

'Yeah. That won't be an issue.'

'Good.'

'Keep in mind that it goes both ways,' he told her. 'Raf likes to keep his life private. It could be weeks until you arrive in Manila, so the pair of you need to find some common ground.'

'I'm aware of that.'

'In the meantime, I hope to God things go to plan. But if they don't, just do whatever Raf says. I can't think of anyone I'd rather have by my side if things turn to shit.'

The words gave Angelina a measure of comfort. 'I'll remember,' she said. The thought of what lay ahead was only starting to dawn on her. And with it, a sense of foreboding.

After Theo left, she peeled her saturated clothes off like a wetsuit and left them in a heap on the tiles, wasting no time in stepping under the shower. To her relief, the water was piping hot, and she uttered a sigh of relief as the warmth slowly returned to her body, like the sun's first rays, and her fingertips turned rosy pink.

Angelina wasn't the only one to have an extended session

in the shower. The water was still running in the main bathroom near Raf's room when she headed to the laundry at the end of the small hallway, carrying her dripping clothes.

The small plane they would be flying in had strict baggage requirements and she was forced to pack lightly, settling on the essentials – clothes that could be mixed and layered to suit varying conditions, plus a weatherproof jacket. Most of her possessions remained in her large suitcase at Docklands: clothes, make-up, toiletries and accessories. On top were her credit cards, containing five and six thousand dollars respectively, passport and boarding pass. For a moment, she pondered how long the police would leave them undisturbed on the off-chance of her returning. It mattered little. Angelina had two fake passports, taken with the light brown and blonde wigs purchased in A Coruña, and two credit cards topped up with substantial amounts from existing offshore accounts. The most difficult thing had been parting with favourite outfits that she turned to time and time again to impress. The crimson, off-the-shoulder, slinky number, for instance. The one guaranteed to turn heads. She'd yet to see another like it. And she doubted her chances of doing so in Manila.

Maybe when I reach Europe, she thought.

¶

When she returned to the living room, there were no signs of anyone, but the TV was still on. With a shrug, she sat down, elevated her feet on a nearby stool and flicked channels with the remote.

Raf appeared shortly afterwards, his bulk framing the doorway, dressed in ripped jeans and a black T-shirt with a logo she'd not seen before. It was only now, that he no longer wore a jacket, that she noticed the thick neck, broad shoulders, and tattooed arms and wrists. It wouldn't surprise her if he'd done a stint in security.

'Where's Theo?' she asked.

'He's gone out for takeaway.'

'So, what time do we have to be up?'

'Five-thirty. Nadim is picking us up at six.'

'Is he from Lebanon, as well?'

'Yeah, from a village not far from mine. Not that we knew each other. We only hooked up when Nadim joined the gang, not long after he'd arrived in Australia.'

'When was that?'

He scratched his chin. 'Around four years, I reckon.'

Angelina nodded. Theo had told her about the member of Raf's gang who'd be sharing the driving load, arranging motel check-ins and outs, and obtaining food and supplies.

'The less you and Raf draw attention to yourselves, the better,' he'd told her on their second meeting. 'Especially in smaller country towns where locals may not see a passer-by for days. They'll seek any opportunity for a chat, particularly in pubs and cafes.'

'So, you're saying no meals out then?'

'Yep. Nadim will organise takeaway each night,' he told

her. 'And keep visits to toilet blocks brief, okay? There'll be sufficient stops along the way to stretch your legs.'

'And this driver, he can be trusted, right?'

'Yep. He knows how to keep his mouth shut.'

9

Theo stepped into the room armed with a large parcel and bottle of Coke. He set the package down on the kitchen table, ripped back the paper, and they tucked in ravenously after hours in the wintry chill. The waft of hot oil, chips and fish that lingered long after they'd finished, reminded Angelina of the shop near the wharf she passed by often as a child.

Once they'd had coffee, Theo turned to her. 'I suggest you get an early night.' It was more of an order than a suggestion. She gathered the pair wanted time alone to discuss the final details.

Still fuelled by adrenalin from the day's events she was far from ready for sleep when she returned to her room. She turned off the light, climbed into bed, and put her hands behind her head against the pillows, listening to the faint voices in the lounge room and reflecting on the audacious plan that Theo had devised. She'd underestimated his capabilities. There was a lot more to the burly bikie gang member than appearances would suggest. Theo had the contacts and transport available at short notice to carry out such a plan, but he'd emphasised that things would not come cheap. Angelina was ready for that and offered him a more than generous sum.

'And what if there was a Plan B?' she'd asked.

'Like what?'

Theo listened with disbelief.

'Fuck! Are you serious? Do you realise what a risk that is?'

'Yeah. And I'm willing to take that risk.'

'And you know the costs involved in something like that?'

'How much are we talking about?'

'Four times the price at least.'

'I figured it would be something like that,' she'd said. 'To be honest, I wasn't sure you had the means and know-how to carry it out.'

'You'd be surprised what I'm into.'

'Do your sums, then get back to me, and we'll take things from there.'

She'd met with him the following day and he had a Plan B far more complex than she'd envisaged. The time-line was dependent on the arrangements for the next drugs drop, and would involve a tedious and uncomfortable trip to Far North Queensland, followed by a light plane flight to New Guinea, which was not without its dangers, then a short trip on a cargo ship to Manila. Upon reflection, she realised she'd not thought through the complications. She was confident that Theo operated independently of his gang on jobs like this, with the sort of money she was willing to pay. She reasoned he'd be wanting the lion's share.

She revealed she'd been on the run for the past year and had nowhere to go, but did not mention why. He didn't ask. Angelina had to assume that he already knew everything that he needed to know. She'd thought that faking her own death was the ideal solution. A new identity. A new start elsewhere. She hadn't stopped to consider that nowhere was safe, as Theo had been quick to point out. Not in Australia, at least while investigations into her disappearance were ongoing. So, where would she go? And what would she do when she got there? These were questions she asked. But Theo's plan had everything covered, with a twist she'd never have envisaged. Her accomplice was, in fact, his son-in-law, Rafiq Khalil, who worked alongside him from time to time, on clandestine matters.

Rafiq, known to everyone as Raf, was of Lebanese descent and operated in a rival Melbourne Middle Eastern crime gang. They were well known to police, dealing predominantly in drug trafficking, fraud and money laundering throughout South East Asia.

'Raf's had experience with boats if that's what you're worried about,' Theo had said.

'I'll take your word for it.'

'Just one more thing. My son-in-law is on the run, like you are.'

'Oh?' Angelina said, surprised. 'What's he done?'

'I keep things private like we discussed. Let's say a few gang matters. Nothing serious. So, I got to thinking, why not turn this job to the advantage of you both.'

By the time Theo had finished, Angelina's head was swimming.

It was the early morning hours before her eyes became

heavy and she drifted off, dreaming of waves, the cold, and beacons.

¶

The alarm went off in the adjoining room at 5:15 a.m., causing Angelina to start. She let out a groan. Her puffy, red eyes in the mirror as she passed, supported the feeling. She felt as if she'd had an hour or two's sleep at best. She could hear the clatter of crockery and running water in the kitchen as she dressed, and when she entered wearing her light brown, chin-length, straight wig, Theo gave a look of approval.

'Are you keeping that look when you get to Manila?'

'Yeah, till things settle.'

'Good move. You have passport and papers to match?'

'All's been arranged.'

She didn't tell him about the other passport she had taken on the same day. The one wearing a blonde wig...

'Coffee?' he asked.

'Yeah, that'd be good. White. No sugar. And make it a strong one, will you?'

He grinned.

'Is your daughter meeting up with us in Cairns?' she asked as she slipped onto a kitchen bench stool.

'Marnie? No, why should she?'

'I thought she might head to Manila with Raf, that's all.'

'No, she's joining him once he's settled.' He paused for a moment. 'Who knows, I may join them at a later date. Truth is, I'm getting sick of looking over my shoulder. Outlaw bikie gangs like mine are being targeted like you wouldn't believe by the authorities, and I'm not getting any younger.'

'What about your wife?' Angelina asked.

'Cleared out years ago.'

Raf entered the room afterwards, clad in black as was she, and making no mention of her new hairstyle.

'All good to go?' he said to Theo.

'Yeah. I'm just putting together a quick breakfast before we hit the road.'

Angelina declined Theo's offer for a slice of raisin toast, despite the appetising waft of cinnamon, deep in her thoughts while the other two chatted.

Once they'd finished, Theo sent the pair to do a final pack while he tidied the kitchen that reminded him of the small place he'd lived in since he was first married. He thought about the years of struggle raising a young daughter on his own, trying to instil in her the values he wanted her to uphold while he lived a life on the wrong side of the law. He'd felt a deep hypocrisy whenever he packed Marnie's school lunches or took her to ballet classes. But as she grew older, he noticed the same headstrong qualities of his Māori ex-wife and keeping his daughter in hand grew more difficult. Things turned for the worse when she left the safety of the small Catholic primary school and entered secondary school. Unbeknown to Theo the bullying began, and Marnie responded in kind. Theo often spotted her bingeing on chocolate or ice-cream, but he blamed it on the new, much larger environment. His scant few years at secondary school had been miserable ones as well.

Marnie's weight began to balloon, and although she acted as if she didn't care, he knew she did. Gone was the girl with the cheeky smile, who wrapped her arms around his neck as he read the morning paper and made his morning bed, no matter how haphazardly. In her place was a petulant, moody young woman who answered back and moped around the house.

The day he caught her sneaking out her bedroom window as a fourteen-year-old, brought things to a head. However, the almighty row that followed led to nothing. She went off anyway. He had no idea who she was meeting up with and dreaded to think of the possibilities.

The only thing he could think of doing was to take her along when he joined up with the gang. But that didn't sit easily. Women were viewed there as targets and ultimate conquests. Bragging rights were a rite of passage, and no second thought was given.

The six years Marnie spent there were the most worrisome of his life. But he needn't have been concerned. Gang members steered well clear, knowing it would be Theo they'd have to deal with. And he'd underestimated Marnie's smarts. She only became cockier, and her comments more barbed.

But over time, he detected a softness to her, happiness she'd not shown since she was a little girl. And then she began dressing up and going out at night.

'So can I ask who the lucky guy is?' he asked

'You'll find out soon enough.'

It was six months before Marnie brought him home. He seemed nice enough, to Theo's relief. A good fifteen years older than Marnie, but maybe she needed someone mature to look up to. Said he was into real estate, but that remained to be seen.

'Can you set me up in a job somewhere?' she asked unexpectedly one day. 'It's time I started off on my own.'

Theo set her up in a gym frequently used by his gang members. A rough-as-guts establishment, but it was a start. It was soon apparent that she thrived in her role in reception. There was a new confidence in her. Then, after a few months on the job, she moved in with the guy. Finally, Theo had reason to relax.

How could I have got things so wrong? he thought.

7

At 6 a.m. sharp, bright headlights shone through the curtains and Theo nodded for them to head to the car parked outside, engine running. The driver climbed out and walked around to greet them. Under the street light, Angelina noted he was similar to Raf in appearance minus the beard, a year or two younger than his counterpart, perhaps, and somewhat shorter.

After brief introductions the three headed off, driving through the sleepy seaside town of Queenscliff. Angelina wondered if things livened up during the day. Probably not. From what Theo told her, little had changed over the years. Those seeking nightlife and excitement congregated around nearby towns along the surf coast, where once expansive tracts of rural land were being sliced up for housing by young couples or retirees in search of a sea change.

Theo stood on the kerb long after the black SUV pulled out of the kerb and turned the corner out of sight. So far, so good. The pair had survived the deadliest part of the operation. It would only have taken one mistake on Raf's part … but he'd held his nerve like Theo knew he would. However, the rest was unknown territory. Especially the drugs-running side of things in Cairns. It was a matter of fate; of nothing unforeseen cropping up along the way. He only hoped that Raf arrived safely in Manila at the other end. For Marnie's sake.

9

From Queenscliff, the driver headed in a northeast direction for two and a half hours to Seymour before taking the six-hundred-kilometre route along the Great Inland Way to Parkes in New South Wales for their first stopover.

Angelina sat, shoulders slumped, ear buds in, listening to music as they travelled along the endless sealed grey road, hour after hour, passing through one large country town and then another. At one point, she leaned forward to check the time on the dash and groaned inwardly. They'd been on the road only five hours, but it could have been five days. Only now did it dawn on her what she'd let herself in for.

But things could have been worse. Angelina almost decided to make the road trip in two days instead of three. She figured it would have gotten the tedious part out of the way and provided another day to enjoy at the beach resort. It was Theo who suggested otherwise. 'Have you been on a journey this long before?' he'd asked.

'No, I usually take a plane. Why?'

'Then, I'd consider adding an extra night's stay. Believe me, two days straight of eighteen hours in a car isn't much fun. Especially if you're not sharing the driving.'

She'd thought about that. The longest stretch she could recall in a car was six hours on a tour of country wineries with her father. It didn't seem that long. But Theo was right. Taking turns in driving definitely made the difference.

But doing so on this trip was out of the question. It would only take one country cop to pull them up for a routine check to blow her cover wide open. And for that reason, Raf only drove on the most isolated road sections.

'Make it three days then,' she'd said. Right now, she was glad she'd listened.

With a sigh, she leaned back against the headrest and closed her eyes again.

ꝗ

As the hours passed, Raf reflected on his life. On how much he'd changed in the twenty years since he arrived in Australia as a fourteen-year-old immigrant with his parents and three younger siblings. Searching for peace after enduring years of a turbulent civil war.

On their arrival in Sydney, the family was set up in government-backed housing in an inner-city suburb where their neighbours shared similar backgrounds and took every opportunity to make successful starts. His parents took on factory jobs, working all hours, leaving Raf to look after the younger children.

But Raf was impatient for the wealth and comforts he saw around him — the expensive European cars, designer clothes and gold jewellery – things that remained frustratingly out of reach.

He was bored at school and took up with a local gang who offered good incentives to be one of their foot soldiers, stealing cars and breaking into houses. Being a quick learner, it didn't take him long to become entrenched in the gang. One day, he left home and never returned, oblivious of the heartache it would cause his mother. His siblings had always been the favoured ones, he reasoned. There was little use in staying.

A trip to a local gym as a twenty-year-old turned his life around. He watched the bodybuilders lifting weights he could only dream of, and compared their taut, muscled bodies to his own still-underdeveloped frame. From that day, he took to doing weights sessions and self-defence classes. And within a few years, he'd become a bouncer at a nightclub in between jobs with the gang.

All had gone well until he made one wrong move and served a two-year sentence for a brutal assault on a member of a rival gang. By the time he was released on parole, he'd given some thought to the future. Gone was the swagger of the past years, replaced by a desire to stay out of trouble and utilise his quick-thinking brain to scale the ranks of the gang's powerful criminal hierarchy.

An opportunity came to extend the gang's operations in Melbourne, and he took it. In his new role he managed to stay under the radar, but realised that with his fingerprints on the police database he would always be vulnerable. However, it took a tip-off from a prison insider some years later for police to raid his house, where they found various items, including cash, cocaine, and prescription medications. He was cornered with nowhere to go.

Raf glanced over his shoulder at Angelina, who was already dozing, head against the headrest, barely believing his luck that she turned up when she did. She was his ticket out of the country, his start to a new life in his gang in Manila.

He didn't have the financial resources to cover such an unconventional escape and would have loved to have known how she had such funds in the first place, particularly at her age. He was also intrigued about her background. *Was Ava her real name? And why she was going to such lengths to flee the country?*

Theo would know all that, of course. Would have looked into things before he went ahead with his plan. But that information would never be divulged. Years ago, as they shared a beer on the front porch, he'd said, 'I've learned through experience to keep things about other people private. You'd be surprised how a leak can occur by telling one person, no matter who it is.'

Raf took his advice. It had saved his arse many times over.

Manila was a perfectly placed transit point for heroin, cocaine and illicit amphetamines to South East Asia and

Australia. His gang had set up operations there several years ago just as the drug business boomed. After forming links with other transnational crime gangs, they'd branched out into other illegal activities – money laundering, illegal firearms and counterfeit money, to name a few.

There was a fortune to be made. The gang worked closely with their Australian counterparts, and Raf's work had mainly involved the pickup and delivery of drugs once they entered Australian shores. But he mostly wanted to explore the importing of illicit steroids into the country. He could see the potential from years of being around gyms, tattoo parlours and security work. Party drug distribution was another category he'd observed when working in security at nightclubs. But he figured that once in Manila, he'd settle in first, do what was asked and take things from there.

¶

It had taken Marnie months to open up. And Raf let things unfold slowly, sensing that pressing her would only undermine her trust. She'd met the guy on an online dating site. 'Blake,' he called himself, but upon reflection, she doubted that, along with everything else on his profile.

Marnie had never been one to access such sites, and only a prolonged bout of loneliness and self-loathing led her to do so in the first place. Even so, she was aware of the dangers associated with such a practice, and it was a while before she agreed to meet him in the first place. Blake appeared not the slightest perturbed, seemingly content to contact her daily and take things from there. When the meeting eventually did take place, it was over coffee in a busy shopping precinct. And by the time they parted, Marnie was smitten. But it didn't take long for things to change. Blake was jealous, controlling and brutal and she only escaped his clutches by letting him know who her father was.

One day she surprised Theo by announcing she'd secured work in a nearby animal shelter.

'I didn't think animals were her thing,' Raf remarked as he shared a beer on the porch with Theo that evening.

'Try every stray dog and cat in the neighbourhood as far back as I can remember. Even birds. Came home one day to find her with a baby sparrow that had fallen from its nest, wrapped in a blanket with a dropper of water, trying to feed it. I told her it was nature's way, but she'd have none of it.'

'Did it survive?'

'What do you reckon?'

'And what did she say?'

'Knew she'd done her best. I knew there'd be another.'

Raf sipped his drink thoughtfully. He thought he knew Marnie, but he didn't at all.

¶

Raf visited Marnie over the next few months and slowly began to see a change. But it was on a night they were alone, when he made the first show of intimacy that she pulled back instinctively.

'Shit, I'm sorry, Marnie. I should never—'

'Shh …' She touched his face. 'I'm just going to need some time, that's all.'

He nodded. 'You wanna talk about it?'

Marnie stared into the distance for quite some time before she spoke.

As Raf listened to the degradation inflicted at the hands of the monster, his emotions were a turmoil of fury, rage and disgust. If nothing else, his father showed deep respect for women, with an abhorrence of violence towards them, particularly of a sexual nature. This he drilled into both sons at an early age.

It was six months before he and Marnie engaged in sex, and she was the one who made the first move.

Not long afterwards, she asked him to move in with her, and a year later, they married. Not that either of them was a great believer in the institution. It just felt right somehow. Raf hoped it would offer her his assurances of commitment. And he did it for Theo as well. The guy had done it tough. He deserved to know his daughter was in good hands.

'So, how old was Marnie when your wife left?' he'd asked soon after he moved in.

'Six.'

He gave a whistle. 'Shit. That's tough. Did she give a reason?'

'Nah. I should have seen the writing on the wall. Kiri

should never have had kids at that age. She was barely a kid herself.'

'Marnie said she was a Māori from the North Island.'

'Yeah. Came over here in search of a bit of adventure and excitement. Suited me. I was pretty wild myself in those days. We took turns at the tattoo parlour, hit the weed, you name it.'

Raf grinned.

'Kiri fell pregnant not long afterwards. We foolishly thought that getting married might solve everything.'

'Did you love her?'

He shrugged. 'Crazy for her, yes. But love? I barely knew the meaning of the word. I came from a broken marriage. Lived with my mum and my step-dad, who hated my guts. Left home when I was fourteen.' He went silent for a few moments. 'I'm going to tell you something I don't want Marnie to know. Okay?'

'Sure.'

'Kiri didn't walk out on us. I kicked her out.'

'Oh?'

'It wasn't a spur-of-the-moment thing. Kiri never took to motherhood like I'd hoped, and as the years went by, she appeared restless and bored. Not that Marnie wasn't looked after. But she didn't get much affection, that's for sure. I worried it could damage her for life, but ...' He shrugged his shoulders and continued, 'maybe she'd never known any different. Besides, I made a point of making up for it when I got home.'

The words gave Raf new-found respect for the

battle-hardened bikie who looked as ruthless as any he'd come across.

'So, when did it all turn to shit?' he asked.

'I began to suspect Kiri had taken to the booze during the day when I wasn't around. Stopped caring about how she looked. And the place was always a mess. But the tipping point came the day I came home late one night, around nine to find the front door wide open and Marnie sitting alone in the darkness watching TV.'

'Shit. What did you do?'

'Bundled her off to the next-door neighbour and went out searching for Kiri. Found her an hour later shooting up in a St Kilda alley with some scumbag. Too stoned to recognise me. I went home, grabbed a few armfuls of her stuff, drove straight back, and dumped it beside her. The rest's history.'

'Do you know where she went?'

'Nah. Probably back to New Zealand. If she lasted that long.'

Raf thought about that. Marnie never expressed a desire to look up her mother. *Probably a good thing,* he thought. There was an unspoken bond between father and daughter. Something he'd never shared with either of his parents. His mother had been too busy managing her young family, and the only sign of affection he could recall getting from his father was as a seven-year-old when they set out on a day's fishing. Before the bombs started. He wondered if things would have been different if his older brother, laid up in bed at the time, had accompanied them. *Probably,* he thought. *Hassim was clearly Dad's favourite. He and his sisters may as well have not existed.*

Not once had Raf regretted his decision to leave. Family members had made no attempts to contact him after he'd joined the gang. But that went both ways. The truth was, he'd moved on long ago. They were no more than a long distant memory, like snapshots destroyed by fire. Over time, Theo became the father he'd never had. They'd kept their rival gang relationship quiet and formed a successful partnership doing jobs on the side.

¶

It was 5:30 p.m. when they pulled up at the small motor inn at Parkes. Raf and Nadim hadn't stayed in this large town for some time and never at this motel. They alternated routes to avoid suspicion when they travelled north for the drug deals, conscious of their Middle Eastern appearance and the battered van that stood out like an albino among the utes, four-wheel drives and trucks parked outside the shops. Angelina and Raf stayed in the car while Nadim entered the office to check-in.

'I told him we were leaving at six in the morning, so we're to drop our keys in the box outside the door.'

Raf nodded and turned to Angelina. 'I noticed a Thai restaurant on the main drag. Will that do?'

'Yeah. Sounds good,' Angelina said. They'd stopped for

lunch hours ago, and the white bread chicken sandwich oozing with mayonnaise was hardly substantial, let alone enjoyable.

'I'll get Nadim to some order take away, then. Let him know what you want.'

Despite her naps along the way, Angelina felt weary, and after dinner and a hot shower, she fell into bed and woke up with the TV still blaring at 5 a.m.

9

They were on their way by 6 a.m. An hour out of town, Nadim stopped on a remote stretch of road under a clump of gum trees. Angelina leaned forward and enquired, 'Why are we stopping here?'

'To change number plates. Car regos are recorded at every check-in,' Raf explained.

She nodded, suitably impressed. In many ways, Raf handled things in the same manner that Nic had. Little as she would have admitted it a year ago, there were things she could not deal with on her own. She was in too deep …

It was another ten-hour journey ahead, and Angelina had no option but to sit back and suck it up. With a fully charged phone, she inserted her ear pods and tapped on the music streaming channel.

To Raf and Nadim, the long trip was nothing new. They made the journey three to four times a year, depending on the timing of the drug drop, in the trusted old, dark van which served as a pick-up vehicle for the drugs in North Queensland.

An hour into the journey, Raf turned to Nadim and remarked, 'My turn to drive.'

'You're not usually this keen,' came the instant quip.

The conversation resumed in Arabic.

'Yeah, well, seeing as this trip's my last, I may as well take advantage. It's not often we get to go in style like in this baby.'

'Fuck, yeah. At least I'll get to drive it back to Melbourne. Pity the two bastards lumped with taking the van back. My back kills for days after I drive that thing. Have you heard word of when they're replacing it?'

'Nope, but don't hold your breath, mate.' Raf was silent for a few moments then grinned.

'What's funny?'

Raf nodded towards the back seat. 'Just thinking how she would have made the trip in the van.'

'I hate to think.' Nadim reached for a packet of chewing gum from the console and popped several pieces in his mouth. 'Just as well she's got the money to make things easy on herself. Where do you think she gets it from?'

Raf shrugged. 'I couldn't care less. She's my ticket out of here, and if she wants to keep things secret, that suits me fine.'

Nadim nodded. He suspected much more had taken place before collecting the pair at Queenscliff. But he knew better than to pry and changed the subject. 'So, do you know who's replacing you in Melbourne?' he asked.

'Ziad, probably.'

Nadim frowned.

Raf was quick to take note. 'You two don't get on?'

'He can be an arrogant bastard, that's all.'

Raf made no comment, despite sharing similar senti-ments. 'Just remember, if he gets the job you will need to find some middle ground.'

Nadim ran a hand across his head. 'Yeah, I'm aware of that.'

Raf paused for a moment and said, 'Would you be inter-ested in joining me in Manila then, if an opening comes up?'

'Yeah, you bet I would.' The words lifted Nadim's spir-its. He learned all there was to know from his Melbourne counterpart and approached the job with the same sense of professionalism. There'd never been a cross word between them. Raf's presence would be sorely missed.

'I'll see what I can do.'

'That'd be great. Thanks.'

Nadim would face none of Raf's obstacles in getting to Manila. There were no convictions, no arrests. All it would take was a set of false papers, and he could fly straight out. There were no ties. No close relationships.

For a moment, his mind became giddy at the prospect. A new start, far away from the ever-vigilant eyes of the drug enforcement authorities. A release from the loathsome prob-ability of working alongside Ziad.

But everything hinged on Raf's safe arrival, something he'd taken for granted to this point.

Suddenly, his mind turned to what lay ahead for his

counterpart in the coming hours and his stomach clenched into a tight ball. The journey from the remote Queensland airstrip to PNG was fraught with danger. Flying below the radar at such alarmingly low altitudes. If Raf was fearful, he showed no signs of it. Nadim cast a quick glance in the rear vision mirror. *And what about you?* he wondered. *Do you have any idea what you're in for?*

Forcing such thoughts from his mind, he pulled over to the side of the road. 'Your turn to drive, then. Wake me up when we get to Roma, and I'll drop by the supermarket for supplies. Do you think she'll come at a roast chook, rolls and salad for dinner?'

'She'll have to,' Raf said. They'd be arriving late at their final night's accommodation in Injune, a small country town, with no guarantees of food places open at that hour.

8

For Angelina, the final two days' travel was insufferably long. Only so much reading and listening to live-streaming music was possible, and sleep mainly was in brief snatches.

The monotonous boom of rap music that came with the regularity of a metronome from the front, despite her noise-cancelling earbuds, became a sore test of her patience. *Can't you two come up with something different, for Christ's sake?* she thought.

She'd long ago given up staring out the window at the endless miles of parched, shimmering plains, gum forests, and the occasional shed and windmill. Even the picturesque hilly country regions with quaint towns nestled below had lost her interest.

If I ever set sight on another country town or road train, or step inside a crappy three-star motel again I'll go nuts, she muttered between gritted teeth and impatiently tapped the next playlist.

The pair in front seemed oblivious to the tedium of the long journey. Apart from turning now and then to enquire how things were and explaining what lay ahead, they seemed content in their own company, striking up the occasional conversation in Arabic.

She was past caring …

Raf had stuck to his end of the bargain and steered well clear of personal questions. Nadim likewise. Saved having to come up with a swag of lies.

Only when they left outback Queensland, headed towards the tropics, did Angelina's spirits lift, and she made the first effort to strike up a conversation.

'Do you two come up this way much?'

'Mainly when there's a drug drop,' Raf responded.

'So, do you know when this one's taking place?'

Raf shook his head. 'It'll depend on the weather. I'll let you know.'

Angelina nodded. 'And the place you two are staying? Is it far from mine?'

'Around a forty-five-minute drive.'

Raf ruminated on the gang's fibro house that had served them well since its purchase three years prior. Set on a large block, it was screened from the road by a thick tangle of tropical foliage. An old ute parked out the back served as their vehicle during their stay. It was also used to transport drums of AV gas to the airstrip to refuel the small plane that brought in the drugs from PNG. Usually, four gang members stayed there at one time. He and Nadim oversaw the PNG drug-drop operations and the Syrians, Ziad and Omair facilitated the drugs' distribution from the Cairns hinterland to the streets of Melbourne and Sydney.

Conditions in the house were rudimentary, and with only themselves to clean up, its interior was far from ideal. But there was a fridge and air-conditioner that worked. That was the main thing.

Other gang members had access to the facility between drug drops, but only those seeking a week or so of fishing or a boozy weekend away took advantage of it. None dared subject their wives or partners to such substandard conditions.

'So, what's the go from here?' Angelina was used to being given information in small slabs and only when asked. It seemed to be Raf's way.

'We'll drop you off at your accommodation in Trinity Beach,' he said over his shoulder, 'then head to our place. You've already been checked in by Ziad – he's from our gang as well. When we get closer, I'll text him to drop off the key.'

'And will I be seeing you before we fly out?'

Raf shook his head, glad she had her own accommodation, leaving him free to focus on other things. The thought of her staying with them for a week, possibly two, didn't bear thinking about. There were no guarantees about what the uncouth Syrian pair might say or do, particularly after a late-night binge drinking session. Or something more potent, perhaps. He'd often wondered whether the burly, bearded Ziad and his companion siphoned off part of their ill-gotten gains for personal use. There'd been no attempts by the two to conceal the footage of their benders in noisy nightclubs. Proving where the white stuff came from was another matter altogether. But if his suspicions proved correct, the pair were heading for an early demise. Raf had seen that many times over. No gang member was indispensable.

Drugs. Something Raf and Nadim steered well clear of. They'd witnessed the effects far too often. Nonetheless, the irony of what they did for a living was not lost on them.

Raf was used to living life on a knife's edge and accepted the dangers that came with it. But his perspective changed when Marnie entered his life. The thought of moving into a house surrounded by high walls and CCTV cameras, not knowing who was in the car parked on the street when venturing out, didn't bear thinking about.

All the more reason to exit the drugs scene once he was settled in Manila, and press his case to set up the importing of illegal steroids into Australia. With Theo's first-hand experiences of the industry and a well-devised plan, there was no reason it couldn't become a highly lucrative business.

¶

It was dark when Nadim drove through the main street of Trinity Beach. The town, located twenty kilometres north of Cairns, was smaller than Angelina expected, set along a small stretch of sandy beach framed by coconut and almond trees. It was difficult to envisage the place being a mere twenty-minute drive from the bustling CBD of Cairns.

'Who lives here?' Angelina enquired.

'Locals, mainly, in search of a more laid-back life near the beach,' Raf said. 'But that's all about to change.'

'What do you mean?'

'It's like everywhere else, I s'pose. When you see the place in daylight, you'll find holiday apartment blocks and resorts going up all over the place. Before too long, it'll be unrecognisable.'

'A bit like where I come from,' she said. The words came out before she had time to stop herself.

Nadim shot Raf a sidelong glance.

Angelina's apartment sat three streets back from the beach. It was one of sixteen self-contained apartments in the complex, set within well-tended tropical gardens graced by three elegant palms and a saltwater lap pool, culminating in a shallow, fenced-off pool for children.

'Wait here while I get the key.' Raf climbed out and headed to the passenger side of the old ute parked on the street.

Angelina followed Raf along the path to the main building and took the lift to the third floor. Her apartment was the furthest along. Not many people were about, but she noted beach towels draped over balconies and parted curtains in rooms.

The sea air was warm and balmy, as Angelina had hoped, and she gave her tight shoulders a few rolls with a contented sigh of anticipation.

'I think you'll be happy with the place,' Raf said, as though reading her mind when he inserted the key card; the door clicked open. Inside, the air-conditioner was already on.

'Ziad stopped by the supermarket for some basic supplies in case you were after an early night, but the supermarket's open till late if you want to head out for anything else. It's not large but should stock most of what you need. If not, there's a pharmacy, bakery and an assortment of shops in town.'

She nodded.

'Remember, this is a small place. You don't want to make your face too familiar. Go out only when you have to.'

'Yeah, I plan to,' she said.

After Raf left, Angelina took a look around. The contemporary, one-bedroom apartment was compact but airy, its white walls adorned with colourful, tropical murals, grey hybrid timber flooring and teal furnishings.

The well-equipped, self-contained kitchen comprised a cooktop, oven and microwave, and stone bench tops with pull-out drawers. No need to eat out. In the living area was a large flat-screen TV with Foxtel and wi-fi, and outside, a private balcony. *Time should pass quickly enough.*

After a shower and a change of clothes, Angelina stretched her legs by walking to the supermarket for a few extra supplies for dinner and breakfast the following day. Better to keep shopping to a minimum. She could be up and gone on any given day.

A few hours later, she settled on the sofa with a beef stir-fry and wine purchased from a nearby bottle shop. *That's more like it,* she thought, after days of unappetising food from plastic containers and brown-paper bags. She hoped she would never again have to consume a white roll filled with plastic cheese and processed meat. Sometimes, there'd been no alternative.

Given Raf's propensity for a healthy diet and exercise, she was sure he would have shared her sentiments. Yet she never heard him complain. She had a new-found respect for the man whose rough exterior belied the intelligence and professionalism he'd shown to this point. If the way he handled the boat explosion and the ensuing escape was an indication of things to come, she was in safe hands. Another thing, he displayed no signs of sexual intent whatsoever. A refreshing change.

9

Angelina was faithful to her word and avoided going out in public wherever possible. Long walks were restricted to early mornings or after dark. There was a small day spa and beauty salon, alongside a smattering of designer beachwear shops along the esplanade, which she would have frequented under normal circumstances. It didn't matter. She'd have the biggest splurge once they reached Manila.

Raf messaged her daily through an encrypted app, but there was no news of the drugs drop for another five days. Meanwhile, the twenty-nine-degree days were a welcome relief from the bout of relentless cold winds that had swept through Docklands before she departed. It wasn't hard to settle into a laid-back lifestyle, clad in shorts and T-shirts or swimsuit and sarong. She would have liked a wider variety from which to choose, but the journey ahead limited her to the basics.

She did twice daily laps in the pool, tucking her hair under a swim cap. The wig was used only to venture outside. It felt restrictive and annoying, like hands constantly pressing down on her head, but there was no choice but to get used to it. Life in Manila would change all that, she reasoned.

North Queensland's rainy season was yet to come, and temperatures remained temperate. Angelina enjoyed drifting off to sleep with only a sheet as a cover for the gentle breeze wafting through the louvre windows.

9

The text came through late morning: *leaving tomorrow morning at four.*

'You've got to be kidding me, Raf!' muttered Angelina, with a roll of her eyes.

I'll be ready, she texted back.

At least she'd have the day to give the place a last-minute clean and purchase the list of items Raf said she'd need: insect repellent, extra sunscreen, rubber-soled shoes and seasickness tablets.

g

At precisely 4 a.m., a set of headlights appeared in the car park. Angelina gathered her things, locked the door behind her and headed down to the ground floor, dropping the key card in the box on the wall and stepping out into the balmy night air.

In place of the dark-grey SUV was an old black van, engine still running. Angelina was far from impressed.

'You didn't tell me we'd be leaving in this,' she complained to Raf as he reached for her gear to put in the back.

'Yeah, well it'll only be for a couple of hours.'

Nadim gave her a quick nod of greeting as he changed spots to join the driver while Raf climbed in beside her in the back. Despite the wound-down windows, a culmination of bad breath, cigarette and body odour clung to the interior. Angelina's nose crinkled in disgust as she fastened her seatbelt, kicking an empty bottle and food container aside underfoot as she did so. Raf introduced her to the driver, whose Middle-Eastern-sounding name she didn't bother to take note of.

'By the way, you look totally different minus the beard,' she said to Raf, as the van took off.

He gave a shrug. 'That was the plan.'

'I don't mind it, actually,' she remarked. 'It suits you.'

There was no response.

From the outset, the trip was bumpy and uncomfortable. There was little she could do but ride out the jerks and jolts in the darkness, having put aside all thoughts of the nap she'd hoped for. She was already bleary-eyed and feeling the effects of just a few hours' sleep, despite turning in early the previous night. The group conversed among themselves in Arabic, but that was what she had come to expect. She no longer cared.

The early morning light was just beginning to peep through the cloud cover when they turned into the remote, sealed, worn runway. Set in the middle of parched grasslands against a backdrop of tree-covered hills, the airstrip was situated two kilometres from a century-old, once prosperous zinc town of just 250 residents. It served to drop off food and supplies or bring tourists to explore the nearby iconic limestone caves.

The six-seater Cessna, twin-engine 402C, was already awaiting them on the runway when they entered the airfield. Nadim backed the van up to the cargo hold, and they scrambled out. A white ute pulled up alongside, carrying six 44-gallon drums of AV gas purchased the previous day under the pretext of refuelling the light plane of a large cattle property. Raf grabbed their luggage from the van and gestured for her to stay put. Everything after that seemed to happen with lightning speed. Rushed. Urgent. The fuel was unloaded, the plane refuelled in preparation for the return journey, and the empty drums tossed in the back of the ute. From then on, it was all shouts and action, done with the expert precision of a team familiar with the process. The van's back seat was slammed down, and a human assembly line of hands passed the packages of cocaine and cash from the aircraft's cargohold into the van, then covered with a thick tarpaulin. The driver of the ute, whom Angelina never got to meet, secured the empty drums with ropes and took off.

Meanwhile, Raf and the other two remained huddled for a few minutes, deep in conversation. Nadim jumped into the van beside the driver, who fired up the engine and took off for the drop-off point in Atherton, where the drugs would be offloaded into another vehicle and taken to Melbourne and Sydney for distribution.

Raf returned hurriedly and indicated with a wave of his

hand to board the plane. The rancid-sweet gasoline smell of aviation fuel hung heavy in the air and lingered in the cabin as they made their way inside, causing Angelina to frown. Raf was quick to take note.

'You'll find it will disappear after take-off,' he said.

It had better, she thought, irritably, *bad luck if I was an asthmatic!*

The thickset, middle-aged PNG pilot climbed into the cockpit soon afterwards.

'All set to go?' he asked, turning around to face them.

They nodded.

'There's an Esky down the back with cold drinks, sandwiches and snacks. Help yourself at any time. It's a long time before we get there, remember.'

'I thought all of this would have gone on in the middle of the night,' Angelina said to him as they buckled their seatbelts.

'Are you kidding? You obviously don't know Papua New Guinea,' he said over his shoulder. 'Attempting to fly over the Owen Stanleys at night would be suicidal. Ask any pilot.'

Angelina had already been given a fair idea of what to expect from Theo. The tiny plane would fly at an altitude of less than a thousand feet to avoid radar detection before landing at Wau, a makeshift grass runway in a dense rainforest, which was a three-and-a-half-hour drive from Lae, their stopover point.

'The pilot's experienced at this sort of thing, right?' she was quick to ask Theo.

'Yeah. He's been flying over New Guinea for twenty-five years, from what Raf said,' he assured her.

'So how often do the drug drops take place?'

'Who knows,' Theo responded with a shrug. 'That's Raf's business, not mine.'

She would have liked to know much more. Out of curiosity, if nothing else. As she looked around the pokey cabin, not much bigger than the van she'd just travelled in, she suddenly felt very uneasy as the pilot gave the plane full throttle, and it headed down the runway, beginning its ascent into the early morning sky.

She'd not stopped to think of the consequences of such a perilous journey until the small aircraft hit its first bout of turbulence an hour into the flight. The ramifications of what might happen should they crash, assuming they survived, was sobering, sending her heart racing and stomach into spasms.

No way of knowing what Raf was thinking. His face betrayed nothing.

Like it or not, they were in the lap of the gods, with hours to go. With her breathing all but stopped, she closed her eyes, took a few deep inhalations, and focused her attention on a yoga mantra.

¶

The makeshift airstrip was set in a clearing in a seemingly impenetrable dense forest. Not that Angelina could make out anything when she peered down into the pockets of fog as the pilot circled the tiny airstrip to check that all was clear, and then prepared to land. They'd been warned of a bumpy landing, and Angelina braced herself as the plane thumped and bounced along the airstrip and came to a halt. She squeezed her eyes tight for a few moments with an inward sigh of relief.

It took all her will not to rush off the plane and kiss the tarmac with relief.

The pilot motioned for them to get out and pointed to where a PMV was parked, its driver leaning against the door of the dilapidated minibus, blowing rings of smoke into the late afternoon air.

A cacophony of insects buzzed and thrummed as they alighted the plane. Birds shrieked and, in the distance, a constant, low chirrup of frogs could be heard. The scents of damp soil, rotting leaves, and fallen branches hit their nostrils. This was a place where bodies could be disposed of, never to be found.

The pilot opened the cargo hold to retrieve their bags and then shook their hands.

'Thanks,' Raf told him. 'You guys have a far from an easy job. Don't know how you do it.'

The pilot gave him a hearty slap on the back and said, 'You get used to it. So, are you both returning soon to Australia?'

'Not sure,' Raf said, his expression guarded.

'Well, if we don't meet again, good luck to you both.'

As Raf and Angelina approached the PMV, the driver

stubbed the butt out with his boot and stepped over to meet them, introducing himself as Kut. He was lean, no older than his twenties, dressed in a khaki shirt, knee-length pants and thongs. As he reached to take her hand, Angelina could detect a whiff of marijuana. *We've made it this far,* she thought grimly, trying not to dwell on the journey ahead.

Kut wrenched the back door open and motioned them to climb inside, where the seats had been removed and replaced with a wooden bench to each side. A crate was fastened to the driver's seat for their luggage.

Angelina turned to Raf with a groan. 'Tell me this is not happening.'

'Makes our old van look like a limo, hey?'

There was no response.

Raf threw their bags in the crate and sat on one side and she opposite, silent and fuming. A bright spotted lizard suddenly came from nowhere, skittering across the floor, over her feet and under the driver's seat. 'What the fuck!' She jumped with a start.

'You get used to it,' the driver said with a grin over his shoulder as he fastened his seatbelt and turned on the ignition. 'Them lizards, they're everywhere in these parts.' He allowed the vehicle to idle for a minute or two, then swung around in an arc and headed off in the opposite direction.

Little was spoken for quite some time as the vehicle bounced and jolted its way along the road between Wau and Lae, kicking up clumps of mud from the previous night's tropical deluge. Meanwhile, the driver remained focused on what lay ahead, making numerous last-minute swerves to avoid potholes, ruts or fallen branches.

'And this is the main highway, for God's sake,' Angelina remarked.

There was a nod from Raf. 'From what I've been told, millions have been put aside for reconstruction. But nothing seems to happen. They just keep patching up the same stretches. Lucky we're making this trip now, actually.'

'Why's that?'

'Well, it's the rainy season in another two months, and they say much of this road gets washed away.'

Angelina glanced over her shoulder at the road's crumbling edges. She could see glimpses of the steep drop below between the drifts of fog, and quickly looked away, fingers vice-like around the seat.

'Does the road stay this rough from now on?' she asked quickly.

'I'm not sure. It'll be dark for the last hour or so of the journey, so we'll just need to hang on and ride things out,' he said.

Angelina frowned. She didn't know how much more jarring and lurching her body could take. Already, there were splinters in the palms of her hands from the rough wooden bench. She could only hope there was a first-aid kit at their destination. And then there was the evening's plummeting temperatures to come. All she had was a waterproof jacket, and it was hardly warm.

'Kut's been given instructions to take us somewhere for

dinner,' Raf continued, 'then we'll head to a house used by the gang, and in the morning we'll be taken to the port.'

At 7:30 p.m., Kut drove them through the outskirts of Lae. It was hard to see much through the constant drizzling rain, but Angelina cared little what the place was like. All she wanted was a decent meal and a bed to crash on.

The Asian restaurant sat in the commercial area of town and was packed with diners as the waiter ushered them through to one of the remaining tables. It seemed as if as many plastic tables and chairs as possible had been packed into the small space. With voracious appetites after eating nothing substantial for the past twenty-four hours, Angelina and Raf ordered a selection of chicken, beef and pork dishes with rice from the Chinese and Malaysian menu — much to the delight of Kut, who wasn't used to free meals, particularly one so sumptuous.

9

The gang's grey, fibro house was built on concrete pylons above a bare patch of earth, under which, from what she could make out in the headlights, served as a garage-cum-storage dump littered with boxes of all shapes and sizes, and bits of rusted machinery. Steps led to a porch with a rotting rail.

Raf pulled the bags from the crate with one easy movement and waited for Kut to open the back door. Crouched over in the darkness, they edged their way towards the door.

But as Angelina stepped outside, her head slammed into the door jamb above.

'Shit, that hurt!' she exclaimed,

Raf swung around. 'You okay?'

'I'll live,' she muttered, rubbing her forehead gingerly.

The driver had already received payment for the journey, but Raf discreetly slipped a roll of notes in his hand as they departed. The young man nodded a few times quickly. 'Thank you, my friend. You call me any time you are in Lae, okay? I make sure you get looked after.' He pulled a card from his pocket and pressed it into Raf's hand.

'I'll do that,' Raf said.

As the PMV backed out of the driveway and disappeared, a dim light appeared under the house. A man approached.

'That'll be Itu,' Raf explained. 'He'll be taking us to the terminal in the morning.'

'Welcome to Lae.' The man's voice was deep and resonant. After a quick shake of hands and introductions, he said, 'You must be tired after your journey. You've eaten, I hope?'

They nodded.

'Good. Good. I am not much of a cook,' he said with a chuckle. 'You don't have to be at the port until 10:30, so there'll be the chance of an extra few hours of sleep.'

'Sounds good,' Raf said.

'Well, follow me.' He headed towards the stairs.

The house was utilised solely as a place to stay when the gang's drugs were due to arrive in Lae's port, smuggled through in shipping containers. For the remainder of the year, it was idle.

Raf wondered what Angelina's reaction would be when she stepped inside. He'd not set eyes on the place but he had inside knowledge from an Australian counterpart who stayed there when he visited the country.

Raf half expected to find the place trashed when they arrived, as it sat in a notoriously dangerous part of town among a sprawl of squatter settlements on the fringe. Here it was each man for himself, and brawls, violence and murders were common; gangs ruled and machete-wielding men in balaclavas patrolled the streets at night. It hardly mattered. The tacky refurbishments lining its walls could be replaced at little cost, and there was nothing of value inside.

Raf had been uncomfortable about bringing Angelina into such a high-risk area, even for a few hours. He was adept in one-to-one combat, two at a pinch, but there was no guarantee he could protect her. The rape of young women was a common rite of passage amongst gang initiations, with no one spared.

We'll be out of here in a matter of hours, he reminded himself. But it did little to allay his fears.

If they'd stayed in Lae more than a night, he would have booked rooms at a reputable hotel close to the commercial precinct, where it was relatively safe for tourists during the day. But night time was a different scenario altogether. Visitors were advised to never leave their rooms and to answer the door to no one.

It wasn't until they stepped inside the well-lit living area that Angelina got to see Itu clearly for the first time; a wiry man in his sixties, with dark-brown skin, short grey, frizzy hair, wearing a grey grandpa shirt over navy cargo pants and white thongs.

'I stopped by the supermarket along the way,' he said with a grin of teeth stained from chewing betel nuts. 'Would you like some coffee?'

Raf looked at Angelina, and she gave a nod.

'Yeah. Sounds good, Itu, then we'll head off for an early night.'

He nodded. 'The beds are already made, and there are towels in the cupboards.'

Half an hour later, he showed them over the house. Angelina expected the interior to be ordinary but not run-down like this. The place was riddled with dust, and the remaining nylon curtains faded and torn. It wouldn't have surprised her to find no running water or electricity. The pokey bathroom and toilet crammed at the end of the hall-way looked like an afterthought. She felt sweaty and clammy after the long journey and could have done with a decent shower, but there was no way she was about to step into the tiny cubicle with its mould patches. Raf's expression told her he shared her sentiments.

Angelina's bedroom was nearest to the bathroom. She said goodnight, fetched her tote bag, and closed the door. A single, iron-framed bed was against the concrete wall, cov-ered with an old, thin bedspread; beside the bed was a small bedside table and a locker-style, chipped wardrobe. An image came to mind of the conditions she'd been forced to endure in her uncle's gang headquarters. At least that place was given a regular clean and had a functioning air-conditioner.

Her clammy underwear, long pants and shirt were stripped off and hung over the wardrobe door, in the hope they'd be sufficiently dry to pack the next morning. She slipped on a pair of undies and T-shirt. Pulling back the bedspread, she bent over to whiff the sheets. They appeared all right, but she thought, *Who knew when they'd last been changed? More to the point, who'd lain amongst them.* With a shudder, she forced the thought from her mind and covered the sheets with a pair of towels from the stack in the cupboard before climbing into bed. Despite her jetlagged state, she found it impossible to get to sleep. The whine of a lone mosquito, Itu's intermittent snores, and the lumpy mattress had Angelina thumping the pillow in frustration. Sheer exhaustion finally allowed a few hours of sleep.

The early morning sun beating down on her face woke her.

Padding barefoot down to the tiny bathroom, she had a wee, then splashed cold water over her face, glancing at her puffy eyes in the cracked mirror and trying not to dwell on it. A liberal blob of moisturiser and some sunscreen would have to suffice. There'd be no make-up for the next leg of the journey. *I may as well get used to it.* Not the way she dreamed of travelling. Nothing but a few changes of nondescript clothes, some exercise gear, a baseball cap, and large, dark sunglasses.

No one was up yet, so she laid on the bed, arms behind her head, waiting for the first signs of someone stirring. She frowned. Her clothes were still as damp as the night before. They would have to remain that way a little longer, stuffed in a plastic bag, until she had time to launder them.

Dressing in pants, a long shirt and sandals, she packed her things and headed for the kitchen, where Raf was filling up the jug.

'Where's Itu?' she asked.

'He's gone to pick up a vehicle. He'll be back to pick us up at 9:30.' He paused. 'So, how did you survive the night?'

'Barely.'

'Not much of a place, hey?'

'I've seen worse,' she said, managing a grin, 'but not many.'

'Do you want something to eat? There's some cereal, milk, and a loaf of bread.'

Angelina declined after glancing over the smudged benches and handful of old kitchen utensils hanging on the wall. 'I'm not hungry, but thanks anyway. Coffee will do fine.'

They sat at the kitchen table, steaming mugs in hand, concocting a story to tell those aboard. They agreed to be solo travellers with a taste for adventure who'd hooked up in Port Moresby and decided on a cargo ship journey for something different.

Angelina hoped this would prove sufficient to be left alone, acutely aware that their freedom hung in the balance. However, she had little idea of what lay in store within the confined spaces of such a ship; how much time she'd be forced to spend in the close company of others.

Raf looked surprised when she asked about the ship's

fitness facilities. 'I'm not sure,' he said. 'They might have a gym, but the ship's too small for a pool. I didn't know you were into that sort of stuff. I am as well.'

'Oh? What?'

'Weights mainly, a bit of boxing. And you?'

'I like a bit of everything actually, but running's my favourite. Do you know if it's allowed on deck?'

'Not sure. I'll find out if you want.'

'That'd be good.'

'I hope you've downloaded some movies and stuff. There's limited wi-fi, remember.'

Angelina gave a groan. 'Don't remind me.'

10

As the Toyota Landcruiser backed out onto the street, Angelina's attention was drawn towards a skinny dog covered in scabs scavenging through the contents of a nearby overturned rubbish bin. Further along, the road came the shrieks and squeals of several small children, clad in shorts and T-shirts, playing keepings off with a ball.

It was the first time she'd seen her surroundings in daylight. The houses further along the road were like the one she'd just come from: fibro or tin, built on concrete stilts, and spread evenly apart on small blocks. Nothing separated them but tropical foliage, perhaps a few strands of wire, or a high concrete wall.

Raf stole a sidelong glance at Itu during the thirty-minute trip to the port. There was much more to the man than met the eye. The veteran gang member was highly respected by his Australian counterparts. He ran a tight ship, taking no nonsense from those working under him and carrying out whatever was asked with meticulous detail. It was Nadim who'd filled Raf in on his background. Fluent in several PNG languages, Itu also had an excellent grasp of English. His father was a payroll officer in one of the country's largest stockfeed companies, and the family was constantly on the move. When Itu's mother died unexpectedly from liver complications, his father took to drinking, and it wasn't long before he began embezzling company funds to fuel his alcohol addiction. Eventually, he was found out and served a two-year stint in prison, during which time Itu and his younger two sisters were packed off to live with their aunt in Port Moresby. The thirtyish single woman meant well but didn't have the means to support them. While keeping the younger two at school, she could not keep tabs on the wayward Itu, who continually wagged school and was entrenched in a local gang by the time he'd turned fifteen. Besides a brief stint as a warehouse foreman, Itu never took on paid employment again, building his way up the ranks to become the gang's leader. Raf found himself wondering how much longer the older man could go on. Not that he was showing signs of slowing down. Raf could only hope that he didn't come to a violent end at the hands of a rival gang.

9

Lae's port was larger than Angelina had expected. With mountains as the backdrop, the harbour was dominated by cargo ships with containers of all colours, resembling a vast expanse of children's building blocks. A heavy whiff of fuel hung in the air as they climbed out of the car and said their goodbyes. Angelina was unprepared for the cool sea breeze that whipped across the terminal as they crossed the wharf, ruffling her hair and making her reach for the jacket in her tote bag. Seagulls wheeled noisily above, and in the distance a large bulk carrier was preparing to dock.

The ship they were about to board was among the smaller vessels, but carried around a thousand containers. Owned by a Chinese company, it traversed mainly between Malaysia and the Pacific regions, its officers a mixture of European nationalities, and the able-seamen mostly Filipinos.

Angelina glanced up at the drab façade and her spirits plummeted. She hoped the interior was more inspiring. At least passengers had full access to the officer amenities. *That had to count for something. Didn't it? Eleven days, that's all,* she thought. She'd been through far worse.

The large, square-faced customs official gave a perfunctory glance at their passports and waved them through. He seemed more interested in chatting with the first officer. The ship's second officer, a lean, thirtyish blonde man with a pleasant face and blue eyes, awaited them on board, dressed in a crisp white shirt with gold strip epaulettes on the shoulders. 'Welcome aboard,' he said, reaching across to shake their hands with a firm hold. 'It's Ava and Raf. Right?'

They nodded in turn.

'I'm Lars. There's just three more of you to come.' He

glanced down at the wharf and pointed. 'They're just getting their papers checked now.'

Angelina turned to watch a couple in their sixties step onto the gangplank, followed by a slim elderly man. The woman went first, plump and of average height, her orange spiked hair and heavily made-up face reminding Angelina of a parrot. She wore a tight, green T-shirt with the words 'Waikiki' and a palm tree splashed across the front, over a pair of jeans that were far too tight, all the while clutching the rail and talking over her shoulder.

Do you realise how ridiculous you look, woman? Angelina thought with a look of unconcealed disdain.

The man who'd followed her on board was somewhat taller, of solid build and with a full head of silver hair, gold-rimmed glasses, a slight moustache, and a flabby belly that protruded over the belt of his pants. He appeared totally uninterested in what his wife had to say. In fact, he looked as if he didn't want to be there at all.

A slightly built man who followed seemed to be Filipino, perhaps in his seventies.

As introductions were being made, the woman jumped in before the officer could finish. 'My real name's not Candice, you know, it's Eula, but I've always hated that name. Don't know why in God's name they called me that in the first place. My second name's Candice, and that's what I'm known as. But you can call me Candy.'

Are you for real? Angelina's mind was swamped with images of children licking large lollipops, Hershey bars, and brightly coloured skittles. *How on earth will I be able to avoid this woman,* she thought.

'We come from Dallas. That's in Texas, if you didn't know.'

The officer took one look at Angelina's expression and said hastily, 'We can discuss all that when we meet for dinner. I'll show you to your cabins and let you get settled, and then we'll meet up in an hour to take a good look around.' He translated in Filipino for the elderly man, explaining, 'Efren speaks no English. He's travelled with us before. Comes to Port Moresby every few years to visit his son.'

'Why doesn't he come by plane?' the woman asked.

'He has a fear of flying,' the officer said with accustomed patience.

'Well, he could choose a cruise ship instead.'

'You'll find Efren to be a private person, madam. Keeps to himself. Life aboard such a vessel would hardly be his style.'

She gave a shrug. 'So much nicer, that's all.' There was an awkward silence in which she realised her gaff. 'Not that I'm running this ship down, you understand,' she said with a rush, reaching for the gold chain around her neck with chubby fingers. 'In fact, we've been so looking forward to it. Something totally different.'

Angelina would have liked to hear what her husband had to say about that. He looked about as enthusiastic as she'd been when she first set eyes on the hamlet in Spain.

'None of our friends has done anything like this on their trips.' Candice patted the side of the large bag at her side. 'All captured on my camera. Hundreds of photos. Like the tree hut we slept in yonder, in the jungle. Can't wait to show the gals back home.'

Located on the starboard side of the fourth deck, the four passenger cabins had container-free views of the ocean. Each was compact but clean, comprising two single beds, inbuilt robes, a sofa, a small ensuite, and a bar fridge for tax-free drinks, against the backdrop of blue furnishings and matching carpet.

Angelina gave a sigh as she closed the cabin door and surveyed her surroundings, relieved that little could be heard of the engine room's clatter and din. Crossing to the bed, she pressed down with the palm of her hand. 'Shit. I've heard of firm mattresses, but this one takes the cake!' she grumbled.

They were met an hour later by Lars at the stairway near their cabins. 'I hope you found your cabins comfortable,' he said. 'A steward will attend to your rooms and provide fresh bedding and towels. Speak to him if there's anything you require.'

The ship proved more extensive than expected. Lars took them up and down stairways to the different levels, pointing out the bridge, engine rooms, working areas, laundry and shop.

'So, where do we eat?' Candice asked.

'In the officers' dining area, where we're heading next. It's your choice if you wish to dine with the officers or among yourselves. We find it's usually a bit of both. However, tonight being the first night, we'll dine together at the captain's table.'

The room consisted of a spacious carpeted area with groups of evenly spaced tables in settings of four, aqua furnishings and matching curtains. Adjoining the dining area was a shared lounge area for officers and passengers, with a small library, TV, DVD and CD player.

'The officers often hold card games in this area after dinner, in which you're welcome to participate,' Lars explained. 'Well, that's about it. I'll leave you to return to your cabins. Tax-free drinks and cigarettes are available at the shop, but remember, smoking is prohibited in cabins and restricted to the smoking room that you'll find on the next level down.'

Harvey watched his wife puff and pant as she struggled down the two stairways to their cabin, thinking about her long overdue hip operation that was being stubbornly avoided. *Lot of meals ahead, my dear,* he thought, with a wry smile.

¶

The tables had been joined for the traditional opening night dinner, covered with a white linen cloth and set tastefully. Despite the occasion being marked as informal, Candice arrived in a tailored dress, jacket, and high-heeled sandals, which to her displeasure, she was asked to remove and leave outside the door.

'It's a no-shoes rule on all carpeted areas of the ship, I'm afraid, ma'am, unless they're rubber-soled,' the officer pointed out.

'I told you, didn't I?' Harvey remarked. The prominent

sign on the cabin door was the first thing he noticed on arrival.

'Oh, shut up,' she hissed as she struggled to keep her balance, one hand on the door jam and the other fumbling for the tiny clasp on the sandal.

Angelina smirked.

As the couple crossed the room to the table, she couldn't help thinking how ridiculous the woman appeared in her bare feet, pearls, and caked-on make-up. It brought to mind glammed-up women on race day after a few too many drinks, stilettos in hand instead of on their feet. She had to admit the sandals had improved the woman's appearance somewhat. The extra height masked the chubby stature and thick ankles.

'Howdy, y'all,' greeted the Texan woman, glancing at the assembled guests as she pulled out a chair. 'I'm Candy, and this is ma husband, Harvey.'

Angelina stiffened. This was about to become a long night. But things turned out to be better than expected. The conversation was light, and the four-course meal satisfying and meticulously presented. Over dinner, guests were asked about their backgrounds. Angelina said she'd been in marketing for the past eight years and was taking a well-earned break, while Raf mentioned working alongside his father in the family business.

'So, what sort of marketing were you into?' Candice turned to Angelina.

'Imported coffee. Selling to delicatessens, food emporiums, that sort of thing.'

'Did your company operate internationally?'

'Yeah.'

'Oh? Well, you probably deal with Lewis-Tremayne. They're an American company who have a string of department stores with fine food sections.'

'Probably.'

'You *have* heard of them,' pushed Candice.

'Yeah. I've heard of them.'

'Great. We'll have to get together and compare notes. I worked for them for years.'

Candice caught the eye of the officer sitting opposite. 'And Efren? What's his story?'

'Efren's from a farming background,' The officer explained. 'He's lived on the same property for forty years.'

'Does he have a wife?'

'No, she died some years back.'

'Wa'll, now that's a pity,' she said, picking up the remaining piece of roll on her plate and popping it in her mouth.

'So what do you do for a living, Harvey?' the captain asked.

'Well, it so happens, I'm retired,' he began in a slow drawl.

'That's not what the captain asked,' his wife intervened. She turned to the group. 'My husband was an engineer at one of Houston's biggest power plants.' She neglected to tell them that this was twenty years ago. Despite her nagging, he'd made no effort to upgrade his qualifications and had been relegated to Dispatch, where, being the lazy sort, he happily ended his career. Harvey Lewis-Carter seemed not the least perturbed by his wife's irritating manner, which had become more abrasive as the years wore on. He'd married for money thirty years go. Candice was the only child of a wealthy couple and the sole heir to their estate.

After her mother's death from cancer ten years ago, Candice pandered to her father's every need and when his health showed signs of deterioration, she and Harvey moved in to be closer to him, much to Harvey's glee. He quickly adjusted to his life of luxury in the family mansion, waiting for his father-in-law to die.

All the while, he played up to his wife's whims, allowing himself to be dominated while appeasing her sexual desires, happy they were now few and far between these days. In her younger days Candice had been an eye-catching beauty with a trim figure from years of gymnastics. But now he found her flabby body, puffy ankles, and double chin a turn-off. It mattered little. He'd been making discreet visits to call girls and an occasional massage parlour.

He did not know that Candice had been having him traced for the past three years, gathering information for lawyers to prepare for the messy divorce that would unfold the moment her father died. The moment the millions came into her hot little hands. She had the grounds to sue under claims of emotional distress caused by his degrading sex acts on the side. But there was more. The thousands of dollars that her husband had filtered from one of her accounts over the years.

Harvey had been blessed with considerable good looks

and body, attributes that attracted him to her in the first place. His startling blue eyes and a thick crop of wavy hair were all that appealed now. A once taut body was now suffering from a decade of dining out on rich food and expensive wines.

There was a prolonged silence.

Attempting to diffuse the tension in the air, the captain raised his glass and proposed a toast. Once the complimentary drinks flowed, the conversation relaxed once again until Candice turned to Angelina, with a nod towards Raf, and said with a wink, 'So, tell me something, sweetie, are you two an item?'

'No, we are not!' Angelina exclaimed angrily, surprising the assembled group, who'd barely heard from her to that point.

'We're both travelling alone.' Raf was quick to cover up. 'Just hooking up for a few trips. A safety in numbers thing.'

Candice nodded approvingly. 'Now that's what I call sensible. Especially in this part of the world.'

Angelina fought to hold her composure, willing dessert to arrive, so they could make their escape.

Once dinner ended, the American couple quickly accepted the offer to join the officers for cards. At the same time, Angelina and Raf made polite excuses and Efren had already turned in for an early night.

'I know, I know, I shouldn't have snapped at her like that,' Angelina said as they stepped outside. 'But honestly —'

'I doubt she even noticed,' he said.

'Maybe. But I'll try to keep my trap shut next time. Not making any promises, though.'

He grinned.

¶

'There's something about that Australian woman,' Candice remarked to her husband as she climbed into the adjoining bed and turned out the bedside light.

'What are you getting at?' It was in his best interests to indulge his wife's obsession with gossip.

'Well, her perfume, for starters. Chanel number five. It's the only one Mom ever wore. Surely you must recognise it. The house reeked of the stuff.'

'So?'

'Well, didn't those two say they were travelling on a shoe-string budget at dinner?'

'Could have been a gift,' he suggested.

'What about the questions I fired at her?'

'What about them?'

'Oh, come on Harvey, you know as well as I do, there's no such company as Lewis-Tremayne. And didn't you see how she squirmed like a rabbit when I raised the topic of marketing?'

No response.

'I tell you, she's hiding something. Harvey? Are you listening?'

There was a loud snore.

Candice lay awake for some time, arms behind her head, listening to the continual splash of water against the porthole, determined to come up with some answers by the end of the journey. Knowing everyone's business was part of her make-up, along with her three long-time friends with whom she regularly met for a game of bridge. More gossip took place than cards, of which the locals were well aware. Those new to town were under particular scrutiny. Candice pictured the faces of her friends when she boasted how she discovered what was behind the young woman on board. With considerable embellishments along the way, of course.

11

No sooner had Angelina and Raf sat down for dinner the following evening when the American couple pulled up chairs opposite, much to Angelina's annoyance. She'd hoped to be joined by a couple of officers.

'So, where are you heading to in Manila?' Candice asked, directing Harvey to order a bottle of wine on his tab.

'We're not sure at this stage,' Raf said.

'Well, make sure you look us up, you hear? We'll have to get together for a dinner.'

Pig's arse, Angelina thought, resting her elbows on the table, chin in one hand, as she looked around the room, wondering what the officers were discussing among themselves.

As the main courses were placed in front of them, Candice gave a look of approval at the generous servings. She was the only one to consume the meal in its entirety, mopping up the remains of her curry with a chunk of bread.

Only when Harvey brought up the topic of Texan gun laws did Angelina give her full attention.

'You guys are allowed to carry handguns, right?' she asked.

'Yeah. Makes things so much safer. Can't understand why you don't in your country,' Harvey drawled.

'So you both have guns?' she probed.

'You bet we do,' Candice jumped in.

Angelina suppressed a smile. *Considering how they treated each other; it was a wonder someone's head hadn't been blown off by now.*

Harvey turned his attention to Raf. 'Do you know much about guns?' he asked.

'Nope. I've been working too hard building up the family business to think about that sort of stuff.'

The American man seemed satisfied with the answer. 'And you?' He turned to Angelina.

'Me? I've never stepped outside an office, let alone been anywhere near a gun.'

Dessert was apple pie and cream, devoured by Candice with the same enthusiasm as the first course. She glanced at Angelina's untouched bowl.

'Aren't you going to eat that?'

Angelina shook her head. 'I don't do desserts. You can have it if you wish.' She pushed the bowl across the table. Candice's eyes lit up as she pushed her empty one aside. 'Don't mind if I do. Can't let a good thing go to waste. You should reconsider your views on desserts, you know. You could do with some extra meat on your bones. Men like a woman with curves.'

After dinner, the couple pulled up chairs at the table

where four officers had settled for a game of cards. Angelina noticed several stiffen as she and Raf made their way to the door.

¶

With a few private words to the first officer the following day and one of her smiles, it was guaranteed that she and Raf would have a table to themselves at meal times from there on.

She felt pity for the officers who dutifully took turns filling the two vacant spaces at the American couple's table. Candice's incessant diatribe on American politics, in which those around her seemed to show little interest, irked Angelina no end. Grabbing her glass of wine and taking a swig, she leaned forward and hissed to Raf, 'I swear to God, if we'd had to put up with her for another meal time, I'd have throttled her with my bare hands.'

He grinned at her.

Meanwhile, Efren occupied his usual table in the corner with his book, oblivious to his surroundings as he waited for his meal to arrive.

¶

In the days to come, Angelina and Raf distanced themselves from the American couple whenever possible. But Candice seemed to materialise from nowhere when least expected.

She cornered Angelina one morning as she was about to put her clothes in the washing machine. 'So, what are you up to today?'

'I'm about to head off to the gym soon for an hour or so. You're welcome to join me if you want.'

There was a derisive snort.

'And you two?'

'I'm on my way to the lounge to select a DVD, and Harvey's in the cabin watching some movie he downloaded before we left.'

Angelina wondered what kind of movie …

¶

An hour later, when Angelina returned to take her washing from the dryer, she was aware of being watched. She looked up. Candice. Index finger on the camera button.

'What the hell!' she muttered, instinctively ducking her head.

The rudimentary gym, containing basic equipment including a treadmill, exercise bike, a rowing machine and various weights, was far from popular. Not surprising, given the physically demanding regimes endured by most of the crew. The officers dropped in from time to time but usually in the early hours of the morning and after dinner. Angelina and Raf soon found the best time to have the place to themselves was the afternoons.

With permission to run on the boat, so long as she wore

the required rubber-soled shoes, Angelina was quick to take advantage. The early morning jog on deck, interspersed with climbs up and down stairwells, became what she looked forward to most, having adjusted to the pitch and roll of the ship.

As she passed through the working areas below, there'd be polite nods of greeting from the able-bodied seamen, whom she half suspected had been given notice she was off-limits. Not that she didn't feel multiple eyes on her legs as she ran past in her shorts and T-shirt. The ship's circumference was more extensive than she'd envisaged, and her Fitbit indicated she'd done a considerable workout by the time she returned to her room.

Occasionally, she headed to the library or video room to escape the boredom, but only when Candice was nowhere in sight. Late mornings were the safest bet when the Texan couple spent most of their time lazing around on sun lounges, attempting to get deeper tans to their already leathery and wrinkled skin, weathered by years of excessive exposure and coconut oil. She wondered what they'd look like in another twenty years.

Haven't you two heard of skin cancer? she found herself wondering with a shake of her head as she passed.

She and Raf kept to the confines of their respective cabins as much as possible. But Angelina found the sixteen-to-twenty-four-knot journey an infuriating crawl as she propped herself up on the bed, aware of the incessant rocking, and flicking through magazines that far from passed the time. During her stay in Trinity Beach, she'd clicked on several YouTube clips of travellers extolling the merits of cargo ship travel. 'Tranquillity, at one with nature – discovering inner peace' were among the terms they came up with.

What a load of bullshit, she thought as she stared across the vast expanse of blue through the salt-smeared porthole, concurring with Candice on one point. *How could a rusted-up hulk like this be preferable to a cruise ship? Especially the latest state-of-the-art varieties that were being widely advertised.*

What she'd do right now for a bit of nightlife. Not to mention a pool, decent fitness facilities, and some mouth-watering cuisines. Her thoughts turned to the previous week's menu, which, while adequate, was becoming predictable. *Is it too hard for you guys to occasionally dish up a piece of grilled fish, wholesome salad and a bowl of yoghurt and fresh berries?* she thought irritably. Obviously, it was. She interlocked her hands beneath her head against the pillow, glancing up at the ceiling water stains she'd fixed eyes on repeatedly. And yearned for a bathtub filled with hot, scented water with bubbles, a fresh, fluffy towel, and a decent bed.

¶

Angelina was used to being aboard boats and was quick to find her sea legs, despite the ship's constant pitch and roll. However, halfway into the trip, the weather turned for the worse. Deck chairs were hurriedly brought inside, and passengers were advised to bunker down until the storm passed. When the skies finally opened, the waves became choppy, and the swell quickly intensified to five metres as cascades of angry white spray lashed decks and stairways. Below, able-bodied seamen lurched from side to side, holding onto rails, raincoats tightly zipped, rain stinging their faces as they went about their duties.

Angelina remained in her cabin as the ship lurched and rolled wildly. It wasn't long before she was sent rushing for the packet of sea-sickness tablets purchased at Trinity Beach.

Even when the storm had passed, the waters remained rough for the next twenty-four hours. It was what she'd expected, having learned from the officers that cargo ships of this vintage lacked the stabilisers of bigger ships to steady themselves in rough seas. With exercise limited, she headed for the library to look for a book. Along the way, she passed Candice, whose face was a shade of grey-green as she clutched the rail with a vice-like grip.

'Oh my gawd,' she gasped, 'nobody warned me about this. I feel like I'm about to chuck at any moment.'

'Didn't you bring any sea-sickness tablets with you?'

'I didn't think it was necessary. I've never needed them on other cruises. They've just ended up being thrown in the bin. Such a waste.'

'I've got some in my room if you like,' Angelina offered.

'Bless your heart,' she bleated. 'Can I come down right now and get them?'

'Sure. I was about to head back anyway.' Angelina led the way, listening to the woman's laboured breath as they headed towards the stairway.

The moment Angelina opened the cabin door, the woman craned her neck to take a sneak peek, but the door was firmly closed in her face. Moments later, Angelina appeared again, handing out two small white pills that Candice popped into her mouth and downed with the glass of water.

'There's four more here if you need,' Angelina pointed out a small sealed bag. 'I hope you recover soon.'

She stepped back into the cabin, closing the door behind her.

⁋

'I haven't seen Candice around for a while,' Angelina remarked to Harvey as he entered the dining room for breakfast a few days later.

'No, she's still as sick as hell. Lost her appetite altogether,' he said, adding with a smirk, 'and that's a first, I have to say.'

'Strange,' Angelina responded. 'I thought the pills I gave her would have worked by now. They did with me.'

She wondered what Candice's reaction would be if she learned that the pills she'd taken were contraceptives. *Got rid of the old cow for a few days though,* she thought.

As she watched Harvey pile his plate with a stack of pancakes from the buffet, she wondered what was going through his mind. He'd appeared bored by the entire trip, seeking ways to avoid spending time with his wife. More often than not he could be found in the smoking-room, chatting to the regularly assembled crew members or in the lounge area, mainly when Candice was in their cabin. Angelina spotted him a few times on the bridge among the officers.

She was not to know that this occurred only when things between the couple were at their worst. But there were only so many times he could do that. There were always the drinks he kept stocked in the cabin's bar fridge. And the earphones.

Angelina looked at the red veins on his cheeks and the paunch that had extended considerably since his arrival, wondering why he let himself go. He'd told them he'd been a keen sportsman in his day, baseball mainly and a stint in football. There was no reason to doubt him. His recollections as a player were too detailed to fabricate. Plus, he possessed a grid-iron player's powerful build and strong legs.

Perhaps he'd suffered a severe illness or something, she thought. More likely, he was simply lazy.

'I'm just a sports nut these days,' he told them. 'Go to every Dallas Cowboys home match and follow every other kind of sport in the meantime. Basketball, soccer, boxing. Makes no difference to me. If it's on the tele, I watch it.'

Angelina could imagine him sprawled on a couch in the early morning hours, TV remote on his stomach, eating handfuls of peanuts washed down by copious amounts of beer.

There was no mention of shared interests with his wife. *Why did people stay so long in a relationship when they clearly detested each other,* she wondered. There had to be something in it for him. She was glad she pulled the plug on things with Nic when she had the chance. Sure, the sex was good, and they had more in common than she'd had with her previous lovers. But it would never have lasted. Her relationships never did.

It mattered little. There'd never be a shortage of men in her life. She noted how the quiet, good-looking officer eyed her as she passed. She'd seen him in the gym, working out, noting his well-defined biceps and toned legs. Under different circumstances, she could have been interested.

As time wore on, card game attendances after dinner in the officers' lounge dribbled to a trickle. When Candice failed to show for dinner for the second consecutive night, the numbers almost instantaneously returned to normal. *They've probably been holed up in someone's cabin every night,* Angelina reflected.

'Do you know much about poker?' Angelina asked Raf, glancing at the assembled group.

'A bit. Why?'

'I'd like to learn how to play, that's all. Want to join in?'

He shrugged. 'Can't see why not.'

¶

Raf was working out in the gym the next day when Angelina arrived, placing a towel on the bench and stepping onto the treadmill.

'Can I ask you something?' she asked as she reached for the key.

'Yeah, what?'

'I did a bit of thinking last night while we played poker. Is your gang in Manila involved in money laundering?'

'Why?'

'I'd like to learn more about it, that's all.' She paused. 'Call it "safeguarding my interests" if you like.'

He looked at her carefully. 'I'm not sure what they're into. I'd suggest you look into the casino industry.'

'I know all that. I could do with a name or two, that's all.'

Raf went silent.

'Look, Raf, if not for you and Theo, I'd be up shit creek by now. This'd just be a one-off thing between us. I've no intention of doing the dirty on either of you if that's what you're thinking.'

He thought about that for a few moments. 'I'll see what I can find out,' he said.

9

On the final night, Candice had her camera out at dinner, snapping randomly like a member of the paparazzi. Angelina was quick to look away at the last minute when the lens was aimed in her direction, as did Raf, but she felt a sense of unease, nonetheless. *Did the woman have photos stored on her phone that we don't know about?*

There'd been no mention of social media, but other more troubling possibilities trickled to mind. *Maybe the woman was simply camera crazy,* she found herself thinking. Maybe there was nothing in it at all. Even so, there was no certainty where the photos might end up. Her chin-length wig and face devoid of make-up made her look different, but there was no disguising her striking features and olive complexion.

At the night's end, Angelina put her napkin aside and said to Raf, 'You go on ahead. I'll be down soon.'

'Okay,' he said, pulling out his chair, 'I'll see you in the morning.'

Angelina watched him go and headed to the American couple's table, where Harvey was in deep discussion with an officer over the impending Soccer World Cup final.

'Feel like a drink out on the deck, Candice?' she asked, 'It's such a nice evening.'

'Wa'll, that sounds real nice, sweetie,' Candice said, eagerly.

Angelina smiled to herself, knowing that Candice would be keen to get the information she craved.

Not long afterwards, they settled into their deck chairs in the briny, warm air, with bottles of Tequila and orange juice at their feet, paid at Candice's insistence. Angelina deflected Candice's probing questions with a barrage of questions about Texas, and Candice was more than willing to comply. Occasionally, Angelina threw in a lie or two for good measure. It mattered little. She'd make sure the American woman had no recall by morning.

Within an hour, Angelina had plied her with six liberal shots of Tequila while taking her time on the first. But Candice held her alcohol well. Only when the bottle was half empty, her words became slurred, and her eyes flickered, did Angelina rise.

'Come on, time to turn in. We have to be up early.'

She hauled the woman to her feet and placed an arm around her shoulder. 'I'll bring your bag.'

'Thanksh, sweetie.' Candice placed an arm around Angelina's waist and leaned against her, saying, 'It's been such fun. Should've done thish days ago.'

'Yeah, right,' Angelina muttered under her breath.

Manoeuvring the rolling deck and two descending stairways with the tottering, heavy woman in her arms proved more difficult than she'd envisaged. Candice's legs gave way more than once, and Angelina had to hold on with all her might to keep her upright. And that was before they reached the stairs. Not about to take chances, Angelina told her to sit on the top step and manoeuvred her down on her bottom, one stair at a time. Thump. Thump. Crash. She grinned at the spectacle unfolding before her as the gasping woman sputtered and cursed. From there, she half-carried Candice to her room and knocked on the door. When Harvey answered, Angelina pretended to stumble. 'Sorry 'bout this,' she said, feigning a hiccup, 'too mush to drink. Got carried away.'

Harvey looked at his wife with contempt. 'Don't worry about it,' he said, 'par for the course.' He managed to get her into the cabin and closed the door behind them.

12

It was a twenty-minute drive from Manila International Container Terminal to the capital's CBD. They were just pulling into the kerb at Angelina's hotel when Raf's phone buzzed. He picked it up. 'Yeah? No. I haven't. I'll just check with Ava.' He turned to her. 'That was the steward from our boat. Candice misplaced her camera. Have you seen it?'

She shook her head.

'Sorry, we can't help you there. Hope she finds it.'

He pressed the end button.

'She won't be too happy about *that*,' Angelina remarked.

'You're not wrong there.'

§

Raf's eyes swept over the exclusive hotel, wondering just how long Angelina's finances would allow her to remain there. He turned to face her. 'Remember what I said about Manila,

Ava. You'll be fine in a place like this but never go out alone at night. And trust no one.'

He pulled out a piece of paper with the name and number of a high roller who worked for his gang in Manila. 'You didn't get this from me, right?' he said.

'I already told you it'd be between us.'

Despite her assurances, Raf had felt a sense of uneasiness. Next to the gang's drug deals, money laundering was their second most lucrative business. He'd put himself at risk by divulging the contact's details. Perhaps he'd done so because she reminded him of Marnie, who he'd initially thought was well able to hold her own among criminals and thugs. *And look where she ended up,* he reminded himself.

He'd already made it clear to Angelina that she was on her own once they parted ways. She was stepping into one of the most dangerous countries in the world. She'd need all the help she could get.

He watched as she slipped it into her bag. 'Be warned that guys like him keep to themselves and are not likely to give away a thing,' he said. 'The authorities are always making unannounced visits.'

She nodded. 'I'll be extra careful, I give you my word.' She paused for a moment and said, 'Well, that's it, then. Don't get out. And thanks.' She opened the door, stepped out into the blanket of hot, muggy air, and walked towards the front door without looking back.

Once she'd checked in and stepped inside her room, she wasted no time pulling off her grimy wig and taking off the clothes she'd had to wear repeatedly during the last ten days, tossing them in a heap on the floor.

A spa bath sat alongside the shower recess in the ensuite and she smiled, stepping across to turn on the taps. Soon afterwards, she slipped down beneath the bubbles with a contented glance around her spacious surroundings, so different to the spartan conditions of her cabin on the freighter. In no rush to get out, she vowed never again to subject herself to travelling under such substandard conditions. Sometime later, dressed in a skirt and top purchased in Trinity Beach, she headed downstairs for a bite to eat.

It was just on midday, but the café was already starting to fill. Crossing the floor, Angelina studied the array of fresh sandwiches, wraps and salads behind the glass cabinet. She selected a chicken oriental salad topped with herbs, pine nuts, and freshly squeezed juice. The waft of freshly roasted coffee beans filled her nostrils, reminding her how much she'd missed a decent latte after the watered-down, percolated coffee served on board.

Perched on a stool behind the bench at the window, she surveyed the scene around her. A constant stream of people passed through the revolving glass door. Porters pushed bell carts filled with bulging luggage, businessmen with laptops slung over their shoulders hurried by, and guests lined up at the expansive front desk.

Finally, she was free to do as she wished after what had seemed an eternity. There was no rush. She'd spend a week or two in this place and then make the call. Taking a sip of her watermelon, passionfruit and pineapple juice, she smiled, reflecting on the chaos that would have transpired on board after she left. She visualised Candice rushing around the ship, hands flapping, ordering the crew to search here or there, and Harvey rolling his eyes and looking at his watch.

Picking up a fork, she started on her salad, savouring every delicious mouthful. Not long afterwards she slid from the stool and left. Outside she retrieved a small blue camera from her handbag, shoved it in a brown paper bag obtained from the café and dropped it in a nearby bin.

She returned to her room.

9

Had it really been a week since Raf passed on the number? Angelina wondered, looking out into the night sky. Curious, she picked up the phone and dialled his number. The line went dead. She knew it would.

He never made contact again.

Things were buzzing in the games hall of one of Manila's larger casino resorts overlooking the bay. A bombardment of flashing lights and dinging noises and bells were interspersed with ear-splitting music, grating announcements, loud voices and shrieks of laughter. It was 2 a.m., but the place was alive. The dazzling shafts of blue, yellow and green lights, odours of sweaty bodies, cigarettes, bad breath and booze were cleverly disguised by the casino's alluring customised signature fragrance, 'Peach Rose', which filtered through the ventilation system on every floor.

In the adjoining arcade hall, a throng of patrons jostled for position at one of the one thousand or so video and shooting games, and nearby pool tables; and a constant stream of bleary-eyed patrons slipped in and out of the windowless room, returning to the nightclub to drink more as they perched on their chairs and watched performers strut their stuff.

But things were different in the private VIP area three storeys above. Surroundings were spacious and lavish with expensive furnishings, plush carpets and soft lighting. Cashed-up high rollers rotated between card and roulette halls and poker rooms, accompanied by the casino's junket operators who provided them with money and settled their debts as they gambled. Entry was invitation-only, with agreed upon four-to-six-hour daily gambling time and minimum bets of five thousand dollars, the average yearly wage of a Filipino professional.

It was here that Angelina could be found six nights a week, except when she was accompanying Romy Baccay, the casino resort's longest-serving junket operator, to one of the nearby five-star hotels. Their role was to entice prospective high-roller gamblers to their casino's resort. Offers included free limousine travel and accommodation in the best rooms, complimentary drinks and cigars as they gambled, massages and other personalised services. Incentives were flashed before them like diamonds. Good junket operators were worth their weight in gold to casino owners. Competition was fierce. Twenty or so other casino resorts just like his were scattered around the bay, all vying for business, with offers too good to refuse. But Romy had the edge. In one word, 'Angelina', known only as Ava to those around her.

The day she contacted him with a 'proposition', Romy asked, 'How did you get my number?'

'That's for you to find out.'

The response was intriguing. He didn't take any convincing to agree once he set eyes on her. Not that he told her that. He said he'd need time to think about it. Would need to take a photo of her first to show his boss. She'd simply shrugged and said, 'Well, where do you want me to stand?'

Even then, the pout from her full red lips and seductive stance took his breath away, and he felt himself harden as he reached for his phone.

¶

Contrary to common perception, junket operators were not beholden to the casino they worked for, but received a commission for their services. In addition, there were generous, albeit illegal tips from satisfied high-roller clients. Romy could have provided his services elsewhere, but he had a mutual agreement with the casino's owner, Manny Dimmano, to the advantage of both. Romy kept silent about his boss's links to corrupt police officials and politicians, which allowed him to funnel illegal gambling funds on a massive scale. In return, Manny turned a blind eye to Romy's long-term connections to a Chinese triad specialising in money laundering.

The triad ran the large-scale smuggling of Chinese currency into Manila, that was laundered through banks and financial institutions via illegal gambling and real-estate ventures. Chinese gang members disguised as tourists brought in the cash covertly stashed in their luggage and waved through by corrupt members of airport security, the police force or the military.

High-stakes gamblers operated in gangs like theirs in casinos dotted around Manila, with large slabs of dirty money laundered daily. But they had to be careful. Manila had strict anti-laundering laws, and casinos were regularly monitored. Consequently, they remained on the move, shifting from casino to casino, sticking within their established limits. But they also turned to other means – dodgy junket operators, for instance, who turned a blind eye while they laundered far more significant amounts.

Romy was one such operator. But his clandestine dealings with the Chinese triad over the past few years had become less frequent. Although handsomely rewarded for his efforts, he figured it better to be a little less well off than risk lingering in the bowels of one of Manila's notorious prisons.

Nonetheless, it was encouraging to know that his boss had all bases covered should things go awry. Casino operators were expected to protect customers, have a set rate of profit, and prevent criminals from infiltrating the system, and Manny was a stickler for all of that. Employees were trained to watch out for suspicious behaviour, and transactions or gamblers masquerading under aliases, and to report such conduct immediately.

One night, as he and Manny shared brandies, caviar and cigars after dinner, Romy remarked, 'Tell me this much, boss, have you ever stopped to think what you'd do if you were sprung?'

The response had been prompt, with a shrug, 'I'd just tell them it's impolite to ask our valued clients where their money comes from. It'd be on their heads, not mine. They know the rules when they set foot in this place.'

Romy smiled at the memory. Like a pair of dodgy book-makers, they had things tightly sewn up.

¶

Manny Dimmano sat in the leather swivel chair behind his vast desk on the casino's eighth floor, awaiting the arrival of Romy and the girl he was to meet. With fingers steepled, he glanced at the image Romy sent through on his computer screen. *She was stunning, all right*, he thought. If Romy hadn't taken the photo, Manny would have sworn it was photoshopped.

The casino boss was just as intrigued as Romy to learn more about her past. To date she'd avoided all such questions but had not hidden that she'd been operating outside the law and needed a place in Manila to lay low for a while. It only served to make him more curious.

He gazed at the almond-shaped brown eyes and strikingly beautiful face framed by brown, chin-length stylishly layered hair, and oval-shaped glasses, which accentuated her high cheekbones. A trickle of sweat ran down the back of his shirt. The thrill of the chase was already coursing through his veins. He was sure that Romy would have similar designs. *What hot-blooded man wouldn't? It mattered little. She could be bought like all the others.* He knew he had far more to offer than Romy, not that he'd divulge his intentions. The woman was a good thirty years younger than him, and he'd be kidding himself to think she would find him attractive. He'd lived the good life for too many years — late nights, fast women, rich food and heavy drinking. Working out in the gym was a long distant memory.

When Angelina first appeared in the doorway, Manny's eyes moved slowly over the slender frame clad in a tasteful, knee-length black dress and strapless high-heeled sandals. He found himself wondering whether the diamonds she wore were genuine.

She crossed the room, head erect and back straight, to extend her hand. It was cool and firm in his clammy fingers. 'I'm Ava,' she said with a smile. 'Romy has told me so much about you.' She managed to hide her distaste at the sight of the man. She never wanted to set eyes on another age-ing pervert. But she'd make sure things were turned to her advantage.

Manny inadvertently licked his lips, reminding her of a teenager watching porn.

'So, I hear you're interested in joining our staff,' he said.

Angelina's eyes never left his. 'That's correct.'

He gestured to the sofa. 'Well, let's sit down and chat, shall we?'

He waited until they'd settled, offered them a drink, and sat opposite.

Half an hour later, Manny went to rise. 'Well, I think that's about everything for now.' He gave Angelina a direct look. 'We haven't employed anyone in such circumstances, but I'm open to the concept. I'm sure you'll understand if I sit in on the first meeting before making a decision.'

'Of course,' Angelina said sweetly, knowing he'd already made up his mind. *Men were such open books …*

Manny closed the door behind them, headed to the cabinet, and reached for the crystal whisky decanter. She said she'd operated in similar circumstances, and he had no reason to disbelieve her. She'd given away nothing, like the poker players who frequented the rooms three floors below. It was where she'd worked and with whom that intrigued him the most. He'd find out. Or so he thought …

⁊

Three nights later, Romy and Manny arrived early at Angelina's hotel and cut across the lobby to the bar where they'd arranged to meet. She was already there, seated on a stool, shapely legs dangling, sipping a cocktail. Both men approached, transfixed. With a toss of her head, she slipped to her feet in her tight-fitting scarlet dress and matching high heels that made her appear inches taller.

'So where are we off to?' She gave one of her smiles. *This would be so easy.*

⁊

Two hours later, the high roller ordered a bottle of French champagne and the four clinked glasses over the candle-lit table.

'You made a wise decision, Heng. Romy and I will look

after you, don't worry,' Angelina told him as she wrapped things up. 'So, how long will you be with us?'

'A week.'

'Why not make it two?' She tilted her head to one side. 'I'm sure we could throw in some extra incentives. Right Manny?'

Romy did a double take. But Manny continued as if he'd thought up the idea himself. 'I think we could come up with a suitable arrangement.'

'Such as?'

'How does a week's complimentary dinners at a restaurant of your choice sound during your stay? Drinks on the house, of course,' offered Manny.

The high roller turned to Angelina, his hand reaching to stroke her leg under the table. 'I think I can stretch things to two.'

She removed his hand with a demure smile. 'We look forward to your patronage.'

9

At 3 a.m., Romy climbed into the back of the casino's limousine alongside his boss and grinned. 'Told you she was something else, hey?'

That was an understatement. Manny could only wish that women like her would glide into his office every day of the week. He'd make a fortune. The wealthy Chinese high roller they'd met at the award-winning restaurant had been putty in her hands.

128

'We can't lose, right?' Romy persisted.

'Maybe. She's yet to prove herself.'

¶

Manny reached for a pack of cigarettes from his pocket. He'd just offered Angelina a two-month probation and a minimum starting wage with free accommodation in a garden view room, subject to an upgrade based on performance. This came with complimentary buffet breakfasts, and use of two gyms and the wellbeing facility.

He offered a cigarette to Romy. 'So you're still none the wiser about where she came from and what she's doing in Manila?'

Romy shook his head. 'Nope. But I'm working on it.' He lit the cigarette and took a puff.

'You don't think she knows about your dealings with the triad?'

'Nah. What makes you say that?'

'No reason.'

For some reason, Romy felt a sudden sense of unease. 'I've made no mention of them if that's what you're thinking.'

'Best you keep things that way, eh?'

Both were silent for the remainder of the journey, watching the city lights whirl by like shooting stars in the darkness, senses dulled by the final double shots of brandy.

15

Manny was well pleased.

A month had passed, and already Romy and Angelina had secured the custom of several extremely influential high rollers who paid handsomely for the company of such a beautiful woman as they gambled their ill-gotten gains. But that was it. From the outset, she'd stated that her services were in a corporate capacity only. No sex. End of story. It added to the intrigue and only served to fuel Manny's desire. She oozed class, down to the slim-fitting, knee-length dresses and matching high-heeled sandals with fine ankle straps that she wore as she worked. She reminded him of one of those perfectly coiffured female air stewards who attended to his needs on first-class flights. The kind that is strictly out of reach and fuels the fantasy of every man who steps aboard.

§

Angelina sat propped against a large pillow on the leather sofa, clad in the hotel room's thick, white signature robe, and reflected on the past four months. Since her arrival her accommodation had been upgraded, with a modest wage rise, limousine pick-up and drop-off, no questions asked, and complimentary drinks at the bar. She was barely able to believe her good fortune. Occasionally, she extended her services to dinner with a client at the end of a shift. Carefully selected, of course. Off-limits were flabby middle-aged predators who ogled her with their hungry eyes, and men with hands that strayed.

If that's what it takes to keep in the boss's good books, then why not? Angelina reasoned.

This exercise was proving well worth her while, her wealthy companions going all out to impress. A diamond bracelet or gift voucher to a designer boutique was an occasional bonus. Dinner was strictly within the confines of the casino. And Romy arrived at the night's end to escort her to her room. Not that he made it past the door.

She wouldn't be here enjoying the high life, if she'd gone ahead with her original plan, and she thanked God she hadn't. Just as well her Melbourne contact, Theo, had the resources to develop an alternative plan at such short notice. And she the dollars to fund it.

Perhaps she wouldn't have resorted to such measures if she'd had Nic's assurances of venturing with her into a life of danger, excitement and dare-devil schemes. Who better to cover her back than an assassin? Neither owed allegiance to any gang in particular. But between them was a deep pool of underworld figures on which to draw. The thing was, Angelina badly underestimated Nic's fatherly instincts —his all-consuming desire to connect with his baby on the other side of the world. *As for playing happy families somewhere and coming clean. He had to be kidding, right? Your loss, not mine, Nic,* she thought as she straightened her toes, inspecting the newly polished scarlet nails. She missed the sex, but that was about it.

Nic had more than served his purpose. She'd kept a close eye on the media since the hit job on her mother. From what she'd read, there'd been no mention of Nic's involvement; she wondered if the police had put the pieces together yet. *Probably not. Nic had lasted this long in the job, undetected.*

If she wanted to play the bitch, she could have sent the authorities an anonymous letter. But there was no point to that. After all, Nic had done precisely what was asked of him …

She couldn't help being curious about his movements that night on the beach following the explosion. *How would he have made his escape with cops swarming all over the place?* She shrugged. *He'd have figured out something. One thing was for sure, he would have made a beeline straight back to Docklands in the hope I was waiting for him.*

¶

Angelina dressed, detangled and styled her wig with a wide-toothed comb, and slipped it on. And reached for her non-prescription glasses. It never ceased to amaze her what a significantly different appearance both gave. Sophisticated and chic, yet business-like.

She never ventured outside her casino apartment without her trademark disguise, not even downtown for a day's shopping. However, both wig and glasses would be removed once she reached the shopping mall and placed in her bag until it was time to head back at the end of the day.

Occasionally during these visits to town, she let her thick dark hair loose, slipped on a baseball cap and dark glasses and went to local bars to meet with male patrons to have her need for flattery satiated. Always with a vague promise of things to come and made-up phone numbers. She missed male sexual contact but on reflection decided the dangers associated made it not worth her while. Europe would come around soon enough.

The first time she was asked her name, the word 'Cara' rolled off her tongue before she had time to think. She'd smiled at the irony, envisioning the reaction of her sister at being portrayed as a pick-up girl.

§

Angelina stood at Romy's side, watching their high roller client push another handful of chips across the table to the dealer. She was beginning to be restless. She'd been here for

133

five months and hardly learned a thing about money laundering practices. Clearly, Romy was making sure she knew as
little as possible. It was time to push him further.

She turned to Romy. 'Do you feel like a drink in the bar
after work?'

'Yeah. Why not,' Romy replied, curious what this was
leading to, hoping wildly it could be the start of something
more. She'd shown him nothing but professional interest to
this point, which only increased his desire. But he could blow
his chances altogether by making an unwanted advance. A
quick glance at the clock, and he held back a groan. Another
two hours to wait.

¶

At 2 a.m., they headed towards a wine bar on the third floor,
settling at a table among scattered groups of patrons.

'Hungry?' he asked.

'Yeah, I am actually,' she replied.

'Me too. This place has a good selection of Filipino appetisers if you'd like to share a platter.'

'Sounds good.'

'Red or white wine?'

'Red, please.'

'Will this do?' He pointed to one of the most expensive
menu items.

'Yeah. That'll be just fine.' She smiled at him.

He rose and headed to the bar to place their order. A

waiter brought the wine not long afterwards, followed by a silver platter of spring rolls, pinoy pork bar-b-que sticks, longganisa wontons and bang bang, producing tantalising aromas that caused Angelina's mouth to water. The last time she'd eaten was a couple of sushi rolls on the way to her shift.

'So how are you finding things so far?' Romy asked as he reached for her glass.

'I'm pleasantly surprised, to be honest,' she said, biting into a crispy spring roll. 'The casinos I've worked in at home are nothing compared to the scale of this place.'

'Yeah, casino resorts are big business in Manila,' he said. 'They go all out to provide the best.' He paused. 'By the way, I haven't had a chance to say that you've made quite an impression. To be honest, Manny was dubious about your proposal to begin with.'

'And you?'

'Much the same, but you proved me wrong. Which reminds me,' Romy pulled out an envelope and handed it to her. 'You made quite an impact on Lei last night. He asked me to pass on this tip.'

Yeah, and I need every bit of it to make up for the shit wages I get, she thought, wondering what he'd be raking in each week. But it was in her best interests not to complain. Her accommodation was taken care of. And there were always the lurks and perks that came with the job. The other workers received no such thing.

'Thanks,' she said, pocketing it.

'There could be more coming,' Romy told her. 'He's returning in a week before he heads back to China.'

She nodded. 'So, how long have you been here, Romy?'

'Coming up to six years now,' he said.

'Working as a junket operator?'

'Yeah. I've worked in a few places before this, but I have to say this is the best by far.'

She gave a nod. 'So, what's the deal with the high rollers? How do you get onto them in the first place?'

'That's Manny's business, not mine,' he shot back.

'Just curious to know how the place works, that's all. I'd like to think there'd be opportunities for promotion.'

'So you're thinking of staying?' Romy felt his heart race.

'Depends. Tell me something, how much corruption goes on in this place?' She leaned an elbow on the table, cupping her chin in her hand and fixing her eyes on his.

'What are you talking about?' he said all too quickly.

'Oh come on, Romy. Everyone knows that money laundering is rife in Manila's casinos.'

'Well, I wouldn't know about the others, but here, strict anti-laundering rules are in place.'

'Yeah, I know all that.' Her eyes never left his. 'But that doesn't mean it doesn't go on, right?'

He shrugged. 'If it did, I wouldn't know. I do my job and go home. Anyway, what's with all the questions?'

'Oh, no reason. Just curious.'

Instinct warned Angelina not to press him further. Raf had been right. Shady junket operators like Romy were unlikely to divulge their business to anyone. But she was frustrated that the night had left her none the wiser about how he went about it. Unless, of course, he was no longer in the game. But she considered that unlikely, given her knowledge of how gangs and their contacts operated.

'So tell me, Romy, are you married?'

He quickly shook his head. 'No time for that in this industry.'

'No kids, then?'

Another shake of his head.

Angelina watched amusedly at the squirming man with beads of perspiration on his forehead; he resembled a prisoner about to be tortured. *Was he so stupid to think I hadn't at some point glanced over his shoulder during shifts as he flicked through videos of his wife and son, who appeared to be around ten? Maybe there were more. Who knew?*

Romy's wife looked a similar age to Romy, around thirty-five at a guess, a petite woman with straggly long dark hair, dressed in black tights and a matching oversized shirt. Her weary expression resembled that of an assembly line worker after a long day's shift. A far cry from the worldly, sophisticated women in Romy's professional world.

Angelina imagined there'd been a string of affairs over the years. His nocturnal job offered the perfect excuse to stay out until all hours or not come home, given his access to the casino's hotel rooms after a late shift. There'd been no signs of any such thing to this point, but she wondered what went on the two nights he had off.

¶

Romy accompanied Angelina to her room in the faint hope she might have invited him inside. But she gave him a brief kiss and said, 'Thanks for tonight, Romy. I've really enjoyed it.'

'Me too,' he said, quick to add, 'Can we do it again, sometime?'

'Why not?'

He watched her open the door and slip inside. He had to be content with that. With too much to drink, he was glad he didn't have to think about making his way home and made a quick call to reception to book a room, hoping there'd be a smoking one available. He was in luck.

¶

Romy awoke at midday with a dull, thudding head and parched throat, momentarily wondering where he was, as the room was still dark with the heavy drapes. He groaned and waited a while longer before rising and yanking them aside. A thick layer of smog outside hid whatever view his room offered of Manila Bay.

After a strong black coffee, he showered and changed back into his hardly desirable uniform, given the inevitable reek of cigarettes from his visit to the smoking room, interspersed with sweat after the night's shift, but it would have to do. He had no plans of heading home for a change of clothes. It wasn't all that long before his next shift. Besides, he was in no frame of mind to deal with a young family. Just as well he'd arranged check-out time for eight when his shift began. He decided to head down for something to eat and then spend the remainder of the day lounging around his room, smoke in hand, watching the large plasma screen.

But as he reached for his key card and phone, the previous night's conversation came to mind, and he was tinged with a sense of uneasiness. Clicking on his contacts, he tapped on a number.

'Are you busy right now?'

'No, why?'

'I'm here for the day, that's all. Stayed over after my shift. Wondered if you wanted to meet up for lunch.'

'Yeah, where?'

'Your choice.'

'Latin American. Give me twenty minutes.'

It was relatively quiet on the fifth-floor restaurant, but Romy chose a quiet booth tucked into the corner to be safe. The two often shared a meal, where private and personal issues were discussed, along with casino matters. It had taken some time for Romy to build up his boss's trust, and he wasn't about to jeopardise the relationship. Especially with the lurks and perks that were sent his way.

The conversation remained general during dinner. Only when coffee arrived was Angelina's name first brought up.

'So, things still working between the two of you?' Manny asked.

'Yeah. You saw how easily Ava won that high roller over to our casino on the first night. She only seems to have got better.'

Manny whistled.

'There's just one thing, though. We had late-night drinks after we knocked off last night.'

'Don't tell me you two —'

'I should be so lucky.'

Manny grinned, 'It's just when you mentioned you stayed here last night —'

'Nah.' He took a sip of his drink. 'But I'm working on it.'

'So, what were you about to say?'

'She started asking questions, that's all.'

'What sort of questions?'

'Like if this place turned a blind eye to money laundering and stuff.'

'Can't say I'm surprised, given she's been on the wrong side of the law herself. Probably fishing to see if there's an opening for something like that here.'

'Probably. But why wait so long to make an approach?'

'Who knows. Maybe the woman's being as cautious about us as we are of her. She'd have to prove herself for some time yet before I'd consider such a thing.'

'And what if she gets sick of waiting and decides to move on?'

'Well, we haven't lost anything, have we? But let's hope that's not the case. With what we've seen of her, she could well work to our advantage.'

Romy nodded. 'I'm still curious about what she's been into so far. What she's doing here in the first place.'

'That makes two of us. We can't be sure of her motives until we get some answers. But as long as she's got nothing to pin on us, there's little to worry about.' Manny paused. 'Be careful though? I've been fooled by beautiful women like her before.' An image flashed through his mind of Hiraya, his stunning live-in lover. The woman who'd all but destroyed him. The woman who went missing not long afterwards, never to return.

'Nothing will go wrong, don't worry.' No sooner had the words come out than Romy felt a wave of unease, triggering an involuntary shudder.

15

In the days that followed, Angelina befriended the casino staff, hoping to learn about money laundering practices. The information she sought finally came from an unlikely source — her maid, a sixty-eight-year-old grandmother with a penchant for gossip. She'd watched as the large woman huffed and puffed her way around the room, lugging a cumbersome, outdated vacuum cleaner, waiting for her to stop.

'How many years have you worked here, Ivy?' she asked.

'Eight,' the Filipino woman said proudly, with a smile revealing several missing teeth. 'The boss of housekeeping, she say I been one of the best workers.'

'I'm sure you are.'

'Not getting any younger, though. Would've given up work years ago. But jobs don't come easy around here, and my four kids and grandkids are doing it hard. Every bit helps.'

Angelina nodded. She'd noted several women of a similar vintage cleaning and performing other menial tasks around the place.

'They tell me you're from Australia,' Ivy remarked.

'Yeah, that's right.'

'You like working here?'

'I do, actually,' Angelina paused. 'But I've always wondered if things are above board.'

'What makes you think that?'

'Well, everyone knows that money laundering is widespread in Manila, especially within casinos.'

'Don't ask me. I wouldn't know a thing about that stuff.' She paused. 'But I might just know someone that does.'

'Oh?'

A look of hesitation suddenly crossed the old woman's face.

'Don't worry, I'm good at holding secrets,' Angelina soothed, 'plus I'll make it well worth your while.' She rubbed the first three fingertips with her thumb for a few moments.

Ivy grinned. 'Okay. But I need to make call first.'

'Of course. Are you on tomorrow?'

'Yes.'

'You can give me your answer then.'

Ivy wasted no time making the phone call once she'd left Angelina's room and was well out of earshot.

'It's Ivy. Have you started your shift yet?'

'No, not for another two hours. Why?'

'I've got a proposition for you.'

Bayani Cabrera raised an eyebrow as he listened to what she had to say. There was only one young woman of Angelina's description working in the casino, and the opportunity to meet up with her was something he would never have expected. He'd seen her numerous times accompanying Romy to the VIP lounge three floors above. She was all class. He wondered where she'd come from and what she was doing there.

He always felt a pang of envy when the junket operators passed by, knowing full well how much they were paid, having been one himself. But he had to be content with his lowly paid position as a gaming attendant. For now. He'd also made the decision years ago to remain single. Having a wife and string of kids to support didn't bear thinking about. If not for Ivy, a long-term friend of his mother, he wouldn't have secured a job there in the first place. It was one of the best casino resorts for wages and conditions, with vacant positions a rarity. But after years of working in the tasteful, elaborate, spacious settings of VIP lounges surrounded by clients in tuxedos and glamorous women, he found the clatter and din of the crowded, tasteless gaming arcade hard to adapt to. But it was his forced move from a spacious apartment with sweeping views of the city to a run-down, tiny apartment that he resented the most. He'd been used to the high life and the string of women that came with it. All was well until a raid by the authorities on the casino where he previously worked. Books were searched, and arrests were made on junket operators known to aid and abet money laundering practices. He could have been among them if the raid had not occurred during his night off.

He could have risked things and begun work at another

casino under a fake identity. But the event had left him shaken. He had connections to several Chinese triads. He thought it was best to lie low while things settled, but knew it wouldn't take long until he was up and running once more.

¶

The meeting between Angelina and Bayani occurred three nights later in a quiet alcove of the all-night bar adjacent to the pool. From the outset, Angelina knew the fortyish, smooth-talking Filipino would be a pushover. His eyes gave him away, like others before him. But she knew she'd need to be careful. It would only take one too many questions to make him a closed book, like Romy. She'd wait until he had a few more drinks under his belt.

Sitting back and crossing one long leg over the other, she fluttered her eyelashes and kept the conversation general. By the end of the evening, she had all the information she needed on money laundering. Of particular interest had been how Bayani exploited his position as a high roller to assist the high rollers undetected. She waited until he'd sufficiently loosened up to broach the subject.

'You'd have to be careful which ones you worked with, wouldn't you?'

'Yeah. Only the ones sent my way through the triad.'

'How often did you do that sort of stuff?'

'Only occasionally. Safer for the triad, safer for me.'

'So, what are you doing working in the gaming arcade here and not as a junket operator?'

His face became grim. 'It's a long story.'

'Did something go wrong?'

'You could say that. I'll get back to it soon. I don't know about here, though. What's the junket operator like I've seen you pass by with?'

'Romy? Knows his stuff. He's been here six years.'

'So, he's above board, then.'

'Says he is, but I've got my doubts,' she said.

'Why?'

'He's told a few lies that's all. The problem is, I've never seen him doing anything that looks on the dodgy side.'

'You two work together?'

She nodded.

'How many nights?'

'Five.'

'And what does he do on the others?'

'I've never asked. I just assumed he was sleeping around. He's got "womaniser" written all over his face.'

Bayani grinned. 'Well, maybe, it's worth checking if he's working a bit extra on the side those nights. Sometimes I did, when the triad offered me a last-minute job.'

'I might just do that,' she said, wondering why the idea hadn't occurred to her before.

'So tell me all about yourself, Ava.'

For something different, she rattled off a story about being raised in Sydney and leaving home at eighteen to work as a receptionist in a large city hotel.

He nodded. 'Well, what are you doing here?'

'I was forced to leave. Someone had been hacking into the books and siphoning money. Because I'd been shown to work at some of those times, I got the blame.'

'Oh, that's too bad.'

Angelina shrugged. 'I'd been there seven years. It was time for a change anyway.' She glanced up at the clock. 'Oh, look how late it is!' she exclaimed. 'Didn't you say you were on an early shift?'

'Doesn't matter,' he said hazily, having already consumed too many drinks.

'Of course it does. We all need our sleep.' Angelina pulled out an envelope that contained eleven thousand pesos. 'You should find this enough to cover things. I've enjoyed your company, Bayani. And you've answered all of my questions. I promise this will remain between us.'

'Wait …' He reached forward and laid a hand on her arm. 'I'd really like to see you again.'

'What, you mean like a date?'

'Yeah,' he said quickly.

'I'm afraid that's not possible, Bayani.' She extricated herself, rose, and said sweetly, 'You see, the fact of the matter is, I'm gay.'

She left him sitting with his mouth wide open as she headed towards the door.

ᵍ

Two nights later, Romy joined Angelina at eight in the VIP lounge. 'Lei has asked if you'd be interested in joining him for dinner at the end of the night. It shouldn't be a late affair. He's flying out in the morning.'

'Yeah, I can manage that,' she said. The late-sixties, polite businessman seemed harmless enough. And with a bit of luck, another envelope might be coming her way.

A table was booked at the most exclusive restaurant on the same floor, with expansive views of the city night lights from the floor-to-ceiling glass windows.

'Thank you for agreeing to join me this evening, Ava,' Lei said as he pulled out her chair for her to sit down. 'I'm a lucky man to have been in the company of such a beautiful young woman.'

'You are too kind, Lei,' she said, lowering her eyes. 'I hope everything here was to your satisfaction.'

'Most definitely. And I assure you, I will seek your services and book a room upon my return.'

'So when is that likely be?'

'Another few months, I imagine.'

'So, what business are you into in China?'

'Manufacturing electronics for international markets mainly, along with shares and property investments.'

'Sounds impressive,' Angelina said. 'So, what are you doing in Manila?'

'I'm checking out several properties with a view to development. And what about you? How long have you worked here?'

'Five months.'

'And you're enjoying it?'

'Absolutely. Years working in corporate management back home were beginning to get to me. It was time for a break.'

'A sensible move. Let's order, shall we?' He summoned the drinks waiter and ordered the most expensive wine.

As the night progressed, Angelina found the conversation stimulating. Lei was an intelligent man, with a wealth of knowledge within the business sector to impart.

'So, tell me about your family, Lei,' she said, nursing the fluted wine glass in her fingers.

'I have a wife, Hong, and three daughters, all grown up now.' He produced his phone and clicked on the camera roll, selecting some images and passing them over for Angelina to see.

'This one's Huan, the eldest – she's a scientist; this is Mei, an accountant; and the youngest, Wen, manages one of my companies.'

'You must be proud of them, Lei.'

'I am,' he beamed. 'They are good girls.'

'And grandchildren?'

'Four and another on the way.'

She nodded. 'So, tell me all about China. I've yet to go there.'

'What would you like to know?'

Over the next two hours, Angelina found herself enjoying the company of this likable man and felt little need to hold back on her drinks for a change. And the words spilled out before she knew it. 'Thanks for not putting on the hard word, Lei. You've got no idea how many clients try to put their grubby little hands all over me the minute we're alone.'

'That's never been my style, Ava. But if I'd been thirty years younger, perhaps I might have hoped you'd show me some interest.'

She grinned.

'Let's say I'm just enjoying the company of a beautiful, engaging woman. It can be lonely dining alone when I do business.' He glanced at his phone. 'Well, best I settle the bill and head back to my room. My flight's at 7 a.m.. Can I see you to yours?'

'No. Romy will do that. I'll send him a text.'

'Oh, I just about forgot …' He pulled an envelope from his pocket. 'A little token of appreciation.' He paused. 'I hope the fourteen-thousand pesos was to your liking?'

Angelina's expression was glacial. 'Did you say fourteen thousand?'

'Yes. Why? Is something wrong?'

'No, no. It was more than generous, thank you.'

'My pleasure.'

Angelina sat fuming as he paid the bill. Fourteen-thousand. Double the sum passed on by Romy.

Romy felt a sense of unease as he accompanied Angelina to her room.

Something wasn't right …

15

It was Wednesday night, the first of two consecutive nights off for Angelina. She waited until 10 p.m. before heading to the casino's VIP room. A quick check of the three private gaming rooms told her Romy was not working. The gaming attendants looked surprised to see her out of uniform but gave her a friendly wave and continued what they were doing.

9

The following evening, she returned, and this time she was in luck. Romy had his back to her, speaking animatedly with a thin, grey-haired Chinese man.

She quietly returned to her room.

9

No mention was made of the incident to Romy for the next

few days, and Angelina waited to speak privately to a gaming attendant who had been on duty that night.

'Tell me, Jerome, I was surprised to see Romy here the other night. I didn't think he worked on his nights off.'

The Filipino shifted uncomfortably. He was aware that Romy worked on rare nights outside his normal hours to facilitate money laundering practices. He had little idea where the clients came from, but they seldom reappeared. He supposed Manny was aware of it but turned a blind eye. If so, it was none of his business. He'd had to work his way up through the gaming rooms to get into the VIP room, and he wasn't about to jeopardise his hard-earned position.

'This wasn't a one-off thing, was it?' she pressed.

Jerome went to respond but hesitated.

'This will stay between us. I promise,' Angelina said.

The response was cautious. 'He works occasionally. Why?'

She looked directly at Jerome. 'I don't like to be lied to, that's all.'

The words came as little surprise. Romy worked to his own agenda and his supercilious attitude and bossy manner made him highly unpopular among his peers. But everyone knew of his close ties to the boss. To challenge to confront him risked instant dismissal. Times were tough, and jobs too hard to get.

'So, the high roller with Romy,' she pushed on, 'have you seen him before?'

'Once or twice.'

'And did he spend up big both times?'

'Why are you asking me all this?'

Angelina sidled up to him. 'Because I suspect Romy might have given him a helping hand. Would I be right?'

There was an awkward silence. Angelina pulled out a wad of tightly rolled peso notes and slipped it into his palm. 'Would this help?'

He looked at her. 'What would you like to know?'

§

It was 7:50 p.m. in the VIP gaming room, and Angelina was yet to show. Romy frowned. Angelina shared his propensity for punctuality. He was about to call when the text came through: *Not well. Can't make it tonight.*

Okay. Call me tomorrow.

§

The following day, she'd not contacted him by late afternoon, and she'd not called. Romy was annoyed. He wasn't used to being kept waiting like this. He found himself pacing the floor, but instinct told him not to make contact.

It was 7 p.m. before the call came. 'I'm still feeling like shit, Romy. I went to see the doctor today and he's given me three nights off.'

'What's wrong?'

'Severe stomach cramps that may need further investigation.'

Romy frowned. They had a meeting with a prospective client in two nights' time.

'Well, let me know how things go and look after yourself.' It was all he *could* say, but he was annoyed, just the same.

ҁ

Romy's meeting with the prospective client did not go to plan. There was no guarantee that Romy had clinched the deal. The businessman was about to look at other options first. Romy returned to the casino, tetchy and irritable. Since Angelina had arrived, hooking in the big high rollers had not been an issue, and he realised just how much he'd taken things for granted. If he was to secure her services, he'd need to read-dress her incentives. It was time to have a chat with Manny.

ҁ

There was nothing Romy could do but work alone. He could do with a swag of money to boost his dark mood. In three nights, on his night off, the Chinese triad had provided another client. To Romy's frustration, Angelina sent a text on the day of her next shift, saying she was still not ready to return for the next two nights.

As the night progressed, he felt an inexplicable sense of unease, and at ten, he rang Manny. The phone was picked up after two rings.

'What's up?'

'I rang Ava before to see how she was, and the call went straight to messages.'

'So?'

'Just have a feeling, that's all. Usually, Ava would get back to me.'

'Want me to go to her room and check things out?'

'Yeah, that'd be good. Maybe send an SMS first. I don't think Ava would take kindly to you just dropping in.'

Manny smiled as he clicked the end button. He'd been waiting to make a move on Angelina for a while now. Maybe it was time to mention the extra incentives Romy had suggested. Maybe a few of his own on the side …

He picked up his phone and texted: *Sorry to hear you are still not well. Mind if I drop by?*

The response came soon afterwards: *Sure. Come down.*

Manny licked his lips, hardly believing his luck. He headed to his office's ensuite for a quick brush of his teeth and a liberal splash of his French aftershave, then headed for the door. The lift down to Angelina's level seemed interminable, and by the time he reached her room, his heart was pumping wildly. He rang the bell and waited. Rang the bell again.

'Ava?' he called out. Pressed an ear to the door. Nothing. With a frown, he headed to reception for a spare room card. Upon his return, he found the room empty.

'What the fuck!' he exclaimed in disbelief.

g

The following night, Romy stood bleary-eyed and angry, not wanting to go through with the shift. But big money beckoned. He'd not knocked back a job yet from the triad. They weren't the most tolerant of men. There were plenty of others willing to step in if he got cold feet. There may not be the next time.

Romy didn't see those coming and going through the VIP's elaborate glass front entrance. Didn't see the tall thin man with dark glasses standing in the corner with arms crossed. was not aware of a thing until he received a tap on the shoulder.

ჶ

Sprawled across the king-sized bed of the five-star hotel in the CBD, Angelina smiled as Manny's call rang out; she waited for the next. Three texts later, she pulled the sim card out, replaced it with another, and made a call.

'Elena?'

'Yes, who is this?'

'Ava. Still interested in that job?'

ჶ

It was not Angelina's intention to step outside the hotel too often. She had no doubt that Manny's connections would be scaling the CBD in search of her and she couldn't afford to remain there much longer. At least she was barely recognisable without the light brown, layered wig, make-up and stylish clothes. She glanced in the mirror at her newly washed dark hair that swung around her shoulders; she wore white T-shirt over leggings. She smiled.

Twirling the wig in her fingers, she dropped it into a plastic bag and placed it in her tote bag, then reached for her baseball cap and dark glasses and headed for the door. Crossing the ground floor, she exited the revolving glass door. With an instinctive check both ways, she stepped out into the fume-filled, bustling side street and waited for a cyclist, who was weaving in and out of the slow-moving traffic, before crossing to the other side.

The air was oppressively still and muggy. Her clothes were already sticking to her body after traversing just one block where she found the nearest industrial dumpster, into which she dropped the wig. A group of teenagers were smoking in a nearby doorway as she entered a small, busy café boasting healthy meals and fresh juice, for lunch. Three more days and she'd be gone.

17

It was a twenty-minute taxi ride from the hotel to Manila's Ninoy Aquino International Airport. Three hours later, Angelina was strapped in her seat awaiting take-off on the Etihad Airways flight to Madrid. The journey took fifteen hours but given the time difference of seven hours, landing time was at 8. With four hours to wait before her connecting flight to A Coruña, she cleared customs and took a leisurely stroll around the airport, stopping by a busy restaurant overlooking the vast runway for brunch.

§

Angelina felt a sense of déjà vu as she stepped off the plane in the small A Coruña airport and took a short taxi drive to the hotel where she'd last met with Elena. She recognised the concierge standing behind the main desk; a balding man, small with a smooth voice and friendly smile. She looked to see if there was a flicker of recognition in his eyes, but her blonde wig and fake passport had effectively done their job.

Her plan was to don the wig for travel, hotel check-outs and work purposes only, alternating as needed with the auburn version and a separate accompanying set of false papers. It was 3 p.m. Plenty of time to shower, settle in, then head out for a walk.

¶

It was a pleasant twenty-two degrees outside, a refreshing change from Manila's muggy conditions. Angelina had paid scant attention to the physical attraction of the city on her previous visit and was surprised as she ambled through its historic precinct: at the atmosphere evoked by its narrow, stone alleyways, old buildings, monuments, and Roman ruins. As evening approached, she stopped by a small restaurant for a bite to eat. Wafts of garlic met her nostrils as she opened the wooden door to a welcoming room of dark furniture contrasted with splashes of vibrant colour. Prints of bullfighters and flamenco dancers framed the walls, and the soft strum of a flamenco guitar played discreetly in the background.

She settled at a table by the window, tucking into a large serve of seafood paella and glass of Sangria before returning to the hotel for an early night.

¶

Elena had been at her lowest ebb when she'd heard nothing from Angelina months after she'd left for Australia. She checked her voice mails and messages daily in the hope that there'd be some word of the job, but as time passed her hopes faded. *Why did she come into my life in the first place?* Elena wondered. But feeling sorry for herself had never been her style, although she'd always been made to feel small, even as a small child. The sense of being undervalued and underestimated only stirred her to prove herself; to somehow escape the poverty she'd been constantly reminded was her lot in life.

And finally, she'd escaped. Made a dash with a battered suitcase crammed with as many of her meagre belongings as possible and took the 400-kilometre journey to begin her new life.

Right now, that day seemed a lifetime ago.

¶

The bus arrived early. Elena stepped aboard, paid her fare and moved towards the back, settling in a seat by the window and bracing herself for the three-hour journey ahead. It had been seven months since she'd made the same trip to A Coruña to visit Angelina after her baby was born, and the frosty reception she'd received still weighed heavily on her mind. *Perhaps she's changed since I saw her,* Elena thought hopefully. *Maybe she's sorted out whatever it was she returned to Australia for …*

Nonetheless, she felt a wave of trepidation as she alighted the bus at its destination. She wondered what she was letting herself in for, instinct warning her not to take everything Angelina said at face value.

By the time she'd arrived at the hotel where they'd last met, and reached out to knock on Angelina's door, her nerves were brittle and her heart hammered inside her chest.

'Won't be a moment,' came a voice from inside, and the door opened, revealing Angelina briskly towelling her hair. 'Come in, Elena. I wasn't expecting you this early.'

'There were only a few aboard the bus today. The driver didn't make as many stops as usual,' she responded, stepping into the room.

'You look good,' Angelina looked her up and down with approval. 'I can see you've been working on your weight.'

Elena felt the blood rush to her cheeks but said nothing.

'Grab a seat. I'll just run a comb through my hair, and then I'll be back. Coffee?'

'Yeah, that'd be good.' Elena sat on the sofa.

Angelina returned not long afterwards with two steaming mugs in hand and placed them on the coffee table.

'I'm pleased you're free to take up the offer, Elena,' she said, sitting alongside her. 'You're still at the café?'

There was a nod.

'And you haven't told them you're leaving yet?'

'No, I was waiting to hear back from you.'

'How much notice will they need?'

'A week should be enough.'

'Good. I'm flying to Madrid in the morning. You can join me there, and we'll make a start. Once you've finalised things, contact me and I'll send you my hotel details.' She reached for her coffee. 'Do you have a passport?'

'No.'

Angelina gave a shrug. 'No matter, I'll be arranging a false one in any case. But first, you'll need a blonde wig, similar to this one, for your passport photo.' She clicked on a photo on a camera roll.

'Why?'

'You'll find out soon enough.'

'I wouldn't know where to get one like that.'

'That's all right. There's a shop two streets from here where I bought this one last time I was here. I'll take you there before you leave and I want you to get something as close to mine as possible. I'll wait outside because I don't want there to be any connection between us. And before we get back to the bus we'll stop and get your passport photo taken.'

Elena nodded. 'So, what does the job involve?'

Angelina studied her carefully for a moment. 'You'd be aware, of course, that things won't be exactly above board.'

Elena nodded.

'Good. Just so long as we're on the same page. You needn't worry. There'll be little risk attached unless, of course, something unforeseen comes along. I want to start making money, and we'll operate as a team. I'll explain the process as we go along.'

'Okay, but I wanted to know –'

Angelina silenced her with a wave of a hand. 'I can't tell you any more at this stage. There are things to be finalised, but nothing's altered from what I told you originally. There'll be a chance to visit different countries, stay in some of the best places, dress up and mix in high circles.'

Instinct told Elena not to push things further, and she remained silent.

'Good, that's settled then. All expenses will be covered, with a weekly wage factored in.' She gave a shrug. 'Could end up being more, of course. Depends.' She locked eyes with Elena, who shifted uncomfortably and looked away.

As Elena boarded the bus for the return trip to Viveiro, her mind was in turmoil. She'd spent a considerable amount of her hard-earned money and sacrificed a day's work just to get here, but had learned little. Angelina had not explained the purpose behind the shared clothes and identical blonde wigs, or the need for a false passport. None of it sat comfortably.

¶

Angelina sat on the sofa, reflecting on Elena's visit. Things had gone to plan. The girl was compliant, keen to make a start. *Why wouldn't she be? Those from poverty-stricken backgrounds like hers were destined to a life of low-paid jobs, long hours, and struggling just to make ends meet. Few, if any, would come across an opportunity of this magnitude.* Angelina shrugged. That's the way it was. There'd always be rich and poor in the world. The wealthy took advantage of people like

Elena to make more money. Her father had taught her that. 'If not for us, they'd have no jobs,' he'd reasoned.

Angelina's mind went back to the years spent under her father's watchful eye, learning the ropes in the family company. She was glad of that solid business grounding. But it didn't take long to learn that there were far quicker ways of attaining wealth through criminal enterprises. *Why spend the rest of your life confined to the four walls of an office?* she reflected.

Emboldened by what she'd learned of her father's clandestine dealings over time as things changed, and the money laundering practices she observed in Manila, she figured working alongside another would generate swifter dividends than operating alone.

Her motive was to amass sufficient funds to move into property development, particularly in the poorer communities of European countries, or the Cayman Islands perhaps, just as her uncle had done with his hamlet in northern Spain. Elena's multilingual skills would be gold.

She smiled and leaned back against the sofa, hands clasped behind her head. And once the time was right, she'd resell the properties, using the proceeds to purchase luxury properties on the coast, apartments or resorts.

❡

Elena took one final glimpse of the dingy café where she'd worked the past two years and drew a deep breath. *Had it really been that long?* She reflected on the day Angelina first walked into the café. An encounter that promised to change her life. *Well, there was no turning back now.*

No matter how things panned out from here on, Elena would be able to say she gave it a go. With a momentary pang of guilt, she wondered how the owner would react to finding the key in his letterbox. It mattered little. She'd be well out of there by then. *He's done you few favours, remember,* she reminded herself as she headed out onto the street, drawing the door behind her with a decisive click. She recalled Angelina's words when she first told her of her dreams to see the world: 'That'll take a while, won't it? The pay can't be much in this place.'

'I'm only waiting till something better comes along,' Elena had replied. The words sounded hollow now. Hope was all she had to cling to.

By the time she had settled the month's rent on her flat behind the fisherman's cottage in Viveiro, there'd been little money left. The last few hundred on her card was spent purchasing the wig, obtaining her passport, a new suitcase and carry-on bag, and the ticket for the ten-hour bus trip to Madrid.

18

Elena swallowed hard as she glanced up at the towering modern Madrid hotel where Angelina was staying. Her clammy fingers clutched the handle of the roll-on case as she walked through the main glass doors and across the vast, elaborate foyer where Angelina was waiting.

Two hours later in her six-storey hotel room adjoining Angelina's, the pair sat deep in discussion as Angelina outlined the job. For the first time since she'd arrived, Elena's shoulders relaxed. At last she was getting the information she'd sought since the job offer was made six months ago. They were to spend the next month in Spain while she learned the ropes, before venturing further afield. She felt a rush of excitement as destinations rolled off Angelina's tongue like honey: Paris, Milan, the Greek Islands, the Caribbean.

'You're beholden to me during the time of your employment, with everything staying strictly between us. Understood?'

'Of, of course,' Elena stammered, unnerved by the piercing gaze.

'Good. It wouldn't be worth your while considering otherwise.'

There was an uncomfortable silence, after which Angelina asked, 'You brought the wig?'

'Yes,' she said.

'Good. We'll be wearing them at all times while we work, posing as half-sisters who've met up in Europe to pursue a few business ventures. It's about making money. Big money and not getting caught. There may be occasions where we stand in for each other, cover for each other, perhaps. But I'll go into that when the time comes.'

'So do we work together?' Elena asked.

'Only while you're learning. After that we'll operate independently, making it less likely to attract scrutiny from the authorities. I've several schemes in mind but to begin with, the focus will be on casinos.' She paused. 'Do you know anything about money laundering?'

§

Angelina applied the finishing touches to Elena's makeup as they prepared for the latter's first night on the job, bringing back memories of that first make-up lesson in the café's shabby back room. And the result this time was every bit as astounding. Angelina leaned down, so their heads both faced the mirror, causing Elena to draw a sharp breath.

They could have been twins. 'You won't let me down, now, will you?' Angelina whispered against her cheek.

Elena's skin prickled. 'No, no, of course I won't.'

Angelina smiled and straightened. 'So, let's go and select our outfits.'

¶

Home to more than fifty casinos, Angelina considered Spain the ideal starting point for Elena's training before they ventured further afield. It didn't take long for her to settle into the job, with Angelina watching on nearby, suitably impressed, as Elena switched fluently from Spanish to English as the need arose.

The pair worked side-by-side in VIP lounges, buying up big on chips but gambling sparingly, then cashing in the substantial remainder to be declared gambling winnings at the evening's end.

Accommodation switched between hotels and apartments to avoid scrutiny.

By week two, Elena was using Angelina's identity to open new bank accounts, into which the winnings were deposited. *The girl would be an asset all right*, Angelina thought.

¶

To begin with, Elena had to pinch herself to believe what was happening. The wage was meagre, but who was she to complain? With accommodation and outfits provided, and shared food expenses, except for times spent dining at expensive restaurants while on the job. Yet it was the simple meals Elena savoured the most; meats, cheeses and bread, fruits and vegetables in season and fresh seafood purchased from local markets and village squares that were turned into wholesome, delicious meals, each taking turns to cook.

All the while, Elena was keen to learn, never taking her eyes off Angelina as she charmed and cajoled to get things on her terms. Yet gut instinct warned her there'd be more to the job as things progressed.

She wasn't wrong.

¶

Before long, Elena accompanied Angelina to casino bars and restaurants to meet up with high roller gamblers, who inevitably succumbed to their charms and invited them to the VIP rooms as they gambled.

'It'll be worth it, you'll see,' Angelina assured her beforehand. 'Just lay on the charm, get a few drinks into them along the way, and the odds are they'll hand over wads of cash for you to gamble.' She paused. 'By the way, whatever you make on a night is yours to keep.'

Elena looked dubious. 'They'd have to be after something in return, surely,' she remarked.

Angelina's eyes locked on hers. 'Rich men expect something for their investments, Elena. Remember that. And sex is among them. My best advice is to be classy. Play hard to get. Make promises they want to hear and then dump them before things get to that point. It's worked for me many times over.' Angelina spoke as if she were outlining a football team's tactics. 'Which reminds me, you are on contraceptives, I hope.'

Elena's fingernails dug into her palms. This contravened all expectations. 'I hadn't thought about it,' she said quickly.

'Well, you'd better. Not that it's a worry right now. We won't be in one place long enough to form connections. But you want to make it up the ranks with the rich and famous when we get to the Riviera, right?'

There was a nod.

'Well, that's when sacrifices will be called for; sleeping around a given. But that doesn't mean you sell yourself short. If any man oversteps the mark, no matter his status, you've every justification for getting even.'

'Even?'

She gave a dismissive wave of her hand. 'I'll help you deal with that if the time comes.'

Elena looked at her.

'Well, that's that then,' Angelina concluded. 'It's your turn to cook. Let me know when dinner's ready.' She rose and headed to her room, pulling the door shut behind her.

Settled on her bed, back propped against the pillows, Angelina reflected on the things she'd learned about wealthy men over the years. They liked to be seen with women who were sexy, smart and understanding, who kept things light and playful. They loved it when she dressed in red, particularly tailored, form-fitting outfits. She'd learned not to make the relationship all about money and was careful not to suggest expensive activities on dates, offering to pay for small things and surprising them with gifts from time-to-time. A sure way to impress was showing an interest in their hobbies, her yachting expertise having stood her in good stead on several occasions. She noted how they liked it when she asked for their help. Playing hard to get drove them crazy, as she'd just alluded to Elena. A sure way to success.

Meanwhile, Elena chopped up vegetables in the kitchen for the stir fry, her anxiety rising from the conversation that had transpired. For a moment she paused, reminding herself that she'd been through far worse than this. *You'll figure out something,* she thought.

19

ngelina's expertise in manipulating others to achieve her ends, and Elena's readiness to comply, provided quicker than expected outcomes. Angelina thought back to the day that she'd entered the Viveiro café to be met by the then overweight girl with straggly hair and blotchy skin. Who would have thought ....

It had been well worth the investment.

Few watching the elegantly dressed blonde woman gliding in and out of banks would guess she was opening yet another account with Angelina's false passport and contact details. They'd barely blink an eye if she returned periodically to deposit or withdraw money, or place gold bullion blocks into a safety deposit box, always well below the legal limit to avoid any hint of suspicion.

All of this Elena did without question, much to Angelina's satisfaction. Angelina pondered another option in which Elena could be of use: the smuggling of cash into Macau hidden in her luggage, to be laundered through the autonomous region's infamous casinos. It would only take one coded message to arrange times once there were trusted insiders on hand to wave them through the airports at each end. However, she'd make sure she was waiting at the destination in case something went wrong. A month's gambling in Macau should reap considerable returns, and yet ... There was a limit to how far someone was prepared to go. Elena had once vehemently told her she'd never agree to be a drug mule, no matter the cost. It wasn't that much different. Angelina twirled her ring around her finger absentmindedly. There were always ways and means ...

¶

It took time for Elena to adjust to a life where money was no object. Where dresses were tried on and purchased with scant attention to price tags, French champagne was chosen over chardonnay, and women's immaculate nail extensions would never reveal the chips and ingrained dirt of menial workers. She glanced down at her beautifully coiffured nails that, as far back as she could remember, had been bitten down to the cuticles.

All the while she was curious to learn Angelina's true identity. Where she obtained the money to live such an extravagant lifestyle and the contacts she seemed to conjure up like a magician. Elena had no doubt she'd been on the run like she'd said. It was one of the few things Angelina told her that she believed. *On the run from what?* Not for the first time, she found the thought unsettling.

Elena knew better than to snoop, but curiosity had the better of her as time wore on. One evening, she waited until Angelina left the apartment, and entered her room. Anxiety skyrocketing and mouth dry, she searched Angelina's drawers then proceeded to look around. Nothing of note that she could see. As expected, the safe Angelina took everywhere remained locked in the bottom of the wardrobe. She wondered what, apart from their passports, money and jewellery, was likely to be inside. What she'd give to find out the code … Nonetheless, she was far from discouraged. It was early days yet.

¶

Angelina returned early to the apartment after the Pilates class she'd booked in town was cancelled, much to her annoyance. The moment she stepped inside, she knew something was not right. Her eyes locked on her bedroom door, now ajar, on the far side of the room. There was movement inside, and as she approached, she could see Elena swirling around the room in one of her dresses, oblivious to her presence.

'What in the hell do you think you're up to!'

Elena spun around mid-air, almost losing her balance in the process.

'Get that dress off now!' Angelina shrieked, hands on hips and eyes blazing.

'But I thought you said we were to share clothes,' Elena blurted out.

'The ones *I* give you permission to wear. Don't you ever touch my clothes again without asking!'

Elena nodded quickly, looking down at the floor. She was unaware that the crimson, off-the-shoulder, slinky dress she'd chosen to try on was a replica of Angelina's favourite, purchased in Milan with her father. Forced to leave the dress behind when she fled Australia, Angelina had an identical one made by a designer in Manila.

Angelina's eyes flashed as she turned to the make-up case filled with expensive cosmetics. 'You didn't help yourself to that as well?' she snapped, as if Elena hadn't been through enough already.

Elena could feel herself redden. 'No, I swear.'

Angelina flipped open the case and inspected the contents. 'Just as well.'

Elena's heart hammered. She'd been just about to sample the array of lipsticks and eyeshadows in exotic shades not provided in her basic make-up kit. It was a stark warning to be more careful in the future.

¶

In the early stages of the job, Elena was free to do as she wished on her two days off, with Angelina too engrossed in whatever she was up to on her laptop to care. The first two weeks spent in Madrid were the best that Elena could recall. She spent hours wandering the streets and gazing in shop windows, sometimes venturing into the well-to-do neighbourhoods and glancing up at the apartment blocks she'd spent much of her time cleaning. Her years spent in the slums, just ten minutes away by train, were a distant memory.

Elena wondered if their father was still alive or whether he had drunk himself to death. The only photo of her mother was taken with him before they married. They seemed so much in love. Elena found herself wondering what went so wrong. Why she walked out on her and her two brothers when they were so young. Why she never returned to see how they were, her father wouldn't say. It was some consolation that she was too young to remember her mother at all. Looking back, she admired her father for what he did for the three of them in those early years. He worked long hours on a meagre wage to make ends meet, and they never went without. Nonetheless, the two boys never respected the sacrifices made on their behalf. She recalled how things gradually fell apart; how her brothers turned to drug-related criminal activities, and her father wallowed in a pool of self-pity and hopelessness. Not for the first time, she wondered what might have transpired if she'd remained in the shabby flat where she'd been raised. But deep down, she'd always known she'd leave, the only one in her family with the resolve to rise above her circumstances and make something of her life. She hugged her shoulders. *This is just the beginning,* she thought. *It'll all turn out. I'll make sure of it.*

It was late evening, and Angelina's door was closed. Elena bit her lip thoughtfully. Time to take advantage and head out for a few hours Snatch a bite to eat. She knew better than to bother Angelina when the door was closed. Perhaps she was asleep. *Who knew? Why not a bit of clubbing,* she found herself thinking. *A few hours won't hurt.*

She felt exhilarated as she slipped into her jeans, ballerina flats, and a classy slim-fitting top purchased with her meagre savings. The chance to venture out with her glossy, shoulder-length hair loose, free of the restrictions of a wig, and face devoid of caked-on make-up, dark eye liner, and brightly coloured lips.

Stepping out into the cool spring evening, she headed along the well-lit, busy road. There was a plethora of vibrant, all-night bars and nightclubs in this part of Madrid but she settled on a small dance club set in a cobblestoned side street, reminiscent of those she'd frequented as a teenager on her rare nights off work.

There was an overwhelming urge to do the simple things she'd missed; having fun and dancing among those her age. No pretence. No paunchy middle-aged men. No expectations. Her spirits lifted as she stepped inside the recently renovated, bustling bar set in an old warehouse. It was already ten, but groups were only just settling in for dinner, which could last several hours. It was a time to enjoy the company of others, share stories and tell jokes. Peals of laughter rose intermittently above the boisterous chatter, and waiters navigated the tables with precariously balanced plates of steaming Spanish food. After midnight it was customary for patrons to leave their tables and head to the bar for drinks, joined there by late-night revellers. It was then that the dancing kicked in, continuing until the early hours of the morning or, in some venues, when the sun came up.

Elena felt not the slightest bit self-conscious about sitting down alone. It was not uncommon in Madrid, where bars were an acceptable way to meet people and initiate conversations. She'd barely had the chance to take in her surroundings when a good-looking, tanned young man rose from a group seated at a nearby table and approached her. 'Are you waiting for someone?' he asked in Spanish.

'No.'

'Want to join us?'

'Okay,' Elena said, rising to her feet.

'What's your name?' he yelled over the din.

'Elena.'

'Hi Elena, I'm Miguel.' He took her hand and led her to his table, where seven others sat.

'This is Elena,' he said.

'Hi Elena,' chorused the cheerful group. Bums shuffled along a wooden bench and she squeezed between Miguel and a large girl who looked to be in her early twenties and welcomed her with a warm, friendly smile. The joviality resumed. There were four women and two men around her age, none of whom appeared attached.

Elena smiled. She'd missed mixing with groups such as this, with nothing more in mind than being out for a good time. It kept things uncomplicated and enjoyable.

She learned that Miguel was a builder, hardly surprising given his lean build, strong arms and hands, and that five of the group, two of whom were his cousins, recently moved to the suburb where Elena had been raised, searching for cheaper rent to help get them on their feet.

'You're kidding me!' she exclaimed. 'Whereabouts?'

The girl sitting alongside her named a street just a block from Elena's old home, sharing images on her iPhone of a narrow, steep road full of buildings in varying states of disrepair and another depicting a four-storey apartment block where they had found accommodation. Elena swallowed hard. Nothing had changed. *Who knew? One day, the entire area could be erased and replaced by upmarket apartment blocks and shops. Probably not in my lifetime, though,* she thought.

'So why did you leave?' the girl enquired.

'It's a long story,' Elena said. 'I don't really want to go into it.'

'That bad, hey?'

'You could say that.'

Elena was spared the pain of elaborating further when the waiter appeared, placing their dessert order before them. The fried churros were promptly snatched off the platter, plunged into bowls of Spanish hot chocolate and devoured without hesitation. The platter had barely been emptied when Miguel declared, 'Well then, drinks before we dance?' There was a roar of approval, and the group called for the bill and divvied the amount between them before heading up the stairs to the bar on the next level, where a sign read 'No cocktails no party'. Elena grinned as she passed and perched alongside the group on bar stools as they ordered cocktails of varying hues over crushed ice with slices of citrus fruit and brightly coloured paper umbrellas. She had barely taken the last sip of her potent pink mixture recommended by the bartender when Miguel pulled her to her feet, and the group headed down two levels to the basement dance floor, now filled with patrons.

A live band performed a range of vibrant music with patrons pumped and dancing. Girls and boys danced wildly with whoever was nearest. It mattered little. Soon, Elena found herself lost in time. It was one of the best nights she could recall.

It was 4 a.m. when she glanced at the clock on the wall. 'Shit!' she exclaimed in alarm.

'What's wrong?' Miguel remarked.

'I didn't realise it was that late. My dad will kill me. I've got to go.' She rushed out into the hall, with Miguel close in tow.'

'Can I drive you home?' he pressed.

'No, no, I'll get a taxi.'

'Wait. Will you be back?' He took hold of her arm.

'I'll try. I loved tonight. I really did,' Elena told him. 'And thanks.'

A brief kiss on his cheek, and she was gone.

⁊

All was in darkness as Elena inserted the key card and stepped inside the apartment. Immediately she felt her shoulders loosen. It was a certainty Angelina would have been up and waiting if she'd discovered her not back at this hour. Nonetheless, her heart pounded wildly against her chest as she crept towards her room, each footstep magnified a hundredfold in her ears. All the while praying that Angelina would not awaken. *Why? What does it matter? It's your day off. You can do as you want,* she thought as she changed into her pyjamas and climbed beneath the covers. But instinct told her things weren't about to be that easy.

¶

Angelina announced they were to leave Madrid in two days and Elena mentioned venturing out for some nightlife on their last evening. 'No, that's out of the question. Not while you're working for me.'

The words stunned her like an animal struck by the dart of an immobilising drug. 'But you said nothing about –'

'Now listen here, Elena. What you do with your spare time is none of my business, but I draw the line at you socialising with strangers. It could place us both at risk and jeopardise everything. I've invested far too much time and effort in arranging things. I'm afraid you'll just have to wait until we part ways.'

Angelina was in control mode, and Elena knew it would be dangerous to dispute the issue. Nonetheless she felt a disturbing sense of uneasiness. The last thing she expected when she took on the job was being deprived of the freedom to do as she wished on her days off. *Keep doing what you have been,* she told herself. *Look grateful and do what she says. You'll figure something out.* But deep down, a profound sense of unease persisted.

20

The pair traversed the country for two weeks, staying in expensive hotels and moving from one casino to the next. Sophisticated and stylish, they spent long hours gambling the proceeds of Angelina's ill-gotten gains that had been transferred from offshore bank accounts to credit cards. After a month, Angelina decided it was time to leave Spain and head for Italy and beyond.

Elena looked forward to the journey with great anticipation. She had never been to Italy despite it being only a fifteen-hour bus trip from Madrid. In fact, she'd never ventured far from her hometown before she'd left for Viveiro. Outings were a rarity. Her father barely scraped up enough funds to put food on the table and a roof over their heads, let alone consider holidays. The only memory Elena could recall of a family outing was as a five or six-year-old, when the family travelled by train to Valencia to spend the day by the beach. Before her mother walked out. Memories were hazy. Sandcastles and buckets, Elena's older two brothers tearing down the sand into the water, her mother fastening the sun-bonnet under her chin, and her father rubbing suntan lotion into her baby skin, shoulders and arms with gentle fingers. Being carried out into the warm sea on his shoulders. The squeals of seagulls high above.

She'd not been back since. Perhaps subconsciously she wanted to hold onto the memory of that day and suspend it in time. All of that mattered little now. A new life beckoned. As she strolled through the old town's cobbled covered walkway towards the main square where old men sat playing cards, birds hovered above in search of scraps and artisans peddled their wares, she could scarcely believe what was unfolding. A three-week Italian stint. *Then who knows where they were headed.*

The pair operated at different casinos, now that Elena had learned the ropes, always in their signature blonde wigs and sophisticated attire, staying in apartments away from tourist hubs, where they could come and go without undue notice before moving to the next town. Angelina chose only the best; self-contained accommodation with separate bedrooms and ensuites. Sometimes there would be overnight stays in small B+Bs at remote villages along the way, enroute to larger towns or cities. It was these stopovers that Elena looked forward to the most. She loved chatting with the owners in their native language over coffee. Learning about their lifestyles and history, noting the pride on their faces as they showed pictures of their families or pointed out plants in their vegetable patches and flowers in the garden.

Despite Elena's offers to translate, Angelina could see no point in wasting her time on such unproductive activities. She spent most of her time in her room with her laptop until she was called at meals times.

Elena was not in the least concerned. She was grateful to have her own room, especially in out-of-the-way villages like these. It was like living in another world, gazing around small bedrooms with sloped ceilings, vibrantly coloured furnishings, old lampshades, handmade quilt covers and faded rugs. A stark contrast to the drab flat she'd grown up in with its smoke-stained walls, chipped basin, sticky, green vinyl couch and matching chairs that had been there for as long as she could remember.

¶

They arrived back at their hotel at 4 a.m. following a late-night session at a casino in the nearby town. Too tired to eat, Elena was glad to kick off her high-heeled sandals, shimmy out of her dress, pull on her pyjamas and climb between the covers.

Tomorrow was their only day off, and she looked forward to a sleep-in, brunch perhaps, and a chance to explore the small picturesque village with its pink, orange and red houses set against a mountain backdrop.

It was the presence that awoke her. Standing over her in the darkness. Elena's eyes opened in alarm, but she dared not move. Dared not breathe. She could not see Angelina's face but knew it was her. Elena squeezed her eyes tightly, willing her to leave. But she stayed. Seconds became minutes, and minutes were lost in time. *Why are you here? What do you want?* Elena feared what might be yet to come, thoughts swirling chaotically around in her mind. She'd done what was asked of her. Angelina had seemed pleased enough. *Hadn't she?*

Elena was well accustomed to Angelina's cold demeanour, but this? This was something different …

Her veins turned to ice. A soft click of the door. And Angelina was gone.

The following day, Angelina acted as if nothing had taken place. But the incident unnerved Elena to the core, and she determined that she would lock her room each night. One thing was certain. Things would never be the same between them again …

9

In the coming weeks, the pair crisscrossed the countryside in their hire car, working in casinos and spending leisurely days wandering the streets, watching the world go by on cafe sidewalks while sipping lattes, or biting into crisp cones filled with creamy gelato. Meals were shared dishes in restaurants, homemade pasta shops or crammed corner tables of delis laden with spiced and smoked meats, cheeses, bread, and delicacies.

Occasionally, Elena sneaked out when Angelina's door was closed to sample alone the decadent pastries the marketplace had to offer, or perhaps to a café for some chocolate amaretti crème caramel or a bowl of tiramisu. What Angelina didn't know …

❡

Angelina oversaw Elena carefully. After three weeks in Italy all was going to plan. It was time to put Elena through the first test. A contact had passed on details of an Italian underworld figure who specialised in selling cut-price diamonds obtained through clandestine dealings with an African diamond mine associate. An ideal avenue to launder some cash. From what she'd been told, he had an eye for beautiful women and could be swayed on the price accordingly. The catch was he spoke little English. A perfect opportunity to utilise Elena's multilingual skills.

'Remember what I told you about swapping identities at times?' she asked Elena over breakfast.

There was a nod.

'Well, this is one of them.' Angelina explained about meeting with the contact to haggle over the price of diamonds and secure a deal. Elena looked dubious.

'Look, it's no different to opening a new bank account using my ID,' she added with a shrug.

There was a moment's silence. 'When?' Elena asked.

'In two nights at an exclusive restaurant not far from here. I'll tell you what to do and say beforehand, don't worry. Look, it's no big deal. If I could speak Italian, I'd do it myself,' she said with a wave of her hand as though she was referring to an errand to the shops. 'Who knows, maybe it could lead to more deals before the guy leaves town. So, if there are favours involved you go along with it, understand?'

Elena winced.

Angelina was quick on the uptake. 'You agreed when you took on this job that it may be a condition from time to time. Right?'

Elena was too shocked to respond.

'And this could be one of them. So, you'd better get used to it.' Angelina rose and headed to her room.

9

Angelina attended to Elena's make-up for the evening and chose which outfit she was to wear.

'Now remember everything I told you,' she said as Elena left the apartment for the waiting taxi.

The candlelit table sat in a private room at the back of the elegant ristorante. When the heavy-set man in his early fifties rose to extend his hand, Elena's skin crawled. His lewd eyes never left her, and his warm, pudgy fingers lingered on hers for a few moments too long.

'You're as beautiful as I've heard, Ava,' he said in Italian as he pulled out a chair.

'Grazie.'

The conversation continued in Italian. 'I've been told you're Spanish.' He settled opposite.

She nodded.

'So where did you learn Italian?'

'My father was Italian,' she lied.

'I see.' He paused, clearing his throat. 'I heard you might be interested in further deals if we reach a satisfactory agreement this evening.'

'Perhaps. It depends.'

'Depends on what?'

'How good a deal you can come up with.'

He roared with laughter, revealing a mouthful of yellow teeth. 'I like your style. We can discuss things further over dinner.'

Elena ordered the most expensive items on the menu, reasoning it would make up for the suffering she had to undergo with this odious man. The dealer, conversely, seemed oblivious to the rapidly accumulating bill. His focus of attention appeared solely on her bare shoulders, arms and decolletage.

The vintage, full-bodied pinot noir was one of the best she'd sampled, and she would have liked to enjoy more than the one glass she was taking her time sipping. She thought it best to get the deal over and done with while the dealer was in a fit state of mind. Already, the bottle sat half empty on the table.

'So, let's get down to business,' she said, twirling a blond lock of her wig in her fingers.

'Yes, let's,' he said smoothly. 'So why diamonds?'

'Why not?' she fluttered her eyelashes. 'Can I see them?'

His eyes darted around the room, waiting until the waiter disappeared into the kitchen before pulling out a blue velvet bag from his pocket, releasing the drawstring, and tipping the contents before them.

Elena gasped at the dozen diamonds that glittered under the candlelight on the pink linen tablecloth.

'*Bellissima*, eh?' he said.

'*Si. Sono incredibili.*' She paused for a moment. 'Before we start, you know of course that I'll be getting these independently valued.'

'I expected you would.' He shot her a sardonic grin.

As the bartering took place and a price agreed upon according to Angelina's instructions, she felt almost giddy, taking the roll of euro notes from her bag and peeling off the required amount, just as she'd seen high rollers do. Having such a sum at her disposal was almost inconceivable. She watched as he quickly checked the amount and passed over the bag of diamonds with a nod, then placed the money in his pocket.

'Dessert?' he asked.

The foot stroking her bare leg under the table and the sight of his tongue wetting his lip as he spoke became too much, and the moment the waiter departed with the empty dessert dishes, she glanced at her watch and remarked, 'Oh my god, I didn't realise it was that late. I need to get going.' She reached for her bag.

'Wait. We haven't spoken about more deals.' He placed a sweaty palm over her hand.

'Hm. I'll have to think about it.' She eased her hand from under his. 'What can you offer me?'

His eyes lowered to her breasts, causing her to squirm. 'A slightly better price for a regular customer, perhaps?'

'And that's it?'

'Dinner and evening at my hotel first.'

'I'll think about it.'

¶

Angelina sat on the sofa, tapping her foot impatiently, arms crossed as she waited for Elena to return. The moment the door clicked open, she rose and crossed the room.

'You've got the diamonds?'

Elena nodded and handed over the small blue velvet bag. Angelina headed to the kitchen bench, pulled open the bag's drawstring, and tilted it so that the diamonds spilled onto the bench top. Picking up the nearest and holding it to the light, she remarked, 'Beautiful.' Turning to face Elena, she added, 'So did he mention more deals?'

Elena shook her head. 'No. Not a thing.'

Angelina looked at her suspiciously but said nothing. Elena's legs went to water. *Had Angelina suspected something? It was hard to tell. Her face was emotionless.*

The following morning, Elena was instructed to wear her blonde wig and accompany Angelina to a nearby bank where an account had been set up to place the diamonds in a safety deposit box. Angelina stood on the street outside in case

Elena had plans of her own. Yet there'd been little reason to doubt her. She'd deposited blocks of gold bullion in Madrid without an issue.

¶

Elena sat in her room crunching on a handful of potato chips. She had next to no money of her own, apart from the meagre weekly wage, and that was subject to performance. She couldn't walk away if she wanted to. Not yet. Meanwhile, Angelina shifted tack, stepping away from casinos to focus on picking up wealthy men to be wined and dined in readiness for the sojourn to bigger casinos such as the Casino de Monte-Carlo.

The pair frequented exclusive hotels, never identically dressed to avoid drawing attention to themselves. There was no shortage of wealthy takers, with frequent offers to wine and dine at exclusive places or see the sights; accepted or rejected by Angelina based on their perceived wealth, status and conduct. All the while, Elena looked on intently, absorbing everything. Occasionally they ventured out alone, Angelina trusting Elena to employ the tactics she'd demonstrated to target wealthy and influential men. By replicating Angelina's mantra of playing hard to get, she'd managed to avoid undesirable sexual liaisons to that point, much to her relief. But how long could she continue to do so? The time for stepping into the playground of the rich and famous was fast approaching …

21

Salvadore Costa never intended to leave his hotel room in Milan and head to the bar. He most certainly never intended to pick up a woman. But he'd had a fight with his wife. Again. This time to do with the purchase of a ridiculously high-priced handbag, of which she had several.

'You think I'm made of money?' he'd shrieked.

'Don't come back at me with that one. I'm aware of the Porsche you've got your eye on. Vito told me all about it.'

Without another word Salvadore had stormed out, slamming the door in his wake. The chauffeur was a blubbering mess by the time he was done. Payback for his wife would be silence and a few nights at a five-star hotel until he'd calmed down enough to return to his well-guarded, palatial residence. A ritual he'd performed numerous times over the years.

The sixty-six-year-old belonged to one of Sicily's oldest mafia families; a prominent extortionist in charge of a crew who ran a widespread protection racket over shopkeepers and businesses in the region. His close-knit brother was up to his neck in smuggling and arms running, and his nephew was a hitman.

Wealthy beyond belief, tough and ruthless, Salvador was not one to be messed with and those foolish enough to try learned the hard way.

The hotel was among his favourites – a large, flashy complex set in the heart of Milan's CBD. He often booked in under the alias of Saverio Amato, with the staff worded up on his idiosyncrasies and whims. Generous gratuities made attention to detail worth their while.

It was 10 p.m. when he stepped into his room after a few hours leisurely spent at one of the hotel's restaurants. Switching on the light, his eyes glanced around the elegant but lonely interior. He didn't feel in the mood to settle in and flick channels on the large plasma screen. Restless, irritable , and in need of a nightcap, he closed the door and made his way down to the bar on the fourth floor.

The bar was relatively busy for a weeknight, with couples and small groups seated around the well-spaced, tastefully decorated area, deep in conversation. When he walked through the main entrance and crossed to the bar, he was immediately recognised by the barman, who put down the glass he was polishing.

'Good evening, sir.'

There was a curt nod of acknowledgement.

'The usual tonight?'

'Yeah. Make it a double shot.'

'Take a seat. I'll bring it over to you.'

The bartender tipped ice into a glass and reached for a bottle of cognac on the shelf. Salvador was about to head to a quiet corner when he stopped, riveted by the beautiful blonde seated alone in a leather armchair before a low table.

'Who is she?' he remarked, his eyes not moving.

'I don't know, sir,' the barman said. 'She arrived about half an hour ago.'

Salvadore was not, in general, one to break the mafia family's strict code of conduct by fraternising with strangers in public, but this was an exception.

Angelina was quick to note the gold watch and chain of the man dressed in a tailored grey jacket and pants, whose eyes were on her from the other side of the room, and she looked down coyly as he made his way towards her, drink in hand.

'Are you waiting for someone?' His eyes swept appreciatively over the elegant, knee-length dress and long, lean, crossed legs.

'Yes, no, well, I was. A business associate, but he didn't show.'

'Would you mind if I joined you?' he asked, the voice deep, polite, and with a distinctive Italian accent, his expensive aftershave evoking memories of her days in the Manila casino's VIP room.

¶

'I met someone tonight,' Angelina said when she returned from the hotel a little after midnight and kicked off her sandals. 'An older guy from Sicily.'

'Oh?' Elena reached for the TV remote and turned down the volume.

'He's rich. More than rich, I'd say,' Angelina added with a smirk.

'What does he do?'

'Investments, property development ventures, in particular.' She stroked her chin thoughtfully. 'He might well be of use to us.'

'So you're seeing him again, I take it.'

'Oh, yes. You can bet on it.'

'When?'

'Tomorrow night. For dinner. He wanted to make it tonight. But he can wait.'

Elena nodded. 'And what did you tell him about yourself?'

Angelina gave a sardonic smile. 'Nothing, of course.'

9

Salvadore had little sleep, fantasising about the woman he knew only as Ava. She gave nothing away except to mention being two weeks into a three-month trip around Europe before returning to Australia. She was all class, matched with the intelligence he'd not seen in a woman for some time. When she announced at midnight it was time she went, he felt like a love-struck schoolboy when he blurted out, 'But wait, would you join me for dinner?'

He lay in the darkness, listening to the faint sounds

of distant traffic. Ava had almost walked out of his life. Even when she finally acceded to his request to see her again, albeit on her terms, he couldn't tell what she was thinking behind the cool façade. Salvadore was used to women flaunting themselves for his wealth. The fact that she exhibited no such tendencies made the desire for her all the more potent.

⁋

Salvadore arrived early at the hotel's expensive rooftop restaurant. He'd offered to pick Angelina up, but she was not about to disclose her whereabouts. It created more intrigue.

She glided into the room on time, dressed in the slim-fitting, scarlet dress she always used to impress, and Salvadore's breath caught in his throat as he rose to kiss her hand and pull out her chair. 'You look beautiful, Ava,' he said.

'Thank you, Saverio.'

He pushed in her chair with one smooth movement and sat down opposite.

With an appreciative glance around the room, she remarked, 'The views up here are incredible. Thank you for inviting me.'

'Thank you for coming.'

Initially, Angelina kept the conversation light, feigning a genuine interest in Sicily, which resonated strongly with the fiercely loyal resident. All the while she sought insight into his business ventures, hoping to glean information on how to set up trusts and corporations in tax havens. He gave away nothing, much to her frustration. Even when she lingered over dinner, encouraging him to order more drinks in the hope of loosening him up, she learned little.

Meanwhile, Salvadore sat back, elbows on the table, fingers steepled under his chin as she spoke, all the time wanting her more. Not just for a night but as his mistress. Glamorous young girlfriends, considered a symbol of success and prestige for a man of his standing, were commonplace amongst Sicilian mafia families. And a man with a wife and a mistress on the side was regarded as virile and robust.

Younger married men tended to remain faithful to their wives while establishing their families and accumulating wealth. But as their power and influence grew their wives had no option but to turn a blind eye if they wished to retain their position in the family. Divorce was seldom seen as an option.

Salvadore fitted into this category. Married at twenty to his childhood sweetheart, a common practice at the time, he was content being a family man to his attractive wife, three sons and daughter.

By the time he turned fifty, his wife had begun to lose her looks and their marriage had lost any spark of romance or passion. A series of brief affairs ensued, which his wife sorrowfully accepted as inevitable. She turned her attention to the family home and the expected arrival of grandchildren. Their relationship was frosty, to say the least, but Salvadore ensured that her prestige was protected.

He had the final say with the finances, and there wasn't a thing she could do about it. Conversely, she had the final say in family matters. She'd been a good mother. He couldn't deny her that.

There'd only been one mistress, a stunning, twenty-two-year-old Italian law student. She was only too happy to reside in the classy, spacious apartment and be lavished with expensive gifts and trips away. A twelve-month affair that ended five years ago. He should have realised that she'd move out after obtaining her degree.

He glanced at Angelina's exquisite features in the candle-light, asking himself if it was worth risking things all over again. But he already had the answer to that …

It was already 11:30, and Angelina was still no closer to the answers she sought. With a flash of irritation, she decided enough was enough. They were leaving Italy within days. It was time to fast-track the process.

§

Salvadore had to pinch himself to believe Angelina was accompanying him to his room for a nightcap before she left for home. The touch of her soft hand was electrifying, and he barely took in a word she said as they took the lift to the tenth floor.

Angelina did not expect a penthouse apartment nor one of such opulence. *He'd have to be involved in some kind of racket, surely,* she thought. *All the better.* Crossing the floor, she gazed out the expansive windows across the city lights. 'This is some place, Saverio.' She turned to face him.

'I'm glad you like it. I usually stay here when I'm in town on business. Take a seat, and I'll get you a drink. What would you like?'

'Do you have Campari by any chance?' she asked, settling on the white leather sofa.

He looked surprised. 'Sure. It's amongst my favourites. I thought you'd find it too bitter.'

'I did when I first arrived in Italy, but it's grown on me.' She watched him reach for the bottle from the shelf. 'I'm not one for overly sweet drinks.'

'Me neither.' He returned with drinks in hand and sat alongside her. Angelina sipped her drink slowly, engaging him in intelligent conversation in keeping with her projected persona, all the while feeding his ego. She fluttered her eyelashes when he paid her a compliment and made no attempt to pull away when his arm slid around her shoulders.

A while later, she glanced at the clock on the wall, turned to him, and said, 'Well, it's been a lovely evening, Saverio, but I didn't realise it was so late. Best I get going.'

She carefully removed his hand, which was slowly making its way up her thigh, and rose.

'Wait. Stay, would you?'

Angelina hesitated. 'Well, maybe one more drink.'

'That's not what I meant.'

She took their empty glasses. 'I'll think about it.'

He smiled and closed his eyes, listening to her light

footsteps across to the bar and the ensuing clink of ice, his senses already dulled by the previous three drinks.

❡

Salvadore didn't recall taking her hand and leading her to the bedroom, dimming the lights and taking off his shoes. But Angelina did. It had taken seven minutes for the drink's colourless and odourless infused drug to take effect; the first indication, slurred speech, followed by a lack of coordination and sudden drowsiness. She glanced at the figure sprawled before her on the king-sized bed. If her contact's account of the drug was accurate, he could be well out of it for six to ten hours, waking with little memory of the previous evening. Sex may well have been part of it for all he knew. Something she would attest to if what she uncovered made the relationship worth persisting with.

Wasting no time, she headed to the ensuite, where an array of tailored pants, blazers and shirts hung alongside pairs of handmade leather shoes. A set of keys with the Mercedes logo lay beside a thick rolled-up wad of notes and a gold cigarette lighter on the top shelf. But the black folder on a shelf above the safe caught her attention. As she quickly reached for it and pulled out the contents, a crazed roar from behind jolted her senses, sending her spinning around, the printed documents flying from her hands like roofs in a tornado.

'What in the hell do you think you're up to!' Salvadore screamed, lurching at her, his instinct for survival kicking in despite his drugged stupor, his strong fingers reaching around her throat, squeezing hard.

But Angelina hurled him off balance in one adrenalin-fuelled move, followed by a violent shove that sent him reeling backwards. What followed seemed to unfurl in slow motion, his arms flailing in a desperate attempt to maintain balance, head smashing into the marble bedside table as he fell heavily to the floor. He lay motionless, eyes wide open and looking at Angelina, as if he was thinking, *You bitch, you scheming bitch. I should have known.*

Angelina, stood before him, frozen; she was hypnotised by a single splash of blood on the wall. This was unfamiliar territory. Ever since the failed attempt on her sister's life, she'd kept her hands clean when she wanted to rid herself of someone.

Think. Think. What do I do here? she thought quickly, fighting through the panic. Rushing out of the room, she grabbed her phone off the coffee table and with shaking fingers, tapped Elena's number.

'Where are you?'

'I'm about to get in the shower. Why?'

'Well, you need to get dressed. I need you over here now. Room 1006. And make sure you wear your wig.' There was a click.

'What the hell,' Elena muttered, heart racing. Something was wrong. Very wrong …

With heart hammering, she changed, rushed out and flagged a nearby taxi to the hotel, a five-minute drive away.

No one appeared to notice as she coolly crossed the floor and headed to the lift. The room was the last on the left. No sooner had Elena knocked when the door swung open, and Angelina dragged her inside.

'What is it?' Elena said anxiously.

'There's been a stuff up.'

'What do you mean?'

'The guy was nothing like I thought. He was out for one thing only, and when he put the hard word on, I resisted. Then things turned ugly.'

Elena's anxiety stepped up a notch. 'Wh-what do you mean, ugly?'

'He attacked me. Luckily, the spiked drink I'd given him had already kicked in and it wasn't hard to throw him off balance. The problem was, he fell and cracked his head on something. He didn't get up.'

Elena's face went white. 'You don't mean he's dead?'

'Yeah.' Angelina nodded towards the bedroom, reached forward, and squeezed Elena's chin so hard she winced. 'Now listen to me, it was an accident. A matter of self-defence. Have you got that?'

There was a quick nod.

'Good. The bastard deserved everything he got. Now do as I say, then we'll get the hell out of here.' Angelina released her grip.

Elena, too paralysed to think, swallowed hard as Angelina dragged her into the bedroom.

If not for the deep gash on his temple and blood-caked

face, the thick-set man slumped hard against the bedside table, could be any drunk who'd not made it to the bed.

Angelina's eyes fixed on hers. 'Okay, we're about to make this look like a robbery gone wrong.'

Elena looked at her in alarm. 'I don't understand.'

'Just do as I say. First, you're to go through the pockets. Find the guy's wallet, phone and credit cards.'

'Can't we just go?' came the panicked response.

'Do it!'

With trembling legs, Elena approached the body, trying not to look at his face as she reached to search the pockets. This didn't feel right. Angelina's eyes gleamed as Elena handed over the thick roll of cash held by an elastic band, a Gucci wallet bulging with more money, and an assortment of cards that included two credit cards.

'Good girl. Now remove his gold ring and chain.'

Elena clammed up. 'I-I can't.'

'Do it!'

Elena took hold of the large hand, struggling to get the signet ring off his finger; she tugged until it came free. In a cold sweat, she reached for the clasp of the gold chain pulled tightly around the man's neck that lolled against his chest, fumbling between the folds of saggy, not-yet-cool skin until the chain released. Last to be removed was the Cartier watch.

Angelina imperturbably extended a hand to take the jewellery. 'Good. Good.' Turn off the lamp, and let's go.' In the main room, Angelina said, 'Okay, we can't afford to be seen leaving together. You go first, call a taxi and go back to the apartment.'

After Elena left, Angelina stood for a few moments, furious that she'd underestimated the dosage of the sleep-inducing drug. Everything had been seamless to that point. But it was too late for reproach. With her mind quickly kicking into gear she grabbed a hand towel, wrapped it around her hand and wiped every surface she thought she may have touched. Even if she missed one, it was Elena's prints that were all over the man's body and personal belongings. Not hers.

That was all she needed for now.

¶

Back at their apartment, Angelina nodded towards the sofa, 'Sit and listen.'

Elena did what she was told, still traumatised by what she had witnessed.

'I've got this covered, all right? Don't panic.'

'But what if —'

'Shut up.' Angelina's eyes bored into hers. 'I told you from the outset there could be dangers involved with the job.'

'Yeah but —'

'The guy went to attack me and I defended myself. End of story. Things go wrong from time to time, Elena, and I'm quite used to dealing with them. So, here's the plan. In the morning we check out and find somewhere else on the other side town. I'll do some Google searches and make a booking.'

'For how long?'

'A couple of weeks, until things die down. By the time I

order new wigs online and arrange for new passports, it'll be time to skip the country.' She paused for a moment. 'I know you've just been through a lot. How about we flit around Europe for a bit and take in the sights?'

Elena looked at her in disbelief. 'Really?'

'Why not? Perhaps hook up with a few tycoons; go cruising around on their yachts.'

She stroked Elena's hand. 'It'll all work out, I promise you.'

The touch sent a cold shiver shooting through Elena's body but she was too paralysed to pull away.

ƍ

Elena stepped into a hot shower, lathering herself frantically with soap as if to wipe away all traces of the man. But thoughts of what transpired refused to subside, long after she slid beneath the covers. *It's not as if I was responsible,* she reassured herself. *It had looked like a bungled robbery. Things would act out as Angelina said. And soon they'd be out of the country. Wouldn't they?*

But sleep was fitful, wracked with dreams of the corpse, its eyes wide open, accusing her as she tugged at the ring that refused to budge, its free hand grasping a handful of her hair and refusing to let go. She woke amongst the tangled sheets in a pool of sweat.

ƍ

Angelina was up early, tidying the kitchen and packing her things. The last item she attended to was the contents of the safe. Picking up the diamond-encrusted Cartier watch and gold chain, she scrutinised them closely with a satisfied whistle. *Should bring in quite a packet,* she thought. She'd already counted the thick wad of notes in the Gucci wallet and the two tight rolls of money. Twelve thousand euros. She'd been on the money. The guy certainly was crooked. An image of his short, thick stature, receding dyed hair and lustful eyes entered her mind. *At least I saved myself from sex with the arsehole,* Angelina thought with a shudder. Italians were supposed to be among the best of lovers, but she doubted he fitted the mould.

She'd not considered the prospect of spiking drinks until she stayed in Manila, where the practice was common, particularly in kidnapping or robbing wealthy foreigners. If the possibility of getting caught wasn't high, she and Elena could make a packet sourcing unsuspecting wealthy older men by these means to make off with whatever valuables they could lay their hands on.

When she checked her phone, Angelina stopped dead in her tracks to learn that the man she'd killed had been a prominent member of the Sicilian mafia. She frowned as his face flashed across the screen. This put a different slant on things. A brief report read that the death was sustained in an altercation during an early morning robbery in his hotel room. But that came as little comfort. Angelina had been around gangs long enough to know this wouldn't be the last of it. *Escaping the authorities was one thing but the mafia? If only I hadn't come across him in the first place.*

CCTV footage captured the moments when Angelina and Elena entered and exited the room at varying stages; both were declared persons of interest.

'I think you'd better take a look at this,' Angelina called out.

'Shit!' Elena's eyes were wide with alarm when Angelina flashed the news story in front of her. 'You never said he belonged to the mafia.'

'I didn't know myself.'

Elena snatched the phone and scrolled further, gasping when their images appeared on the screen.

'It's just routine,' Angelina said with a nonchalant shrug.

'But —'

'Get a grip, Elena. Look how grainy those images are. We're in our blonde wigs, looking down. It could be anyone.'

Elena looked far from convinced.

'Nothing's changed. It's a matter of sticking to what I outlined last night.' Angelina's tone was businesslike. 'You've ordered the taxi, right?'

Elena nodded.

'Well, get your things and I'll join you soon.' Angelina stood with her arms crossed. *So far so good. The look of fear on the girl's face when she was shown the footage was as expected.*

The gang boss's death had totally messed up Angelina's plans but things could have been worse. She could have left something behind in her haste to exit the room or may have bumped into a hotel guest in the passageway. Given what she'd read of the man's shady past, there could be any number of potential murder suspects. It was a matter of turning the situation to her advantage. She already had a head start. Elena was petrified from the entire ordeal. Angelina knew she couldn't escape if she wanted to and was beholden for meals and a place to live, with her passport safely locked away. It was enough for now.

It was 9:45 a.m. by the time they left the apartment, donning dark clothes, sunglasses and hair pulled up under their baseball caps. Not long afterwards, they pulled into a large shopping mall where the uber driver parked the car, as arranged. Elena climbed out, handbag slung over her shoulder and fingers clammy on the tote bag handle. She was sick with fear as she walked towards the front entrance and into the complex. She got what Angelina told her about getting straight onto things before the cards were reported stolen. *But was the overall risk worth it?*

With every step she took, and every store she entered, she imagined she was being watched.

Meanwhile, Angelina waited in the car, watching people come and go while the driver sat alongside, absorbed on his phone. She'd given Elena half an hour to max out the two stolen credit cards, which would be used to purchase gift cards and pre-paid credit cards. *Why not?* she reasoned. *Can't let good money go to waste. He wouldn't be needing them now.* She stroked her chin, wondering how much Elena would return with.

As Elena exited the complex with her heart pumping wildly, she couldn't see the car. *What if this was a set up? What if I've been left high and dry and Angelina has cleared out altogether?* To her relief, a large SUV masked the sedan and she uttered a deep sigh.

'Did you get everything you were after?' Angelina asked casually when Elena climbed back in the car.

'Yes.'

The driver, not the least suspicious, started the car and headed towards the main road.

9

Angelina gave a look of approval as the pair stepped inside the third-floor apartment with their things. 'I'm glad I settled on this place. Looks roomy enough, and it's well away from the CBD. So let's unpack, and then we can make up a list of food supplies I'll collect from the supermarket.'

'Can't I go as well?'

Angelina shook her head. 'Too risky to be seen together. It needs to appear as if one person occupies this place. Not that hard. It's simply a matter of sharing clothes and always wearing a baseball cap and dark glasses when we go out during the day.'

Elena's felt her stomach tighten. But there was more to come.

'And you're to remain inside unless I give you the go-ahead to leave.'

Elena looked at her in disbelief.

'For your safety, you understand. Just till things die down. It's in your best interests to cooperate.'

¶

Elena watched Angelina leave, then settled on the sofa, legs pulled against her chest, chin resting on her knees. She'd expected to stay well clear of public scrutiny until things settled. But this? There was a sudden pang of unease in the pit of her stomach. *Still, it was better to be safe,* she supposed. Two weeks and they'd be leaving Italy. She could put up with her wings being clipped for that long. *Europe beckons, remember,* she was quick to remind herself. *But would things be that straightforward?* The last thing she envisaged when she took on the job was rifling through a dead man's belongings, reefing gold rings off sausage-like fingers and mopping up pools of blood. With a shudder, she forced the memory from her mind.

22

Three days passed and things were better than Elena had first feared. The modern apartment was roomy enough to keep well out of each other's way, comprising a self-contained kitchen and separate bedrooms with ensuites attached. She scanned the media daily for further developments of the gang boss's death, but there were no fresh leads. Nonetheless, this did little to ease her mind. Any day she expected the police to come barging in, guns drawn. It was like walking on eggshells.

Meanwhile, Angelina disposed of their blonde wigs, ordering brunette replacements online. Once they arrived, they took each other's photos, which Angelina forwarded to her contact for fake passports.

At night they went for runs at alternate times. It was Elena's only stretch outside, her one source of sanity. She accepted the bit about masquerading as one person, but having to head out minus her phone was another thing altogether.

'It's too easy to track us down if someone gets hold of it,' Angelina told her. 'It won't be for long.'

And your phone? Elena thought.

¶

Elena noted a subtle shift in Angelina's demeanour in the ensuing days. A compliment here and there or an amiable conversation. Could she dare hope that things had finally taken a turn for the better? Nonetheless, after eight days within the confines of the apartment and no word of a departure date, things became too much for Elena. She might as well have been lumbered with an electronic monitoring bracelet. Angelina, on the contrary, didn't seem fussed at all being holed up. She seemed contented on her laptop, performing planks, sit-ups and squats while watching television or participating in YouTube yoga and Pilates sessions.

One night, Elena dreamt of being back in the smoky bar in Madrid with the group she'd encountered and awoke with a burning desire to escape once more, if only for a short time.

'There's a movie I'd like to see at a theatre not far from here,' she remarked at breakfast as she helped herself to some juice. 'I passed it on my run the other day. Can I go?'

'When?'

'Tonight. You can come if you wish, but it's in Italian.'

Angelina looked at her for a moment. This was uncharacteristically forward of the girl, but she risked dissent by pushing things too far. 'Very well then. But you're to leave your phone behind and take only enough money for the taxi and movie.'

Elena nodded, spirits plummeting as she turned to go. But the words to follow caused her skin to crawl: 'I know the place you're talking about, Elena. It wouldn't be worth your while me having to check up on you.'

Elena took an early dinner to her room, but it remained untouched on her bedside table. Once she'd heard the swish of the dishwasher followed by the click of Angelina's door, she crept to the kitchen, wrapping the contents of her plate in foil and shoving it under a pile of rubbish in the bin.

At 7:30 p.m., she was met by Angelina in the living area. 'Show me.' She held out her hand. Elena handed over her tiny shoulder bag that contained a small make-up bag, brush, and purse with fifteen euros.

Angelina inspected the contents with a nod. 'The taxi's booked both ways?'

'Yeah.'

'Enjoy the movie, then.'

As if, Elena thought as she slipped out the door and pulled it behind her.

The theatre was adjacent to a large shopping centre two kilometres from the apartment. Being a Friday night, the place was abuzz with people. There was a throng of patrons in the foyer waiting to be admitted, and Elena stood among them for a moment, absorbing the comforting waft of popcorn that brought back memories of happier times. She strained to remember the last time she'd seen a movie. Perhaps when she'd accompanied her friend, Damita, to a chick flick as a sixteen-year-old. Her distinct recollections of the day had little to do with the film but with the two boys they met up with afterwards at the ice cream parlour.

With a wry smile, she headed to the counter to enquire what time the movie ended and then made her way to the toilets. Waiting for the last person to leave, she removed her hair tie and shook her hair loose around her shoulders, then applied eyeshadow, red lipstick and mascara. Lastly, she pulled the credit card out of her bra and tucked it into her purse.

The nightclub sat further along the road amongst a set of late-night eating places. Music throbbed and pulsed as she drew close, and a line of patrons stood on the pavement waiting to be admitted. She joined the queue. The moment she entered the building, she could feel the electricity. Heading to the bar, she slipped onto a stool and surveyed her surroundings. A live band played in the background before a throng of packed bodies, hands in the air, gyrating in a frenzied rhythm beneath a stream of psychedelic strobe lights.

Her cocktail had barely arrived when a tall, lean Italian youth, drink in hand, quickly spotted her and weaved his way through the crowd to join her, eyes fixed all the while on her tight-fitting jeans, white designer T-shirt, and her mane of thick, dark hair.

'Mind if I join you?' The conversation took place in Italian.

'No, go ahead,' she said with a smile.

'Haven't seen you around these parts,' he said, shouting to be heard.

'No, I've been travelling around.'

'Are you here for long?'

'Another week or so. And you?'

'I live nearby.'

'And what do you do?'

'I just finished school. I'm working in my uncle's café until I figure out what to do.'

She nodded. That made the youth around five years younger, but it mattered little. She just wanted someone to dance with. As luck would have it, the young man shared the same sentiment.

Not long afterwards, they stepped onto the dance floor, and Elena soon became lost in time, exhilarated by the freedom denied over the past two months.

'Aren't you tired?' he asked, his brow a mass of sweat and shirt saturated following a lengthy stint on the dance floor. 'How about we sit down for a while?' He went to take her hand.

'No.' Elena's eyes shone with excitement as she spoke. 'I've only gotten started.'

An hour later, she faked an excuse about having to leave, telling the boy her partner would be furious if he found out what she'd been up to.

'You're not happy with him, then?' he dared ask.

'No.' She shook her head.

'Then why don't you leave?'

Elena sighed. 'It's a long story.'

'I'd like to see you again,' he said. 'Can we meet here tomorrow night?'

'No, that's too soon.'

'How about next Friday?'

'I'll see what I can do.'

It was an hour past the arranged taxi pick-up time, and Elena gave a gasp of alarm when she glanced at the clock on the wall. She rushed outside and back to the theatre to find it all in darkness, and the mall closed. Further along the street, she stopped under the cover of some trees, opened her make-up bag, grabbed a cleansing wipe, hastily removed all make-up traces, and tied her hair back in a ponytail.

Glad that she'd built up a considerable fitness level since departing Viveiro, it didn't take long to jog along the well-lit street to the apartment.

Angelina checked her watch and sat drumming her fingers on the table. The girl should be back by now.

Elena had barely stepped inside when Angelina crossed the room to meet her. 'I'm going to ask you a question, and I'll know by your answer if you lie. So think very carefully. Were you at the movies tonight, or did you just make it up?'

The words hit like lightning, giving Elena little time to think. 'Of course I was,' she said quickly. 'Where else would I be? I waited for the taxi to come, but it didn't arrive.' She raised her chin and looked directly at Angelina. 'And without a phone, there was no choice but to walk home.'

Angelina's expression didn't alter. 'So, tell me about this movie. Beginning to end.'

Elena rattled off the plot of an Italian Netflix series she'd recently watched in her room to hone her multi-lingual skills. 'Look, what's this all about?' she demanded.

'Just making sure that we're on the same page, that's all.'

'What's that supposed to mean?'

'Just remember it would be your word against mine what happened that night in the hotel. Your fingerprints all over the body, not mine.'

Elena froze, too stunned to respond.

'Assuming we were caught,' Angelina continued mercilessly, 'but that's not about to happen, now is it?'

'You're not suggesting —'

'I'm not suggesting anything. Just keep doing as you're told, and things will be fine.'

Angelina crossed the floor to her room and closed the door without another word.

Elena squeezed her eyes shut for a moment and forced herself to breathe. She knew she remained safe while she was of use. But how long would that be?

¶

Deep in thought, Angelina lay on her bed, propped against the pillows. She'd sensed signs of unease on Elena's part, and her fear of being arrested was palpable. Continuing to keep her locked up like this would hardly guarantee her willing participation from here on.

The more Angelina thought about it, the more convinced she was that she needed to get rid of Elena sooner rather than later. Initially she considered a discreet push over a cliff in the Cinque Terre or the Amalfi Coast. *But was that really worth the risk? No, I need to remain at arm's length from jobs such as this.* She reached for her phone and began to compose a text to her contact.

¶

The response to Angelina's SMS took longer than expected, jolting her from her slumber. Fumbling for the light switch, she grabbed her phone, anxious to see what the message contained.

I've found someone and he's thinking about it, the message read.

When will I have an answer? she tapped back impatiently.

Late tonight some time.

What followed were the details of an encrypted messaging app that Angelina downloaded on her iPad.

The message showed promise. Given the fee she was prepared to pay, she didn't expect any major issues.

23

At breakfast the following morning, Angelina chattered on as if nothing had taken place at all the previous evening. 'There's been some good news, Elena,' she said, pulling up a stool. 'Our new passports are on the way so you can make a start on your packing.'

'Really?' Elena was barely able to contain her excitement. 'Have you decided where we're going?'

'Not yet.' Angelina poured herself a juice. 'I'll do some checking around. In the meantime, I think this calls for a celebration don't you?'

Late in the evening, Elena settled on the sofa next to Angelina, watching with intrigue as Angelina poured herself another drink. It was uncharacteristic of Angelina to loosen up like this, and given they'd not eaten, she wasn't holding her drinks as well as usual.

'So let's talk boyfriends.' The words interrupted Elena's thoughts. 'How many have you had?'

'A few before I moved to Viveiro. To be honest, there

wasn't time. I was too busy working.'

'Hm. Photos?' Angelina ran her finger around the rim of her glass.

'Just one, taken when we were fifteen.' Elena rolled her eyes. 'I look disgusting. I don't know why I haven't deleted it.'

Angelina grinned. 'Show me.'

'No, I don't want to.'

'Go on.' She picked up Elena's phone and thrust it at her.

'Only if I see one of yours,' came the resolute response.

'Deal.'

Elena clicked on the camera roll, tapped on a photo, and handed it over.

Angelina looked at the photo of the overweight girl with a round face and badly applied lipstick, dressed in a low-cut top and all-too-tight jeans. The pimply-faced boy with his arm draped awkwardly around her shoulders appeared every bit as uncomfortable. She shrieked with laughter. 'This is priceless, Elena. Don't delete it. Use it as a reminder of how far you've come.'

Elena quickly snatched back the phone. 'Your turn.'

'Okay, let me see.' Angelina scrolled through the photos on her phone and said, 'This one's Omari. He's African.'

Elena stared at the strikingly handsome man who was every bit as good as any movie star she'd seen. 'How long were you together?'

'Around a month, I guess, and this one's Ty …'

Elena watched as image after image flashed before her eyes, all good-looking and fit young men. She couldn't envisage Angelina choosing otherwise.

'Not bad, some of them, hey?' Angelina said as if she could read the other's mind.

'God yeah! Were any of them long-term?'

'You've got to be kidding. Who'd want to be tied down?' Angelina reached for a bottle and topped up their drinks. 'Let me give you a bit of advice, Elena; it's only when the thrill of the chase is over that men show their true colours. They either dump you or want to stifle you. Don't get me wrong, men are exciting. Sex is exciting. But you need to be one step ahead. Make sure that things are on your terms, not theirs. Got it?'

Elena nodded. It was the first time she'd got a glimpse into the woman behind the façade, and there may not be another chance. She dared to venture further.

'So which one's the baby's father?'

'Who, Nic? I haven't got to him yet.' She tapped on a photo of a dark-haired man. For some reason, Elena felt drawn to it. Something set him apart from the others but she couldn't decipher what.

'Not bad,' she said, passing back the phone. 'He looks European.'

'Greek, actually. Yeah, not half bad, is he?'

'Do you still keep in touch?'

'Nope. He was ditched long ago.'

Elena paused, curious to know more but hesitant to push things too far. 'And the baby?' she ventured. 'Have you ever thought about going back to see it?'

'You've got to be kidding. My uncle told me I'm never to go near her again and that suits me.'

'What uncle?'

'None of your business.' Suddenly, Angelina glanced at the clock and jumped up. 'Shit. I didn't realise it was that late. I'll be back in a moment. I'm expecting a message.'

Returning in a matter of minutes, she glanced down at the coffee table with a frown. She could have sworn her phone was before her when she left. *What was it doing on the armrest?*

'Did you touch my phone?' She swung around to face Elena, who was assembling a platter of cheese, dips and assorted meats on a platter in the kitchen.

Elena nodded. 'It fell on the floor as you got up, and I picked it up.'

Angelina looked dubious. But it mattered little. The deal had been clinched. A little more than she would have liked to pay and another five days to wait until he finished his current job, but that's what came with hiring a professional. An inconvenience more than anything. A matter of rescheduling flights and accommodation and extending the rental. And thinking up excuses to stall Elena.

She sat down, eyes fixed on a moth in its frenetic path around a light globe as she waited for Elena to bring the food.

¶

Elena did not feel the least bit sleepy as she lay in bed. Images of picture-perfect Greek Islands, the French Riviera and the

Bahamas drifted in and out of her mind like lazy clouds. The prospect of sailing across endless stretches of clear blue water now seemed tantalisingly close. *Things would fall into place when their new passports arrived. Wouldn't they? A new identity, a new look. Another country ...* But a ripple of uncertainty swept across her as the words of the previous night's thinly veiled threat reverberated in her head.

What else was going on in Angelina's mind and can I believe a word she said?

24

When Elena returned from her run, she quickly slipped into her room before Angelina took her turn. Nerves jangling and barely breathing, she waited, ear pressed to the door until she heard Angelina's light footsteps cross the room, followed by the click of the front door. Wasting no time, she kicked off her runners and climbed on the bed, her hand clutched tightly around her phone. It was 5 a.m. Australian time, far from ideal but the only safe time to talk was when Angelina was out on her run. And there were no guarantees about how long that would last. She frowned. No guarantees about anything. The call may go unanswered. And the response could well be hostile. But she had nothing to lose.

Clicking on her contacts, she scrolled down with shaky fingers until she reached the number.

The call was answered after four rings.

'Am I speaking with Nic?' Elena's heart hammered so hard it felt like it was about to jump out of her body.

'Who is this?' The voice was thick with sleep.

'My name's Elena. I know it's late, but I'm calling from Milan. It's concerning Ava.'

The words jolted Nic upright into an immediate state of high alert. He'd expected to be tracked down at some point by Angelina's contacts when he first landed on his brother's farm, but after seven months he dared to hope the trail had run cold.

'What's this about. Money?' he demanded.

'No, Ava's holding me hostage and I'm in fear of my life.'

'Bullshit. Ava's dead.'

'Dead? What are you talking about? I've been working for her the past two months.'

The words sent Nic's heart racing. 'I don't believe you.'

'I've a selfie of us taken by Ava a few weeks ago.'

'Send it.' The voice sounded hard.

Seconds later, Nic stared at the image, chilled by the resemblance between the women, his mind reeling over the staggering prospect of Angelina still being alive.

'Are you still there?' Elena said anxiously.

'This could have been taken any time.'

'I know, but it's all I've got. Will you at least hear me out?'

'All right, starting from how you got my number in the first place.'

'I searched for it on Ava's phone last night when she slipped out of the room. She mentioned your name.'

'And said what?'

'Not much. Just that you two had been an item, and things didn't end well.'

There was silence at the other end.

Elena faltered. 'Look, I'm only calling because you know her, and I desperately need advice.'

Instinct warned Nic against getting involved, but the words spilled out before he could stop them. 'Advice on what?'

'On what I should do,' Elena said, her voice strained. 'Ava's lied to me several times, and I don't know what to think anymore.'

The words struck a raw nerve. 'So what makes you in fear of your life?'

'Two weeks ago, Ava accidentally killed someone. She made sure my fingerprints were over the body, and I think she has plans to frame me for the murder.'

'What makes you think that?' he said all too quickly.

'A passing comment two nights ago about what would happen if I went to the police.'

'Why wait so long to do that? Did you say something?'

'No. Nothing. Until then, things were okay as long as I did as I was told.'

Nic's jaw hardened. This sounded all too familiar.

'But things are different now. I can't put my finger on what it is, but I'm frightened.'

Nic was silent. The caller sounded genuine, but what's to say she wasn't a damned good liar, that this wasn't some elaborate extortion plot or a trap designed to lure and kill him.

'So, let's begin with the murder then. When and where did it take place?' he probed.

'June 12th at a hotel in Milan's Corso Venezia. It was all over the media. You can check it out for yourself.'

'I'll be doing that all right.' There was a hard edge to his voice.

'Look, I can only talk when Ava goes out for her run at night, and she's due back at any moment. Can I ring you tomorrow at the same time? Please.'

'You can. I'll have done my homework by then.'

There was a click at the other end, and Elena slumped back in the chair. Maybe this had been one big waste of time.

9

Nic's mind was in turmoil as he logged on to his laptop and tapped the search engine. Within seconds the information he sought appeared on the screen: "Sicilian mafia capo killed in botched robbery".

'What the fuck!' he gasped in disbelief. *What was Angelina doing in mafia circles if the caller was to be believed?* he thought. *And implicating herself in a robbery? That was definitely out of character.* He knew she kept her wealth a guarded secret, and he had little interest in knowing what it was. But from what he gathered, it was considerable.

He read on quickly. CCTV footage depicted two blonde women of similar build and clothing entering and leaving the murdered man's hotel room at different stages. But the image was not clear, leaving him far from convinced. It was only when he clicked the play button that his veins turned to ice. The woman in the first footage could be anyone. But the glide and the erect stance of the second was indisputable. A cold fury hit his gut as he replayed it … again and again. From the outset, he'd harboured a doubt that Angelina died in the boat explosion and he knew he'd never have closure until there was word of a body. But as time passed and no information was forthcoming, there was no option but to put things behind him.

However, nothing could stop the images of the boat explosion that constantly haunted Nic's dreams, nor of Angelina's exquisite features seared deeply into his subconscious. He coped in the best way he knew by throwing himself into his job and insisting on offering his brother a hand around the place on his days off. There was always something of interest on the sports channels when sleep was elusive.

But nothing could have been prepared him for this. As the reality of Angelina's ultimate betrayal sank in, a rage boiled up inside, the likes of which he'd never experienced. And only thing was on his mind. To hunt down and wipe from the face of the earth the woman who had all but destroyed him.

He had nothing to lose.

But things were far from that straightforward. Nic had finally extricated himself from 'The Family', found a place to reside with some semblance of safety, and was planning at last for the future. *Was she really worth putting all that at risk?*

An early morning run through the rainforest with mist on his face, and streaks of sunlight streaming through the canopy of green overhead, gave him the clarity of mind he sought, and by the time he'd returned, he had a plan in mind. He changed into pants, lightweight shirt and boots in preparation for the long shift ahead and sat with a coffee, resuming his website search for further information. But little was forthcoming. So many unanswered questions. *Where did Angelina come up with the girl in the first place and what was her reason in doing so?* He deduced it had to be something to do with the stark similarities in their appearance. *And what was with the blonde wigs and identical clothing? More to the point, what was the role of the girl in the bigger scheme of things?*

Nic reached for his phone and tapped on the photo she'd sent through. Granted, she lacked Angelina's striking features but she bore a natural beauty. There was something about her eyes, the long dark hair that hung loosely on her shoulders. Yet he detected an air of uncertainty and vulnerability.

A hard knot formed in Nic's gut. Exactly the type Angelina would seek to fulfil her needs. And he knew only too well her penchant for discarding those who'd served their purpose.

And he assumed Angelina would know that if she couldn't get Elena framed for the killing, she would be hunted down by the mafia. He'd not personally had dealings with the victim's Sicilian gang but from what he already knew, Angelina had chosen the wrong mob to become involved with.

There *was* no time to waste.

¶

The call came through at 5:05 a.m., but this time Nic was wide awake.

'It's Elena,' came the anxious voice.

'Are you good to talk?'

'Yes. Ava's just left for her run.'

'I've looked into things, and from what I can see your story adds up.'

'Thank God. I've been at my wit's end. So, what do you think I should do?'

'I'm willing to offer advice for what it's worth, but I need to make it quite clear that I've moved on as far as Ava's concerned. I've no intention of becoming involved.'

'I wasn't expecting you to.'

The instant response caught Nic off guard, somewhat allaying the niggling doubts about the validity of her story that had sat in the back of his mind.

'Going by what you've told me, I suggest you waste no time in getting yourself out of there.'

'But I can't. She watches everything I do. I'm allowed out once a day to go for my run. But that's without anything – phone, credit cards —'

Nic frowned. 'And what time's that?'

'Six-thirty.'

'When does it get dark there?'

'Around eight. You're breaking up. I can't hear you.'

'Damn!' Nic swore and punched his hand with his fist, rising quickly and heading outside.

'Is that better?'

'Yes. I can hear you now.'

'All right. Tomorrow night think up some excuse for postponing your run till then while keeping your phone and credit cards hidden. Do not stop, just keep going. Are you near a station?'

'Yes, it's ten minutes from here.'

'Good. Head straight there and catch a train to the city. Do you have a travel pass of any kind?'

'No but I can download one quickly.'

'Okay. When you arrive call me.'

Elena's breath caught in her throat. 'Okay.' She dared not ask what was behind it all.

'Is there a lift code where you are?'

'Yes.'

'Send it along with the address.'

The line went dead.

25

Late afternoon the following day, Elena stepped out of her room with the rubbish bag from her room and headed to the kitchen to collect the other. Angelina looked up from her magazine. 'I forgot it was rubbish night. You can grab mine if you like.'

'Okay. Look, I'm not feeling the best today. I've got a bit of a headache. Can we swap times for our runs tonight? I might feel better after a lie-down.'

Angelina shrugged. 'Suit yourself.' She flicked another page. 'And remember to take out both bins.'

❡

The moment Elena heard the door click open, she squeezed her eyes tight, squared her shoulders and then stepped out of her bedroom,

'So you're better then?' Angelina gave a perfunctory glance as she entered the room and pulled off her runners.

'Yeah, much. Thanks.'

'Well, I'll see you when you get back.' She headed to her room.

Pulling the door softly behind her and stepping out into the passage way, Elena was filled with trepidation as she went down in the lift and out onto the street. She anxiously scanned her surroundings to make sure there were no passers-by before she lifted the lid to the rubbish bin and hastily removed the rubbish bag containing her bum bag with her phone, charger and credit card. And ran.

At one point she heard footsteps behind her. She glanced over her shoulder but it was just a fit-looking young woman gaining ground, earphones on. She vanished down a nearby street.

The incident was unsettling, nonetheless.

9

Darkness was settling in as Elena darted across the park to the road leading to the station. The next train was only a five-minute wait, and she jumped aboard a carriage full of young people heading to the city for a night out. Within twelve minutes the train arrived at the CBD. Elena quickly made her way through the throng of passengers and up the escalator towards the main entrance. Finding a secluded corner, she unzipped her bum bag with shaking fingers and pulled out her phone. She could feel the throbbing of her temples when she stopped and, crouching in the shadows, tapped on the number.

The call was picked up immediately.

'I made it,' she said.

'Good girl.' The voice was calm. Reassuring. 'Now go and find somewhere to stay for the night, and don't move from there. Expect to hear from me in the morning.' Nic ended the call and made another.

'Si?' came a gruff voice.

'Do you speak English?'

'Who is this?'

'That's none of your concern. I know who robbed and killed Salvadore Costa and where to find her.'

'There were two women,' came the quick response.

'Yeah, but she's the one who did it.'

'How am I supposed to believe all this?'

'Well, how do you think I got your number in the first place? I'm in the business like you are. Let's just say she's ruined my life as well.'

There was a brief pause at the other end. 'Go on.'

'You're in Milan, right?'

'Yeah.'

'Well, she's hiding in an apartment ten minutes from the CBD, but not for long.'

'How long?'

'Forty minutes, max.'

'Send the details.'

Nic hung up and did as he was asked. For a few moments he sat, unmoving, jaw tight. Gaining access to the phone number of someone affiliated with the close-knit Sicilian gang had been far from easy. It took three calls to connect with someone with the means to do so. In the end, things had gone down to the wire. He could do no more.

ꟗ

Shortly after nine, two men burst into Angelina's apartment and into the bedroom where she was about to change out of her running gear. Acutely aware of what was about to take place, Angelina watched in stunned silence as the larger of the pair reefed the Glock pistol and silencer from his belt, took aim at her forehead and fired at close range. Within a split-second Angelina crumpled to the floor, where she lay, eyes wide open and looking upwards, a thin stream of red flowing into the carpet behind.

But it wasn't enough for the assailant, who rushed forward and stood over her. 'This one's for you, Uncle.' He fired a shot that hit her in the chest. 'And this.' Another shot followed. He went to fire again, but his accomplice stepped in and laid a hand on his arm. 'You've got your revenge, Aldo. We've gotta get out of here.' Glancing at the beautiful face, which in repose could have been a Raphael portrait, he shook his head. 'What a waste.'

ꟗ

The call came through at 7 a.m., and Elena came to with a jerk.

'Yes?' she said quickly.

'It's Nic. You can move on now.' The tone was grim. 'Ava's been taken care of.'

Elena's hand flew to her mouth.

'Are you there?'

'Y-yes I'm still here.' The words sounded distant in her head.

'Have you found somewhere safe?'

'Yes.'

'Good. Best to remain there until you've had time to think. Are you right for money?'

'I'll figure something out.'

Nic paused. 'Well, once you're settled, text me so I know you're okay?'

'All right.'

The line went dead.

⁊

By midday the following day, Elena was walking through the uptown shopping complex, still in a daze; passers-by were but a blur, their voices merely a disjointed mumble, and her feet seemed to be detached from her body. *This won't do,* she told herself. *Ava's not waiting for you and you have shopping to do, so get a grip.* She sat for a few moments on a bench seat outside a fashionable-looking boutique to gather her thoughts, then stood up and moved off with a determined look on her face.

By four, she'd returned to the small but neat one-bedroom studio apartment, armed with several designer bags that she placed in the corner alongside her bed.

Energised by the double-shot expresso and bowl of pasta she'd enjoyed on the return journey, it was now time to go in search of a supermarket.

26

At 9 a.m. the following day, Elena slipped into the slim-fitting black dress, aqua high-heeled shoes and matching accessories that she'd purchased. She glanced in the mirror behind the door. Little remained on her card, but undeterred and resolute, she swept her hair up in a bun, meticulously applied her make-up and, armed with a piece of paper that had five addresses on it, stepped outside. For a moment she wondered what felt different. And then it struck. The absence of fear.

Within an hour, she'd secured a three-month trial position as a receptionist at a nearby hotel; her elegance, poise and multi-lingual skills proving too much for the manager to turn down. Only too glad to remove the newly purchased shoes the moment she arrived home, she rubbed the toes that were red and already showing signs of blisters, grateful there'd been no need to head to the next hotel on the list.

Parting the curtains of her first-floor room and looking onto the bustling street close to the CBD, she scanned her surroundings. To each side were identical apartment blocks, and directly opposite was a boarded up six-storey building about to be demolished and replaced with a large office complex. Hardly a peaceful environment to return to at the end of the working day but it would suffice until she was in a stronger financial position.

¶

All was quiet when the Syrian hit man turned up at the park near the apartment at 6:30 p.m. The only sign of movement was a young couple driving out of the car park. He waited. Watching in the shadows for the target to show for her run. He didn't know which apartment she occupied.

Another thirty minutes passed. The man reached impatiently for his phone, signed in to his encrypted app and sent a message, but no response was forthcoming. Not prepared to wait any longer than he had to, he remained until the agreed time, plus an extra ten minutes, and headed to his car parked in a nearby side street. After he climbed in, he sat to reflect for a few moments. It hadn't been a wasted trip. The woman known as Ava had deposited half his fee into his account, and there'd be no refund if there was further contact. And there'd certainly be no dealings with her in the future.

He reflected that it had been some time since he'd had a break, and what better place to spend a few days.

27

Sam Walsh sat in the living room of Kilkenny with David Zielenski, Cara and Will.

'You said on the phone you had information regarding Angelina,' David began.

Sam took a deep breath and looked at each of them in turn.

'Yes, I have. Angelina's body has been discovered in an apartment in Milan.'

'Body?' Cara gasped.

The three sat in stunned disbelief as Sam outlined the sketchy details he'd so far received from Interpol.

'But I don't understand!' Cara exclaimed in disbelief. 'We thought she'd died in the boat explosion.'

'That's what she wanted you to think. Wanted us all to think.'

'But how was she able to fake her own death?' Will shook his head incredulously.

'That's something we may well never know,' Sam

responded. 'Nor how she got to Italy in the first place. However, one thing is certain; she had help. It isn't easy to completely drop out of sight like that and get out of the country – it requires planning and organisation. Interpol is working with us to put the pieces together.' He looked at Cara. 'And the money she embezzled from your family's company should be rightfully returned.'

'Well, that's something we haven't thought about,' she responded. 'What I'm feeling right now is relief, to be honest.'

'You mentioned Angelina's death was gang-related,' Will said. 'Was she involved in one?'

Sam shook his head. 'No, it appears she accidentally killed a prominent mafia member, and this was a case of reprisal.'

Carla slumped back against the sofa, arms folded across her chest. 'Call it karma,' she said with a grim expression.

No one spoke for a moment, and Sam got to his feet. 'Well, I must get going. I just wanted you to have this information as soon as possible, and doing it by phone seemed to be too impersonal.'

'Can I get you a coffee first?' David asked.

'No, thanks. Another time, perhaps.'

'Well, I'll see you out then.'

Outside, David turned to Sam and said, 'Thanks for delivering the news, Sam. It's what we needed to hear. Finally, we can move on with our lives. I don't think either of us will ever shed the guilt of not being there with Jennifer that night.' With a deep sigh, he ran a hand over his neck.

Sam looked at him. 'I've always wondered why she was out alone that night.'

'Hm. Well you see, she loved her 5 p.m. walk down to the beach. From what Cara told me, it had been a daily ritual from when she and Angelina were old enough to look after themselves. Jennifer said it cleared her mind and provided her with a sense of inner peace. She was too unnerved to venture out alone when Angelina's threats began. But as the months passed with no signs of imminent danger, she insisted on resuming the walks, despite our apprehension.' He gave a shrug. 'Who were we to deny her that happiness after all she'd been through. So we agreed, as long as there was at least one of us to accompany her. And once, just once …' He ran a hand over his forehead as if trying to wipe the memory.

'Go on,' Sam prompted gently.

'Cara had been invited to give an afternoon recital at the local school. She was expected to be home by five when Jennifer set out for her walk but was delayed because of calls for encores. She didn't arrive home until close to six and, finding Jennifer not at home, set out immediately to look for her.'

'And you?'

'Will and I got held up collecting building materials for the final renovations on my house before it went on the market.'

'I see.'

'So if anyone shoulders the blame for Jennifer's death, it should be us, not you. I just wanted you to know, that's all.'

A lump formed in Sam's throat, and he could think of nothing to say. David went on. 'I saw the accusing look Cara gave you that night; her way of deflecting the blame away from herself, I guess. And I was too overwhelmed with grief to say anything. We've discussed it since, and she doesn't hold you responsible.'

Sam took a moment to respond. 'Thanks for telling me, David. It means a lot. I know the police are supposed to remain detached and objective, but I really liked and admired Jennifer.'

'You needed to know. The chilling thing is, Sam, Angelina would have found a way to do this, I'm sure of that.'

Sam was choked by emotion as he shook David's hand and climbed into his car. 'You'll learn more in the coming days,' he said, fastening his seat belt.

'Okay.' David paused for a moment. 'Cara's been through more than enough. Could you keep things as low-key as possible in the media?'

'Of course. I'll do what I can.'

As Sam drove away, he reflected on what David had said, and suddenly, an image came to mind that caused his blood to run cold There may have been two bodies in the bushes that evening. Not one. *What if Cara had returned home in time to accompany Jennifer?*

28

Nic was about to make lunch when a message came through on his phone: *I landed a job. E.*

Nic's pulse quickened. He half-expected not to hear from Elena again and definitely not so soon.

Good. I'm glad things worked out. Where? he responded.

Elena texted through the name of the hotel, hoping there'd be a response. There was none.

§

Elena arrived for work at her customary early time and was met with a smile from the concierge. She was by far the best receptionist he'd encountered in his ten years on the job. Attractive, stylish, good-natured and efficient, he gauged it was only a matter of time before promotion was in the wind.

'By the way, something arrived for you this morning,' he said, reaching for an envelope under the desk.

One glance at the Australian stamps and Elena's heart

skipped a beat. 'Thanks, Riccardo,' she said, slipping it into her bag.

The two hours until her break couldn't come soon enough. Scanning the café for a quiet spot, she ordered, pulled up a chair, and tore open the envelope in which was a cheque for fifteen hundred euros and a note: *Something towards the rent until you're settled. Look after yourself. N.*

She stared in disbelief for a few moments. The money couldn't have come at a better time. She'd all but wiped out her credit card, with another five days until her first pay. Reaching for her phone, she texted: *I'll be repaying every euro.*

The response came fifteen minutes later as she was about to leave. *My pleasure. Don't leave town.*

Elena smiled. She didn't know why her heart leapt at hearing from him. After all she'd never met him and knew little about him. He'd made it clear he'd moved on after Ava. Could well be in another relationship and if that was the case, she wished him well. She knew it was best to put all thoughts of Nic behind her. She'd already received an invitation to dinner but she wasn't sure a relationship was what she needed so soon. She looked thoughtful as she rose to pay the bill.

Two nights later, despite her better judgement, she reached for her phone and dialled Nic's number and left a message, but there was no response. She expected as much.

⁊

Nic sat on the faded director's chair, sipping a beer outside his modest quarters on his brother's farm. It was a pleasant twenty degrees – a far cry from the muggy, oppressive conditions of the hinterland's recent rainy season. It had been two weeks since Angelina's death, but it could have been a month. Nic had felt suspended in time, senses numb, reminiscent of the week preceding his father's funeral. He coped in the only way he knew by throwing himself into his work and downing an extra drink or two at night. This time, there'd be no baring his soul to his brother. *Will I ever be able to do so?*

Coming to terms with death had come with the job. The inner turmoil that consumed him would subside over time. It always did. But whether the wounds Angelina inflicted would ever heal was another matter. *Will I ever find true peace?*

Nic felt his stomach tighten as he reached for his phone and scanned the news for updates on Angelina's murder. To his relief, no further development or mention of Elena was forthcoming. He took refuge in the knowledge that the story didn't get as much coverage as expected from the outset, with only a few lines stating that the woman responsible for Salvador Costa's murder had been killed in a contract hit. No reference to Angelina's criminal history or her audacious escape from Australia. Doubtless that would come once a formal identification was made, and the Australian Federal Police became involved.

It wouldn't take them long to tap into her clandestine activities and follow the money trail. At least the surprise attack would have given her no time to delete any incriminating evidence on her laptop. Nic had noted Angelina's well-hidden, locked safe, which it was safe to assume, contained false papers, fiscal documents and bank details. He was curious about the amount she'd amassed. Not that he cared.

Nic leaned back in his chair and ran a hand through his hair. There was no way of making amends for his role in Jennifer Lorenzo's death. He'd been blind-sided, captivated by Angelina's charms. And he had to live with that. But even when he was at his lowest, he was able to take comfort from knowing that Angelina would have found other means of bringing about Jennifer's death if he'd refused her. If nothing else, he exacted his retribution, and the Lorenzo family would have the closure they deserved.

Nonetheless, Nic couldn't stop feeling like he'd wasted the last year of his life. Perhaps he should have cleared out when he had the urge following the boat explosion. But upon reflection, he'd been in no fit state of mind to do so. Taking up work on his brother's farm was probably the best thing he did. The peacefulness of the hinterland property proved the perfect antidote for the turmoil he'd endured, the ideal place to collect his thoughts and regroup. All the while he yearned for some semblance of normality like his brother enjoyed. But it was a dagger to his heart when he set eyes on the mischievous faces of his blonde nephews and his brother's adoring wife. Nic considered the tranquil vista before him and felt his heart miss a beat. This is the life he would have wanted for his daughter; perhaps it had been at the back of his mind when he set about heading to Spain to retrieve her. He downed the remainder of his beer. There was an emptiness in the pit of his stomach. He hadn't even learned his daughter's name. And now she was gone.

There was nothing here for him now. It was time to move on. He was surprised he'd stayed as long as he had. Perhaps it was the contentment of working alongside his much-loved brother after years apart. The satisfaction that came from seeing the results of their hard physical labour. Yet all the while, fears and uncertainties plagued his mind. First and foremost was the safety of his brother and family. He'd taken all measures possible to keep his whereabouts hidden, yet every time a stranger stepped onto the property he was instantly on edge. He wondered if there'd be a time when he wouldn't be looking over his shoulder.

There were things he knew he'd miss – the heady early morning fragrance of lilly pilly and jasmine; the intermittent tweets and warbles of birds as he jogged along the now well-worn track; the comforting sound of rain on the tin roof as he drifted to sleep; and the one-eyed old heeler that appeared from nowhere and attached itself to him.

29

When Nic left Australia, he had no specific plan in mind, but something drew him to the small Greek island of his birth. He experienced a sense of relief as he ditched his old false passport with the alias surname of Drakos, used as a cover when he worked. It was as if he was drawing a line through his previous life. Conversely, his new passport under the family name, Diamandis, gave him a feeling of freedom, of renewal.

The island of Nic's birth was one of the Cyclades group's minor and less crowded, due to its isolated location and inaccessibility to the towering cruise ships that frequented its larger neighbours. Nic's first view of the place was from the deck of the Blue Star ferry as it approached the harbour. He was transfixed by the rows of whitewashed houses that gleamed and shimmered on the hillside under the relentless midday sun. Nothing could have prepared him for the stark beauty of the place. At that moment the felt that he was truly home.

Making his way to the luggage area, he searched through the myriad of cases, bags and boxes of all sizes until he spotted his worse-for-wear black backpack. Flinging it over his shoulders, he joined the line of passengers impatient to disembark. The warm salty air filled his senses as he headed down the gangplank and stepped onto the ancient cobblestone path leading to the harbour. The place was abuzz with tourists, decked out in beach gear and hats, exploring the narrow streets or relaxing over drinks in bars and outdoor cafes. The whiffs of suntan lotion came in waves, evoking memories of the beaches back in Australia. It was the height of summer, when the locals made the money to sustain them through the winter months. Further along was a sandy stretch with sunbeds and umbrellas, all occupied, and turquoise waters with heads bobbing, swimmers splashing, and others playing games of keepings off with coloured balls; shrieks of laughter carried in the wind.

He didn't know what to expect when he enquired about the only relatives he knew were still on the island. Speros was a cousin of his father and Nic knew the two had been close friends as children and as they grew into young men. They had corresponded for several years after Nic's family migrated, but that had become less frequent over the years and eventually stopped altogether. Nic realised he didn't even know if Speros was still alive or the tavern he ran still existed. However, the first person he asked – an elderly lady who looked more like a local than a tourist – pointed to a taverna further along the waterfront. Nic thanked her with a smile.

The first thing he noticed about the blue shuttered taverna bearing the name *Thalassino Aeraki*, translated as Sea Breeze, was the crowd of patrons seated on blue wooden chairs on the paved white cobblestones; tables were covered with blue and white checked tablecloths. Rows of terracotta pots filled with flowers lined the edge of the nearby low wall that dropped down to the sea, and a ginger cat was sunning itself, contentedly licking a paw. It was lunchtime, and there was hardly a spare place to be found inside and out. The interior's whitewashed walls contrasted with various shades of blue and small windows limited the sun. Seascapes, family photos dating back years, and ornate religious icons adorned the walls.

Nic guessed that the thickset, tanned man who appeared to be in his sixties bustling around behind the counter was Speros. Nonetheless, he waited until he'd been ushered to his seat and things had quietened before rising and heading over to introduce himself. There was a loud whoop of excitement, and the man rushed around the counter to give him a few hearty slaps on the back that made his eyes water, followed by a warm embrace.

'Athena, come quickly,' Speros called over his shoulder. 'It's Yiannis and Adriane's boy Nic, from Australia.'

Within seconds, a short, solid woman of approximately the same age, with dark hair flecked with grey tightly pulled back in a bun, emerged from the back room, hastily wiping her hands on her blue and white striped apron as she dashed across to greet Nic, her face wet with tears.

Within an hour, word had gotten around, and Nic sat surrounded by locals, drinking ouzo and tiny tumblers of Greek coffee; the appetisers before them were replenished the moment they were consumed amidst raucous laughter and chatter. Celebrations continued well into the early morning and Nic was only too happy to roll up his sleeves and pitch in behind the scenes as the night wore on and the customers poured in.

Upon Athena's insistence, Nic stayed in the couple's quaint whitewashed house facing the village square, that had been purchased when Speros and Athena married, until he secured a short-term rental. This took a couple of days, and in that time, he learned much about his parents when they were young, with Speros eager to show him the places they frequented as children.

Athena was a spontaneous, kind-hearted and generous woman who was hard not to like, despite occasional displays of tactlessness that were met with reproach by her husband. Not that she was in the least deterred.

'So tell me, are you married, Nic?' she'd asked not long after he arrived.

'I was years ago, but things didn't work out,' he replied.

'So you're divorced then.'

He nodded.

Children?'

Nic's stomach knotted. 'No children.'

'Pity. Well, don't leave things too long.'

'Athena, that's enough,' Speros remarked sternly.

'I'm only telling things as they are,' she shot back. 'How old are you, Nic, thirty-two?'

'Thirty-eight.'

'See?' She glared at her husband with crossed arms.

Nic grinned. He wondered what conspiratorial schemes might follow. The family came above all else to the Greeks, and he had noticed Athena's eyes light up at a baby cradled in someone's arms or children seated around a table at mealtime.

9

In barely two weeks, Nic had decided this was the place he wanted to settle and confided in Speros that he wanted to look around for a suitable business. Speros responded by saying, 'Look, I know one that is on the market. It's run-down but you should get it for a good price. It's basically boat hire and all that goes with that, and I reckon it would be a winner with some hard work and a bit of money spent on maintenance.'

Nic was enthusiastic and the agreed price was too good to resist. He quickly set to, replacing the tin on the rusty boat shed and taking a ferry to the mainland to order new kayaks, snorkelling gear, and replacement of catamaran sails. Next came the patching up of an ageing fleet of small boats until they were placed in drydock for servicing in the off-season.

Meanwhile, he kept an eye on the property market, eventually purchasing a whitewashed house set on the hill overlooking the port and with commanding views of the glimmering Aegean. It was invigorating to jog up and down the steep paved cobblestoned path, and he was relieved to find the emerging paunch from Athena's piled-up plates of delicious Greek fare slowly turn to muscle.

Gradually, thoughts of Angelina dissipated as long hours of physical work followed by uninterrupted sleep took over his time. Neighbours became family, as was the Greek way, and there was never a shortage of offers to home-cooked dinners coupled with the welcoming Greek hospitality he grew up with.

During the summer high season numbers swelled with families, island hoppers, and those searching for a restful holiday without the glitzy resorts and incessant clubbing of the larger islands. Not that there was a lack of bars and clubs to choose from. Inland, however, was another matter. Quaint, traditional villages dotted the stark terrain, and small farms and ancient olive groves abounded.

The faded photos in the old family album shown to him in Australia did little justice to the island.

Tourist numbers swelled to capacity in August, forcing Nic to put on two locals to deal with the demands, and his business showed solid profits. Crowds gradually dispersed until the winter months when the ferry schedule was reduced to a trickle, businesses closed, and shop owners took a well-earned rest to enjoy the peace and serenity surrounding them. It was also a time when the locals gathered for traditional feasts, festivals and celebrations.

Nic didn't mind shutting down the business for five months. He hadn't taken a break for over a year. It allowed time to explore the island and search the crumbling ruins Speros spoke of.

As the biting wintry winds set in and the locals gathered in cafes or the comforts of their homes, Nic set out on foot in a windproof jacket and sturdy hiking boots, feeling the powdery white dirt yield under his footfall. He traversed age-old donkey trails past ancient olive groves and small-scale farms, through traditional villages to windswept, barren mountains. What struck him most was the diversity of the island's beaches. While the most popular were noted for their white sands and crystal shallow waters, perfect for families and swimming, others could only be reached by boat and were frequented by snorkellers and divers. To the north lay several small coves surrounded by rocky outcrops and white pebbled shorelines beneath imposing cliffs.

After a few months of particularly cold weather, the bleak, cloudy skies turned blue, and the early rays of spring sunshine seeped into his bones. Summer was again on the way.

Nic and Athena's only child, Leonidis, his wife Selene and their two sons lived in a traditional village set into a mountain on the far side of the island where they operated a well-established olive grove. It was customary for Speros to give a hand during the winter months and Nic, not being one to sit around, provided his services as needed.

'Did Leonidis show an interest in the taverna growing up?'

he asked Speros one evening as they headed home after a long day's work.

'Perhaps for a while, but he and Athena proved too similar, both feisty and wanting things their way. And we made the mistake of working him too hard over the years. When I look back on things, we put a man's responsibilities on a young boy's shoulders.'

'Tell me about it,' Nic muttered.

Speros gave him a sidelong glance. 'Are you referring to Yiannis?'

Nic nodded. 'Yeah, Alex and I did it hard for years, juggling school and the shop. It was expected that we were there to share the load, and I suppose we were both burnt out in the end.'

Speros gave a sigh of resignation. 'I had hoped my son would change his mind and take over the business, but it wasn't to be. I told Athena not so long ago that perhaps we should sell up and retire, but she'd have none of it. Cooking is her life.'

Nic nodded. Athena displayed exemplary culinary skills, producing the best of traditional Greek fare with finesse and subtle touches, using fresh ingredients sourced from local fishermen and farmers, and vegetables and herbs from the restaurant's garden. The resulting dishes were tantalising to the palate.

ꝗ

Once the Greek Orthodox Easter passed in April, ferries resumed and tourists began to arrive. Despite the busy, long days spent at his business, Nic sometimes felt lonely. He often stirred during a deep sleep, expecting to feel Angelina's smooth skin beneath his fingers, the rhythm of her soft breath against his cheek.

He sometimes lingered at the boatshed at the end of the day rather than facing the steep jog to an empty house. Feet dipped in the fine sand, he'd watch the sun's last rays slip below the horizon just as things were starting to liven up in town. On occasions, he'd stay the night on his makeshift bed in the shed or carry his mattress onto the sand and drift off to the sound of waves gently lapping against the shore, the warm breeze caressing his skin. On one of these nights, when he was at his lowest and about to start a second can of beer, he bolstered the courage to make a call he'd been contemplating for some time.

Elena was dining at the hotel's top-floor restaurant with the CEO's nephew when her phone rang. A quick glance at the number, and she rose quickly. 'Sorry, I have to get this, Stefano. Will you excuse me?'

He looked at her for a moment and nodded. She moved across the room out of earshot and pressed the phone to her ear. 'Nic. Are you still there?'

'Yes. I hope it's not an inconvenient time to call.'

'Not at all,' she lied, her heartbeat quickening.

'I was just wondering how you were getting along?'

'I'm well, thanks. And you?'

'I'm fine. Are you still working at the same hotel?'

'Yeah. I've been here a year now and just been offered a promotion.'

'That's good news.'

'So, how're things in Australia?' she asked.

'I'm no longer there.'

'Oh? Where are you calling from?'

'The Greek islands.'

'Really? Why didn't you tell me? I'd have arranged to meet you.'

The words caught Nic by surprise, and he struggled for a response. 'I've been rather busy actually, setting up a boat hire, snorkelling and kayaking business,' he said.

'Well, I wish you every success. When you're settled, let me know, and I'll come for a visit.'

'I'd like that,' he said more quickly than he would have liked.

For some time afterwards, Nic sat on the steps of his boathouse in the dark. He'd provided her with his whereabouts, but only time would tell whether he'd see her again. And he doubted if he could summon the courage to contact her a second time.

9

Elena sat aboard the Aegean Airlines plane awaiting take off for the two-and-a-half-hour flight to Athens. It was her first trip to Athens, and she'd booked a hotel near the Acropolis for the night, enabling her to visit the ancient monument before she headed to Piraeus the following morning to board the ferry for the eight-hour trip to the island. A middle-aged Japanese couple acknowledged her with a polite nod as they buckled their seatbelts, and she was glad she wasn't burdened with a companion's incessant conversation. As the plane took off, she rested against the headset and closed her eyes, barely taking in that she was at last having a break from work. She didn't know why, but she felt on edge. After all, things were looking up. She'd established herself as a respected member of the hotel management team, with an improved salary that allowed her to move to a more upmarket part of the city. Unsettling thoughts about Stefano had begun to creep into her mind two weeks ago when Nic's call interrupted their dinner. When she returned to the table that night something in his eyes led her to hastily fabricate a lie about a sick family member.

Why couldn't she tell him the truth? After all, she was only going to the island to thank Nic for giving her the belief and courage to escape when she did; the chance to clean the slate and begin a new life free of Angelina's clutches. She would have gone to Australia if the opportunity had arisen.

Stefano had made his approach a month ago, much to the envy of her female colleagues. Unattached at thirty-five, wealthy, good-looking and suave, he'd be anyone's dream catch. His string of affairs was hardly a secret, and initially, Elena was surprised that he made a move at all, considering her employee status and unremarkable background. She'd been flattered at the time and up to the challenge, as Angelina had taught her how to win men over by playing hard to get.

It was early days yet, and Stefano treated her with the affection and attention she'd long craved. It was hard to resist the beautifully wrapped French perfume awaiting her on the counter one morning or the elegant sapphire ring he'd produced several nights ago that she'd removed that morning and left in its box in her bedroom drawer. She wondered what he would say if he knew. She thought, *Wasn't this the main reason she took on the job with Ava? The chance to dress up, look glamorous and meet someone like him?*

Perhaps her instincts had been wrong. Stefano didn't seem too bothered by her announcement of taking a six-day break in the Greek Islands. 'It'll do you good,' he'd said. 'You've been working far too much lately.'

And yet …

¶

It was eight o'clock, closing time, as Nic hauled the last of the kayaks across the sand and into the shed. In the distance, he could see a woman's slender figure clad in a loose white dress heading in his direction, and as she drew near, he did a double take. Everything about her, from her heart-shaped face to olive skin and hair falling softly around her shoulders, reminded him of Angelina. But as she approached, he could see she radiated a naturalness. Perhaps it was the face devoid of make-up or the simple sandals that bore no resemblance to the high-fashion footwear that Angelina always wore.

She stepped across and held out her hand to his. 'Hi Nic, it's good to meet at last.'

His breath caught in his throat. 'I didn't think you'd come.'

'I told you I would.' Her accented voice was surprisingly soft.

'I didn't think it would be so soon, that's all.' The words

came out with a rush.

'It was a last-minute decision, to be honest,' she said. 'I haven't taken a break from work since I began and could sure do with one.'

'Well, you've chosen the right place to do it,' he said. 'How long are you here for?'

'Four days. I'd like it to be longer, but it's our busiest time of the year.'

'Same here. So how did you know where to find me?'

'I asked in town when I first arrived, but things looked busy down here, so I decided to have a bite to eat and wait until you closed for the day.'

'So where are you staying?'

'At a small guest house on the edge of town.'

'Which one?'

'Xenos.'

'I know the one. It's one of the island's most popular. You should enjoy it. Have you had a chance to settle in?'

'Not really. I plan to unpack and have an early night.'

He nodded. 'Give me a few minutes to lock up, and I'll walk you back.'

'I'll give you a hand.'

'No need.'

'I'd like to.'

She set about collecting pairs of flippers and snorkels for him to wash.

¶

The bars and restaurants were quickly filling as they headed along the path into town.

'Have you got a minute to stop by a taverna to meet my father's cousin and his wife?' Nic asked her. 'I'm sure they'd like to meet you.'

'Yes, of course.' Elena followed his glance to the white-washed, well-lit façade opposite with a look of appreciation. 'It's lovely, Nic. Postcard stuff,' she said.

He nodded. 'Yeah, it's pretty special. The one that the locals turn to as their regular. I'd highly recommend it if you're looking for a place to eat,' Nic said as they crossed the street and stepped inside.

They waited at the counter for Speros to settle a bill before Nic made the introductions.

'Welcome,' Speros said, giving her hand a warm shake with both of his. Athena, meanwhile, had her back turned, placing a platter of calamari before a couple on the far side of the room. Nic frowned. Their full-time waitress had left without notice, and the backpacker kitchenhand proved slow and unreliable, leaving the couple struggling to find replacements for the busy months ahead.

When she turned to see them, Athena looked surprised and quickly crossed the floor.

'Athena, this is Elena,' Nic said. 'She's over from Italy for a few days.'

He noticed the look of instant approval on Athena's face as she stepped across to kiss Elena on both cheeks, then turned to face him. 'You didn't tell me you had a girlfriend.'

Nic's heart pounded. 'No, that's not the case, Athena. We —'

'We just happened to bump into each other in town.' Elena quickly completed the sentence, as does a twin to their sibling, sensing his awkwardness. 'Nic helped me out some time back when I needed a hand.'

Nic shot her a look of gratitude.

'I see,' Athena said. 'Is it your first time on the island?'

'Yes, it is.'

'And what do you think?'

'I've not long arrived, but from the little I've seen, I like it very much.'

Athena beamed. 'So, how many days are you here for?'

'Just four. I wish it was more.'

'Well, I insist you stay for dinner.'

Elena glanced around. 'Are you sure? It looks hectic.'

Athena gave a shrug. 'No worse than any other night at this time of year. It will be a matter of joining you when we can, of course. We're rather short-staffed at the moment.'

Nic was barely listening. He'd not stopped to think about the barrage of questions Elena might have faced had she not intervened when she did. And how he would have dealt with the situation if she hadn't. And now, there was dinner to contend with. Nic was in a sweat just thinking about it. Perhaps it was a mistake introducing the couple to Elena in the first place.

To his relief the tables filled quickly, and Athena and Speros barely had a moment to spare until the end of the evening when they joined them for coffee. Elena deflected any questions that came her way by redirecting the conversation towards Athena and Speros, their taverna and life on the island. By the time they'd arrived back at her guest house in the early morning hours, he realised he still knew nothing about her.

'It's been a wonderful night, Nic.' She reached for his hand and his heart skipped a beat. 'Oh, by the way, I have something for you.' She pulled out an envelope and handed it to him. 'I said I'd pay you back.'

'No, no, consider it a gift. I don't need the money,' Nic said.

She smiled with a shake of her head and reached for her key card.

'Wait,' he said. 'Can we meet again tomorrow? I can try to organise someone for the day.'

'You don't have to do that. Perhaps I'll drop by.'

'That'd be good.' He watched her go inside.

At 3 a.m., Nic arrived home, shed his clothes, showered and climbed into bed. Opening time was seven, but he knew he'd have little sleep. His mind was in turmoil. He'd seen the stark resemblance between Angelina and Elena in the image she'd sent. But nothing could have prepared him for the shock of meeting her face-to-face. It was like seeing Angelina all over again. But she was not Angelina, he reminded himself. There was a softness about her, a vulnerability. But it didn't stop the memories of Angelina he'd tried so hard to suppress from flooding back. The lengths she'd taken to bring him to his knees. The steps she'd forced him to accept that he'd have to live with for the rest of his life. His jaw hardened. *Would Elena always have this effect? What did it matter? After four days I'll probably never see her again.*

¶

At 2 p.m. the next day, Nic looked up to see Elena carrying two souvlakis and takeaway coffees. His heart skipped a beat. 'I called by the taverna, and Athena insisted I bring you these.'

He shook his head and grinned.

For the remainder of the afternoon, she sat on a deckchair alongside his, watching as he tended to a stream of tourists, fitting flippers and adjusting goggles, or assisting them climb aboard one of the small boats moored nearby.

'I didn't realise it would get this busy,' she remarked. 'I'm happy things have worked out so well.'

He was about to make a comment when her phone rang. He watched her body tense. 'Aren't you going to answer it?' he asked.

She quickly glanced at the number. 'Yes, will you excuse me for a few minutes?'

'Of course.'

She rose, brushed the sand from her legs and headed further along the beach, back turned, phone pressed tightly to her ear. Every now and then she gave a quick nod.

'Is anything wrong?' he asked when she returned.

'No, everything's fine,' she said, resuming her seat. 'It was my boyfriend, Stefano. It's the first time I've been away from him, that's all,' she explained.

Nic's spirits plummeted, but he feigned a smile and nodded. Soon, the crowds thickened on the beach, giving him little time to spend with her. At six, when there was a quiet moment, she rose and headed across to the water's edge where he was collecting a pair of oars. 'You don't mind if I head back now?' she asked. 'I could do with an early night.'

'Not at all. Rest up and enjoy the break. That's what you're here for.'

She nodded. 'Thanks. I'm looking forward to having some time to myself. I'm not sure if I'll see you again before I leave.'

Nic's stomach tightened.

'That's okay.' He paused for a moment. 'If you want someone to talk to, you know where I am.'

¶

Long after she'd left, Nic sat alone in the darkness, his heart heavy, wondering why the thought hadn't entered his head that she might be in a relationship. Perhaps because there'd been no mention of it when he rang her in Italy; and the fact that she'd arrived alone. Ever since he first set eyes on her, he'd harboured a glimmer of hope that she'd come with the intention of getting to know him better. He realised that he should have heeded the warning bells when she knocked back his offer to show her around the island. He wondered who the boyfriend was. *Lucky bastard,* he thought, rising to his feet.

¶

Nic didn't hear from Elena until the day prior to her departure.

'Hi Nic, I've been wondering how you are. You haven't called.'

He struggled for a reply. 'You needed your space. Besides, things have been busy.' He cleared his throat. 'So, did you have a good time? That's the main thing.'

'Absolutely. But it's gone way too fast. Maybe next time I'll stay a little longer.'

'That would be good.' His voice sounded hollow in his ears. He wanted to ask, 'When will that be?' but he remained silent.

'Well, I suppose I'd better get going,' she said. 'I've got to start packing. I'm catching the earliest ferry in the morning.'

'Well, have a safe trip and look after yourself' was all he could think of to say.

¶

It was late and Nic draped his towel on the sand and sat, unmoving, watching the lights of the distant fishing boat approach the harbour. He'd thought of calling Elena again and asking her to join him for a final night's dinner but was in no fit state of mind. He rubbed the back of his neck and looked up at the sky. Life would go on. He'd simply immerse himself in his work. The sooner he pushed on the better. He hardly remembered walking up the pathway to his house.

In the morning, he dragged himself out of bed when the alarm went off at six and threw cold water over his face, fighting the exhaustion that was welling up inside and groaning at the bleary eyes and drawn face that met him in the mirror.

9

Nic ran into Athena on the way to work.

'Did you get to see Elena off yesterday?'

Nic felt his cheeks redden. 'No, I didn't, actually.'

Athena went to respond but stopped herself. 'Well, I'll miss her. I don't know what I would have done without her these past few days.'

'What do you mean?'

'She didn't tell you she'd been working for us, front of house and in the kitchen when I needed a hand?'

Nic was astounded. 'No, she didn't.'

'And I suppose you didn't know she had a hospitality background and ran a café? That she's Spanish, not Italian, and is multi-lingual?'

He gave her a blank look.

'Men!' she said with a snort and headed up the path towards the taverna.

ℊ

It was another two weeks before Nic felt as if his life had returned to some semblance of normality, and he dropped by the taverna for a late evening meal. It felt good to immerse himself in local chatter once again and get stuck into Speros' home-brewed retsina. The taverna was jam-packed, and they'd found a temporary replacement for Elena, much to his relief.

At the end of the evening, he stopped by the kitchen where Athena was stacking the last dishes.

'It's about time you dropped by,' she said. 'I was beginning to think you'd fallen off one of your boats and drowned.'

'You're unreal, Athena,' Nic said, grinning. 'I just called to say goodbye.' He patted his stomach. 'Dinner was delicious as usual.'

'Just as well.'

There was a moment's pause. 'Have you heard from Elena since she left?'

'No. Why?'

'I thought you might have, that's all.'

Athena watched him go, with a thoughtful look.

31

Elena was unsettled. Upon her return, she'd struggled to readjust to the rigours of Milan's fast-paced city living and found herself missing the island's simple lifestyle and friendly faces. But with new staff to train and an abundance of paperwork, she was sure it wouldn't take long to get back into the routine.

Why then, after a week, am I still restless and unable to sleep? she pondered, and wondered if she was missing Athena's friendly chatter, or if Stefano's constant presence and overt displays of affection was causing her uneasiness. While it was easy to be swept away by his charm and promise of things to come, something didn't sit well. Something that Elena couldn't pinpoint. The previous night, for instance, when he announced a weekend away together in Paris the following week to celebrate his birthday. Paris. A place she'd always wanted to visit. A romantic getaway, presumably in a five-star hotel, as was his style. But the fact that she'd been told, not asked, annoyed her. She'd pretended that their first night together at an exclusive Milan hotel on her first day off was better than it was. His lovemaking was about him, feeding his ego, saying and doing what was expected of someone of his status.

'I'm sorry, Stefano, but that's not possible. It'll have to be another time.'

'What are you talking about?' he'd exclaimed incredulously.

'I won't be here. I've decided to return to the island for a few weeks to give Athena a hand.' The words had come out of nowhere.

'Everything's booked, Elena.' His voice was cold.

'You can always reschedule, can't you?' she suggested with a tilt of her head. 'I told you I'd —'

'I think you've said enough.' He cut her off with a sweep of his hand, then turned on his heels and stormed out of the room. Elena chewed on her lip, arms crossed, and watched him go.

She'd arrived at work that morning to find a box of long-stemmed red roses with an envelope. She opened it. *I was out of line and I regret it. Go and have a good time. I'll rebook. S*

She brushed a lock of hair from her face with a smile. Perhaps she'd judged him too harshly the previous evening. Maybe he'd been overdoing things at work, as he'd mentioned one day in passing. Come to think of it, she could hardly blame him for flaring up after the time and effort that would have gone into arranging the trip. She sent him a text: *Thanks. The flowers are beautiful.*

When they met for dinner the night before she flew out, Stefano was charming and attentive. No demands. No requests to stay the night. And for that, she was grateful. Perhaps this couldn't have come at a better time. She needed time away. Time to think.

'So what time is your flight to Athens?'

'Early evening. It works out well, actually. There are a few loose ends to tie up at work in the morning, and by the time I finish packing, it'll be close to five o'clock when the bus leaves for the airport.'

'No need to do that. I'll drive you.'

Elena shook her head. 'Thanks, but you're busy enough.'

'When it comes to you, I'm never too busy.' His voice was soft as he reached for her hand. 'I'll miss you.'

She wondered why she couldn't bring herself to say, 'I'll miss you too.'

That night, she tossed and turned, trying to put aside the conflicting thoughts that kept creeping into her mind. Athena wasn't the only reason she was returning to the island. Nic bore none of Stefano's classical, refined looks and impeccable style. Still, periodically she found herself thinking about his expressive eyes, jawline dark with stubble, and tanned, lean physique. But she'd observed no spark of interest whatsoever on his part. Perhaps the sight of her reminded him too much of Ava. Or maybe an Australian girlfriend was waiting in the wings to join him once his business was established.

For now, it was enough to know she'd be seeing him one more time.

¶

Stefano felt a surge of anger as he exited terminal one and headed to the nearby carpark where his black Porsche was parked. He was used to being the one in control, used to calling the shots. Ex-girlfriends had quickly learned to be compliant and do as they were asked if they wanted the relationship to last. Not that any of them had lasted long. Elena's knockback had left him in a cold fury and it had taken every bit of self-restraint not to end things there and then. He asked himself, *What is it about her that won't allow me to let go? The classiness, perhaps? The looks of admiration sent her way whenever we ventured out or her natural warmth that drew people to her?*

His playboy lifestyle held less appeal with his mates settling down one by one. Perhaps his mother was right, he thought. Maybe it was time he did so as well. He wasn't getting any younger, and being the only son between two sisters, there was the family name to carry on. His parents made no effort to hide their disappointment about not yet being grandparents, and their patience was running thin. He couldn't afford to fall out of favour. Not with the wealth and status that would come his way when they died.

His mother had high expectations of the type of woman who'd fit the role of wife and mother, and Elena ticked all the boxes from what he could see, apart from her unremarkable background. But that could be dealt with. Therefore, it was frustrating to him that Elena remained as elusive as the day he met her. And the harder to get she played, the more determined he became. Her decision to return to the island had only strengthened his resolve. He'd not seen Elena's face as radiant as when she kissed him goodbye and made her way to customs. Suddenly he felt jealous. And threatened. *But I'll win out in the end.*

There was a steely glint in his eyes as he pressed the remote to his car and climbed inside. *I always do.*

9

It was 1 a.m. when Stefano put down his glass of whisky, turned on the mute button and made the call. 'Hey, Zeta. It's not too late, I hope.'

'No, no. I was just finishing off something from work,' came the eager response.

Stefano smiled and put his feet up on the coffee table. 'I'm sorry I haven't been in touch for a while. I've been away on business,' he lied. 'Mind if I came round?'

32

It was midday and the summer sun was at full strength when Nic turned from the water's edge to find her there. His heart all but stopped. 'Elena. It's good to see you,' he said, happier than he let on. 'Why didn't you tell me you were coming?'

'It was a last-minute thing. I decided to put things on hold and take up Athena's offer to work here for the remainder of the summer season.'

'I'm glad. She could do with a hand. Where are you staying?'

'With Athena and Speros. Free board and meals. I couldn't knock it back,' she said with a smile. 'Well, best I get going. I'd like to get started.'

'No worries. Let me know how things go.'

ς

Elena immersed herself in her front-of-desk role at the

taverna for the next two weeks. Although the hours were long and the atmosphere hectic, it was nothing she hadn't faced before. Athena had managed to employ a young British waitress and her German backpacking boyfriend. Both were grateful to have a chance to bump up the finances for their oncoming journey and proved to be hard workers.

Meanwhile, Speros at last had the opportunity to step back from the taverna. An outdoor man at heart, he'd never been comfortable spending his summers behind a counter, trying to juggle bookings and seating or smooth over issues with tetchy tourists. Content to do the ordering and put away the supplies, he spent his days working in the small plot where the taverna's herbs and vegetables were sourced, or sitting in the town, smoking, drinking Greek coffee and playing cards with friends. Nonetheless, with his generous, hospitable nature, Speros was happy to mingle with the taverna's patrons, well into the early morning hours.

From time to time, he'd glance across at Elena as she worked. There was an elegance about her, a welcoming manner that put patrons instantly at ease. They were lucky to have her. *But for how long? She'd no doubt be missed at the hotel where she worked. On any day, a call could come requesting her to return. Yet Athena stubbornly held that possibility at bay.* He'd not seen his wife as content in a long time. *How can I deny her that? The time would come soon enough.*

¶

Nic had barely caught sight of Elena since her arrival. She worked at the taverna most days from 11 a.m. until the early hours of the morning, while business had never been more hectic at his boat shed. However, he harboured a glimmer of hope she'd show, if just to let him know how things were going.

One morning, he dropped by the taverna, in the hope of seeing her, but it was one of her rare days off.

'Can I pass on a message?' Athena said.

'No, just tell her I called.'

She nodded. 'She's been a wonderful help, Nic. I'll hate to see her go.'

Nic's heart sank. 'Did she say how long she'll be here for?'

Athena shrugged. 'Another few weeks, I guess. She told me she couldn't afford to be away from her job too long.'

Nic's stomach tightened. He spoke before he could stop himself. 'And has she mentioned her boyfriend?'

'Occasionally. His family have something to do with the hotel chain she works for. I'd say they're far from being short of money.'

Nic swallowed. 'Did she say whether things are serious?'

There was a pause. 'How would I know? It's none of my business. But I noticed he calls her often at work.'

Nic remained silent and Athena's eyes fastened on his. 'I just have one thing to say to you, Nic. Ask yourself this. Is she worth fighting for?'

33

The phone rang. Elena wasn't about to answer it. She was tired of Stefano calling when she was at her busiest. And despite her requests for restraint, there'd been little let up. His calls seemed to be getting longer and she would find herself fidgeting impatiently as she listened to his small talk, anxious to get back to work.

Things had quietened somewhat by the time the next call came and there was no point in ignoring it a second time.

'Why didn't you answer when I rang before?' The voice was that of a sulky child.

'We were busy,' she said, trying to remain calm. 'Look, I'm really tired, Stefano. I don't feel much like talking right now.'

'I don't understand why you're working such ridiculously long hours in the first place, Elena,' he shot back. 'Or working at all for that matter.'

Elena felt the blood rush to her cheeks. 'What I do with my life is my business, Stefano.'

There was a moment's pause. 'Of course it is,' came the

rushed response. 'I'm sorry, I was just being selfish. I miss you, that's all. I'll let you get back to work. Try to get some downtime, okay?'

'I will. Thanks.' She ended the call and stood with her back against the window for a few moments. That was what she wanted to hear. Perhaps the time away would get him thinking. For the next three days, she heard nothing from Stefano and for the first time since she'd arrived, she began to unwind and relax.

¶

As Athena and Elena headed down along the paved narrow street towards the taverna to open for the day, Elena glanced at her surroundings, enraptured by the simple life, the beauty of the place and its welcoming, friendly people. But the spontaneous, happy family life seen in spades wherever she looked was something she'd never experienced. There'd been no looking out for each other in her apartment. She had been the slender thread that kept the family together. It had always been that way. And with it came responsibility.

And now, it was like living in another place and time. Elena embraced all things Greek and, with her multi-lingual competence, picked up the language sooner than she expected. Meanwhile, Athena had become the mother she'd never had, and the locals her family. She looked sideways at Athena, striding alongside her, muttering something about a supplier who'd not delivered on time. And smiled to herself.

Athena was a contradiction; a woman who could match it with the most outspoken and determined of the locals. But there was an inherent sensitivity behind the bossy façade. Elena had mentioned only once in passing about her background in Madrid, and Athena had sensed her discomfort. 'Not the best, eh?' she'd remarked. 'No,' Elena had responded quietly and there'd been no mention of it since.

¶

Nic reached for another beer, stroking the soft fur of the stray moggie sitting on his lap that had made his house its own. It was easy for Athena to challenge him about fighting for Elena. But he'd visited the website of the hotel where she worked. Five star and classy. And her boyfriend had the money and lifestyle he'd never be able to offer her. He could only wish her well. Given the little that Athena had told him of Elena's background, she deserved everything she fought so hard to get. She could do so much better than him.

¶

It was 3 a.m. and the night was particularly warm. Elena swung her legs to the floor and crossed to the window to open the shutters. The paved village square was bathed in silver moonlight and all was quiet except for the distant bark of a dog. Summer was drawing quickly to an end. Tourist numbers were thinning and she was running out of excuses for not returning to Milan, with Stefano pressing for a specific date to arrange a two-week break with full pay before she recommenced her duties.

It was a thoughtful gesture that she could certainly do with after the past hectic five weeks. Since she'd confronted him over the phone calls, he'd backed right off. If anything, she'd began looking forward to his calls. He was sounding like the charming, caring man she first knew and she missed the feel of arms around her waist as he drew her close. And there'd been the unexpected offer to move into his impressive Milan apartment with floor-to-ceiling windows, plush leather furniture and spa, emphasising there was no need for her to work at all. An enticing prospect, considering the unrelenting years of long days in any job she could lay her hands on. But she could not see herself giving up work completely. She'd never been one to sit around and do nothing. A day or two less perhaps …

Even so, would she really be happy living such an existence? Accompanying Stefano to business functions or dinner parties with his friends? Keeping up appearances with his privileged parents, whom she'd yet to meet? As it was, his preoccupation with looks and appearances was a source of frustration for her. She knew how to step out with the best of those in Stefano's circle after months alongside Angelina, and the admiration in his eyes was unmistakeable. Yet, even when they ventured out for a casual outing, she felt the need to go the extra yard with outfits that flattered, and pay attention to detail with her hair and make-up.

He'd never got to see the girl who slouched around in her apartment, devoid of make-up in her favourite tracksuit pants and windcheater. *Am I prepared to sacrifice who I really am for the glamorous lifestyle I've craved, now so tantalisingly close?* She chewed on a thumb nail. *Maybe I've gotten things all wrong,* she thought. *Maybe he doesn't care a stuff about what I get up to at home. The only way to find out was by giving things a go. Who knew, maybe I could encourage him to venture with me to places like this, show him there was more to life than city living, parties and making money. Perhaps we could purchase a villa in the Mediterranean somewhere.* She smiled at the thought and gave her shoulders a hug. But deep down, she sensed that nothing was about to be that easy.

9

It didn't take long for the calls to resume. For the third time that day, the shrill ring came, causing her nerves to jangle. With a deep inhalation, Elena squeezed her eyes shut for a moment then reached for her phone.

'Stefano, I told you not to ring me at work.'

'Yeah, but I'm about to drop by the hotel. Have you come up with a return date to pass on.'

'No, I haven't,' she snapped. 'And I'm sick of you asking.'

There was a frosty silence at the other end. Elena anxiously looked across the room to where Athena was reaching in the basket for another tablecloth, and turned her back. 'I can't keep this up any longer.' Her voice was strained. 'I can no longer keep up the pretence.'

'What's that supposed to mean?' he barked.

'Trying to be the person you want me to be. You think you know me, Stefano, but you don't at all. I can't imagine living in your squeaky-clean apartment, having to dress up to go out when you want me to. I just want to slouch around in my pyjamas at night if I so choose. Wear a charcoal face mask around the house if I feel like it, fill the house with dogs and a cat or two.'

'This is beginning to sound ridiculous, Elena.'

'Is it?'

'Oh, for fuck's sake.'

'Stop yelling.'

But he wasn't finished. 'I can yell if I want.'

'Well, in that case, I'll ring you back later and we'll resume the conversation when you've calmed down.'

'Don't bother.'

There was a click at the other end.

Elena stood for a few moments in disbelief. There. She'd finally said it after three weeks of doubts and uncertainties. Perhaps, deep down, she'd known all along it would come to this. Right now, she felt drained and exhausted. She'd confide in Athena eventually. But it was Nic she wanted to talk to the most. And couldn't bring herself to do so.

§

It had been a sweltering day for September, and Elena took advantage of the balmy evening for a late-night stroll through town and down to the marina. She'd heard nothing more from Stefano since she'd broken things off, to her relief. The ordeal left her drained and needing time to consider her immediate future. One thing was for sure. There'd be no going back to the hotel. Perhaps she could venture to another country and find work in a similar venue. After all she had the credentials and experience.

Or maybe she could apply for a job as an interpreter in a court or a hospital. In the meantime, she'd stay another few weeks, determined to enjoy the last of the summer season before she came to a final decision. She was glad to have entered a short-term rental arrangement. It was simply a matter of gathering her few possessions and moving on.

Few were about on the well-lit marina as she strolled along the pier where a profusion of blue fishing boats in various states of repair bobbed in the water amidst chartered and privately owned yachts. Three mega yachts were moored side-by-side at the furthest end of the dock, and she could hear the clink of glasses and chatter from below as she approached.

From what she'd been told, the small marina was particularly busy throughout the tourist season, as yachties and boat owners vied for well-protected berths for their water, supplies, a place to refuel, perhaps with a more extended stopover.

When she'd finished her leisurely stroll, she removed

her sandals and headed down to the water's edge for a walk along the beach before turning back. *Nothing stopping you from coming back some time,* she thought to herself as she wandered, wondering why the sentiment did little to raise her spirits. She'd miss the feel of moist, firm sand beneath her feet, gentle waves that lapped her ankles, and the heady smell of salty air in her nostrils.

The boat shed was perhaps thirty metres away when Elena detected a flicker of movement and, as she neared, she could make out the outline of Nic in the moonlight, seated on the sand. She stopped for a moment, debating whether to approach him. *What if he'd dozed off or simply needed some time to himself?* But it had been over a week since he'd called in at the taverna. And she'd been too busy to speak to him.

She bit her lip hard, something she did out of habit when unsure of herself and made her way across the sand. Nic's heart skipped a beat when he caught sight of Elena in the distance, and he rose and crossed the sand to meet her. 'I thought you'd be working,' he said.

'It's my day off, but I felt like a walk along the beach. I wasn't expecting to find you here this late.'

'Yeah, I've usually left by now, but there won't be many more warm nights like this. May as well make the most of it. Do you have time for a chat?'

She nodded. 'And then I'll drop by the taverna to see if Athena needs a hand.'

'I've some beer in the fridge if you'd like.'

'Sounds good.'

Nic grinned.

For a while they sat in silence, looking out over the still water bathed in moonlight, sipping their drinks and listening to the voices drifting across from the town. Nic wanted to ask about Elena's boyfriend, but decided to let it go.

'You must love it here, Nic,' she said, picking up a handful of sand and watching it funnel through her fingers over her toes.

'Yeah, I really do,' he said in a sincere tone.

'Any thoughts of returning to Australia?'

He shook his head. 'Unless it's to visit my family. I've made this place my home.'

Elena waited a few moments before responding. 'So, tell me about your family, Nic. Are you close?'

'Yeah, we are, I guess.'

'Well, you're lucky.'

He noted the pain on her face and said, 'Feel like talking about it?'

Elena hesitated, then proceeded with an account of her early years in Madrid. When she got to the abuse suffered at the hands of her brothers, she stopped as tears welled in her eyes. 'I'm sorry. It's just that I've never spoken about this to anyone before.'

Nic reached across and gently wiped a tear from her cheek with a thumb, and she quivered at his touch.

'We all need someone to talk to, Elena.' His voice was gentle. 'You can come to me at any time.'

'Thanks,' she managed, hastily pulling a tissue from her

pocket and wiping her eyes. *But the thing is, I won't be around here for much longer, Nic, or have you forgotten?* she thought.

There was an awkward silence, after which she placed her empty can on the sand and rose.

'Well, I'd best be going,' she said. 'Athena must be close to finishing by now.'

'Okay. Give me a minute to lock up, and I'll see you back.'

They walked side-by-side in silence, and when they neared the taverna, Elena stopped and turned to face him. 'Remember what you said the first night I arrived, about taking an afternoon to show me over the island —'

He nodded.

'Well, could we arrange a time before I leave? I've seen so little of the place since I've been here.'

The words were bittersweet, and Nic swallowed hard.

'Sure. I'll get someone to look after the boat shed,' he said, doing his best to sound nonchalant. 'Let me know when you're ready.'

'Okay. Would you like to come inside to see Athena?'

'No, another time,' he said quickly. 'I've got a few things to attend to.'

At midnight, Elena walked home with Athena, deep in thought. Nic was the only person in her life she'd confided in. And he hadn't judged. Hadn't made suggestions. Just listened. There was an easiness about him.

But there was something else. Being close to him was different to any moment she'd spent with Stefano. She wanted to lie side-by-side with him on the sand under the stars.

Envisaged the warmth of Nic's hand in hers as she snuggled close. Wanted to get to know him better. Hoped he'd feel the same.

But there'd been no sign of reciprocation on his part, nor of a glimmer of emotion on his face when she'd raised the topic of returning to Milan. Elena's heart was heavy. She'd been on the island long enough for him to have shown at least an inkling of romantic interest. *Perhaps it was time to look to the future and book a flight back to Milan,* she thought.

34

It was 8 a.m., and Nic was about to jog down to the boatshed when his phone buzzed. He dug it out of his pocket and swiped it open, smiling at the number.

'Hey little brother.'

'Hey, Nic. Good to hear from you. Are you at work?'

'Nah, just about to leave. Why?'

There was a moment's pause. 'Is everything okay?' Nic asked.

'Yeah, we're all good. Look, a letter arrived today for you, redirected from your Docklands apartment.'

Nic groaned. 'Probably another bill.'

'I don't think so, mate. It's from Spain.'

Nic's stomach turned and his mouth went dry. There was a short silence at the other end. 'Do you want me to open it?'

'No. Send it through, would you?'

g

Athena was in the town's small supermarket paying for a few ingredients needed for the evening shift when she saw Nic pass by. She frowned. He wore an expression she'd never seen before, and she immediately sensed all was not right.

'Have you spoken to Nic lately?' she asked Elena, who was busy resetting the tables when she returned.

'A few days ago. Why?'

'How did he seem?'

'Fine, from what I could tell. Why?'

'I saw him not so long ago, and he appeared troubled, that's all.'

'Would you like me to check on him?'

Athena nodded. 'Why don't you head on down now while things are quiet.'

'Okay.' Elena picked up her phone and clicked on his number. 'Hi. Are you at the boatshed?'

'Yeah, I just arrived back. Why.'

'Feel like a coffee?'

'Since when do Greeks knock back a coffee?'

She smiled. 'Expect me soon.'

The day was cool, and not many were on the beach. Nic was inside the boat shed, moving a few things around when she arrived and greeted her with a smile. 'Not working today?' he asked.

'Yeah, but I thought I'd drop by while it was quiet.'

'Well, come inside. It's a bit cold to be sitting out here.'

She nodded. 'Thanks.'

'So how are Athena and Speros?' he asked, pulling up a

couple of chairs and sitting alongside her.

'They're fine.'

'I feel guilty that I haven't dropped in for a while.'

'They know how busy you are,' she said, handing him a coffee.

'Thanks. This'll hit the spot.'

She looked at him. 'It's not the only reason why I came, Nic. Athena saw you in town today and said you looked worried. Is everything all right?'

'Yeah, yeah. I'm waiting for a letter, that's all.' The response was quick.

'From Australia?'

'No, Spain.'

Elena chewed the side of her lip and paused for a moment. 'I know it's none of my business, and you don't have to answer. But does it have anything to do with the baby?'

Nic gave a start of incredulity. 'How do you know about the baby?' he demanded.

'Ava and I first met at an internet café where I worked in Spain. She was pregnant then and came in most weeks, almost to the time she gave birth.'

'So that's where you came across each other.' Nic's eyes fastened on hers.

She nodded. 'I've never brought it up. You made it clear you'd moved on.'

'So, did you get to see the baby?' The words caught in his throat.

'No. Ava had left the hospital when I last saw her and was

about to depart for Australia. The baby was already with her adoptive parents.'

Nic's heart raced. 'Did Ava mention who they were?'

'No. A Spanish couple. That's all I know.'

'And the baby ...' His voice cracked. 'Did Ava tell you her name?'

Elena shook her head. 'I'm sorry, Nic.' Her words were soft. 'You know how secretive Ava was.'

Nic's expression hardened. 'It doesn't matter anyway. The baby's dead.'

'Dead?' Elena looked at him in surprise. 'What gave you that idea?'

'I got word from a contact.'

'When?'

'Over a year ago.'

'Maybe he got his facts wrong. It's certainly not the impression I got from Ava.'

'What do you mean?' Nic's heart was racing.

'Well, she never mentioned anything of the sort to me. In fact, I asked Ava not so long back if she'd consider returning to see the baby, but her uncle had ordered her to never go back.'

'And what was her reaction to that?'

'She said that it was fine by her.'

Nic winced.

Elena looked at him in concern. 'I'm sorry. Perhaps I shouldn't have said anything.'

'No, I needed to know.'

She reached out and laid a hand on his arm. 'You turned to me when I needed help the most, Nic. I'd like to think you'd do the same.'

'I'll see if it comes to that, but thanks.'

'So, will you tell me when the letter arrives?'

'Look, the whole thing's complicated. Not something I want you to be involved in.'

'Perhaps leave that up to me to decide.' She rose. 'Promise?'

'We'll see.'

He watched her go, his thoughts in turmoil. First and foremost, in his mind, was the baby. *Could she still be alive, as Elena believed? If so, why had his contact lied? He'd always been reliable. Always a first time,* he thought grimly, reaching for his phone, and swiping it open. He tapped on the number, slumping back in his chair as the automated message told him the phone had been disconnected.

Fuck,' he raged, scrolling through his contacts and trying another. 'It's Nic. I'm trying to reach Bernardo.'

There was a moment's pause at the other end. 'Bernardo disappeared somewhere in Russia months ago. I thought you would have heard. Anything I can help you with?'

'Nah, not now. Maybe some other time.' Nic ended the call and exhaled wearily. Now there was nothing to do but wait for the letter to arrive. Despite its priority postage, Nic had no way of knowing how long that would be on a small island relying on ferries for its mail deliveries. He wasn't one for patience in such matters and didn't like to think about his state of mind should things drag on. But Nic was also an optimist at heart. *The letter had to be a good sign, didn't it? There must be a chance that the baby was still alive.* His brow creased. But why did it take this long for him to be contacted? And there were other questions yet to be answered. Antonio's gang headquarters was based in Rio de Janeiro. *So what had Ava been doing in Spain in the first place? How long had she been there, and where had she stayed? And what was she doing spending her time in an internet café? Did it matter? Elena seemed no wiser than him. Antonio would be the only person with the answers to any of it.* Nic's face hardened. *And I'll get those answers, you bastard,* he thought.

35

It was another six days before the letter arrived. Since Nic's brother's call, he dropped by the post office every day on the way home from work to check his post office mailbox, and as time wore on, he'd become more on edge. So, when he caught a flash of white as he opened his mail box, his legs felt weak beneath him.

Quickly pulling out the crumpled letter, Nic closed the box, headed down to the harbour where no one was about, and sat on the ancient stone wall, legs dangling. With fingers shaking, he opened it, careful not to rip the contacts. The typed letter was short and to the point:

> *You don't know me. I'm Joaquin Cardoso, the nephew of Filipe and his wife Rosa who adopted Ava Ferreira's baby, Talita. Filipe speaks little English so I am writing on his behalf. He believes you could be the father of Talita. If that's the case, could you ring me on this number.*
>
> *Yours*
>
> *J*

Nic read the message over and over until the words blurred, overcome with raw emotion, and wracked by sobs. Wiping the tears that stung his eyes with the heels of his hands, he shoved the letter in his pocket and jogged back to his house. It was 7:30. Not too late to make the call. Half-expecting to reach voicemail, his heart raced when a voice with a thick Spanish accent answered. 'Yes?'

'Am I speaking to Joaquin?'

'Yes. Who is this?'

'My name's Nic Diamandis, and I'm calling about the letter I received from you.'

'Are you Talita's father?'

'Yes, I am.' The words echoed strangely in Nic's ears. 'How did you get my address?'

'Aunt Rosa found it hidden amongst Ava's belongings before she went to the hospital. I tried the number first, but it rang out.'

'It's been changed since then. Is everything all right?' Nic asked anxiously.

'Yes. I felt the need to contact you because Aunt Rosa died recently and my uncle is struggling to look after Talita. He's sixty-seven, you see. I'm sure he'd be relieved to be freed from the responsibility of raising such a small child if the opportunity arose. Would you consider coming to speak to him about this?'

'Yes, yes, of course!' Nic's heart raced. 'When?'

There was a moment's pause. 'I'm not sure if you are aware, but Talita's great uncle, Antonio, has a vested interest in all of this. He can't know that this call is taking place.'

'I've had dealings with Antonio before, don't worry. Leave me to handle him. So where is he now?'

'He's currently staying with us on his property near Viveiro.'

'What sort of property?'

'A fifteen-acre hamlet that he purchased several years ago. Filipe's been his caretaker.'

Nic was thinking fast. This was no simple matter of waiting until Antonio returned to Rio and then absconding with the baby. He'd be hunted down by Antonio eventually. And he wasn't prepared to give up his chance of fatherhood a second time.

'Have you any indication how long Antonio will be there?'

'No. He comes and goes from Rio.'

'If he mentions anything, let me know. Otherwise, expect to hear from me soon when I've confirmed a flight.'

'Okay. I'll pass this on to Filipe.'

Nic pressed the end button and sat for a few moments. Viveiro. He'd have to google the place. There was no way of knowing how far and wide Antonio's assets stretched. In no fit state of mind to think of immediate plans, he hastily typed and printed a sign, stuffed it in his pocket, jogged down to the boat shed and attached it to the door.

And when he arrived back, he settled on the sofa, bottle and glass in hand, and wiped himself out …

It was 6 p.m., and Elena cleared the last tables and placed the dishes on the sink in readiness for the kitchenhand, who was soon to arrive. 'I haven't heard from Nic for a while,' she said, turning to Athena. 'Mind if I slip out and drop by the boatshed to see him?'

'No. I've been worried about Nic myself.'

Few were about when Elena headed along the beach. As she neared the boatshed something fixed to the door caught her eye. She quickened her pace.

The sign read: *This boatshed will be closed today. Normal hours will resume tomorrow. We apologise for any inconvenience.*

Elena frowned and headed back to the taverna. 'He wasn't there. The boatshed's been closed for the day,' she told Athena.

'Why?'

'There was no explanation.' She paused. 'Do we have many bookings for this evening? I'd like to check on him, just in case things aren't okay.'

'Of course. I can manage easily. We only have a table of two and one of six. Do you know where Nic's house is?'

Elena shook her head. Athena gave directions and said, 'If you get lost, just ask someone.' She glanced down. 'Are those shoes suitable for a steep walk?'

'What, my work shoes? I'm in them for hours every day, remember.'

'And what about a jacket? It may be warm now, but —'

'I have one with me, don't worry.' Elena looked at her with affection.

'Wait.' Athena laid a restraining hand on her arm. 'I cooked a tray of moussaka this morning. I'll prepare a few servings and a salad for your dinners.'

The labyrinth of narrow, winding, paved pathways reminded Elena of the rural Italian villages she'd meandered along with Angelina. As she made the steep climb to Nic's house, carry bag in hand, the locals she passed exuded the same welcoming appeal. Birds chirruped noisily as wily cats made their rounds, and occasional crimson petals from a bougainvillea-festooned verandah floated past like feathers.

Nestled amid a profusion of whitewashed houses set close together in a narrow alleyway, Nic's small house with its blue shutters and balcony was an unexpected and welcome surprise. Ascending the narrow stone steps leading to the front door, she rapped several times and waited, hesitant about Nic's response to her uninvited arrival. She needn't have worried.

'Elena. What a nice surprise,' he said as he opened the door. 'How on earth did you find the place?'

'With much difficulty,' she replied, adding, 'Just kidding. Athena told me. Speaking of … she insisted I gave you this. Said it was for our dinner.'

He took the bag with a grin and waved her inside. Elena cast her eyes around the cosy space with its whitewashed walls and traditional simplicity. 'It's beautiful, Nic. I love it.'

A blush crept up Nic's neck. 'Not much, but it's home.'

She pointed to a blue door on the far wall. 'Does that lead to a balcony?'

He nodded and placed the bag on the kitchen bench. 'Come, and I'll show you.'

The moment they stepped outside, Elena's eyes shone as she clasped the blue railings and scanned the plethora of white sugar-cubed houses bathed in a soft pink glow that stretched out below as the last of the sun dipped beneath the horizon of the harbour and the Aegean waters beyond.

She turned to face him. 'It's magical.'

'I was lucky to hear about it, actually,' Nic remarked. 'The steep walk became too much for the previous elderly owners. They sold up and bought closer to town.'

She nodded. 'I suppose you know why I'm here.'

'You dropped by the boatshed by the sound of things.'

'Yeah. It's not like you to close for the day.'

He rubbed the side of his neck. 'Tuesdays are normally quiet so I decided to take some time out.'

Elena met his eyes. 'You've received the letter, haven't you.'

He hesitated, then nodded.

'Can I see?'

Nic pulled it out of his pocket and handed it to her.

She quickly scanned it and turned to him. 'See? I told you the baby was still alive. So, you've made the call, obviously.'

'Yeah, last night.'

'Tell me about it.'

When he'd finished, she remarked, 'I'm so happy for you, Nic. I really am.'

She observed him stiffen. 'Everything's all right, I hope?'

'Yeah, Talita's safe.' His jaw hardened. 'And I'm going to Spain to fetch her.'

'When?'

'As soon as things can be arranged.'

'So what is it then, Nic?' She touched his shoulder in concern.

He paused momentarily and when he spoke, his voice bore a steely edge. 'It won't be a straightforward process, that's all.'

She looked at him. 'What do you mean? What did Joaquin tell you?'

Nic drew a deep breath. 'Perhaps we should discuss things inside. Could you do with a coffee?'

'Yeah, I could, actually.'

And as they sat on the sofa, Elena listened without interruption until he'd finished. 'That explains what little Ava told me about her uncle,' she said, eyes thoughtful. 'Have you met him?'

'We've crossed paths before.'

'And does he know you're Talita's father?'

'That's debatable. There's been no mention of it to Rosa and Filipe, and yet —'

'Go on.'

'Antonio reveals nothing unless it's a means to an end. I guess I'll find out soon enough.'

There was a tense pause, after which she turned to him and said, 'Can I come with you?'

Nic gasped. 'What?'

'I'd like to be there to support you in all this. Two is far better than one in juggling luggage and a young child on a long trip like that, let alone one you've yet to get to know. I'm familiar with Viveiro. I know the language and can interpret it for you. I can —'

'No way, Elena.' He cut her off with a wave of his hand. 'You have no idea of the seriousness of all this. The danger involved.'

She met his eyes. 'I've worked alongside Ava for two months, remember. I know what danger's all about, believe me.'

'You don't know a thing about me, Elena,' he cried out in anguish. 'A thing about my past.'

'Listen to me, Nic. Do you think your past matters? Ava told me you'd worked alongside her, and I couldn't imagine that being a squeaky-clean arrangement in some corporate business or something.' She paused for a moment. 'Maybe you might want to talk about it someday, and if not …' She gave a shrug. 'I don't care a stuff.'

Nic wondered if he could ever bring himself to do such a

thing. Perhaps some things were better left unsaid.

'Look at me, Nic. I want to go because I care about you.'

He flinched. 'Thanks, but I'll be fine. I'm sure your boyfriend will want you back now that the season's almost over.'

She looked at him. 'I won't be going back.'

'What do you mean?' Nic's heart started to race.

'I called it off with Stefano a week ago.'

It took a split second for the words to register.

'Why didn't you tell me?'

'I wanted to but couldn't. I needed time to get my head around things first. Let's say it wasn't pretty.'

He wasn't sure how to respond. Sensing his awkwardness, she said, 'Stefano was nothing like I first thought. He was domineering and demanding, and I couldn't cope with all of that. I've sent through my notice. It would be too uncomfortable to remain there. Stefano's father is the hotel's CEO.'

'So what are you planning to do?'

'I haven't thought about it, to be honest. I'll get a reference easily enough, but I don't know if I want to return to the hotel industry. I no longer want to be part of a world where people are judged by their bank balances. Being here on the island has made me see things differently.'

'You wouldn't consider staying?' The words rushed out before he had time to stop them.

For a moment, she looked thoughtful. 'I thought about it. I'm sure Athena would be happy for me to continue on there but the work's seasonal. It wouldn't be enough to keep me going through the winter.'

Wondering if he'd said too much already, Nic hesitated. But the thought of losing her altogether was too much to take, and he said, 'And what if something could be worked out with Athena and Speros?'

'What do you mean?'

'Just a matter that Speros brought up a while ago. I'll have a word with him and get back to you. But keep this from Athena until he's had a chance to discuss things with her, okay?'

She nodded with a puzzled look.

'Well, perhaps we should have dinner. I don't want to get you back too late.'

'There's no rush. I could stay longer if you wish.'

Nic's heart lurched. There was no way of knowing what that meant. 'But Athena will be worried about you,' he blurted out.

'I'll give her a call.'

'Why not stay the night?' The words spilled out before he knew it. 'I can make up a bed in the spare room and walk you back in time for work in the morning.'

'Well, as long as I'm not putting you out.'

'Not at all.'

Elena glanced down at her work clothes. 'I'm a bit unprepared. Would you have a spare T-shirt for me to sleep in?'

'Sure.'

'Thanks.' She paused for a moment then said, 'So, getting back to Spain, what will you tell Athena and Speros? You can't just rock up with a small child.'

'I know, I know,' his voice was tense.

'And the sooner, the better. Why not first thing in the morning once we get back.'

Nic looked alarmed. 'I don't know what I'd say, Elena. I've hidden everything about my past from them and don't want to go there.'

Elena chose her words carefully. 'And you don't have to. Athena knows you value your privacy. It's your daughter only you need to mention.'

'I suppose.'

'If it helps, tell them as much as you'd want the locals to know. It'll make it easier all around when you arrive back.'

Nic thought about that.

'All good to make the call, then?' she persisted.

Nic rubbed his hands over his face and said, 'Yeah, may as well do it.'

Elena swiped open her phone and tapped on the number.

'Hi Athena, yes, yes. Things are fine with Nic. He's been waiting for some news, that's all, and it's all good. He wants to tell you both on the way to work tomorrow. Look, we're about to get dinner ready. It could be a bit late to head back afterwards, so I decided to stay the night.'

'I'm glad you said. I would have waited up otherwise,' came the response.

'I figured that. We'll see you in the morning then.'

She ended the call and said, 'Okay. That's done. Now let's have some dinner. Can I give a hand?'

'No, all good,' he said, rising.

'Well, I'd like to be useful in some way. Show me where the sheets to the spare room are kept.'

Not long afterwards, she settled on the sofa, one foot tucked under her, and her lips curved in a smile as Nic busied himself in the tiny kitchen, tea towel over a shoulder. 'So, tell me about the neighbours,' she said, and listened in amusement to the colourful depictions of the families who resided along the narrow, cobbled alleyway.

'And then there's Hermia next door. You think Athena's a mother hen.' He nodded to the left as he placed the piping hot dish of moussaka before them with gloved hands.

'Go on.' Elena tilted her head with a hint of a smile.

Nic stopped, his breath caught in his throat. There was something infinitely natural about her, reminiscent of his ex-wife Kelly when they first began dating. An elegance and dignity about her. 'Where do I start?' He blurted out the first words that came to mind. 'She'd be well into her eighties, lost her husband years ago and…'

The words washed over Elena as they dined, lost in time, talking about nothing in particular. And after Nic had cleared the dishes, they settled side-by-side on the sofa, sipping the remainder of the wine.

'So tell me about your family, Nic,' she said.

'My dad passed away not long ago, and Mum lives near my brother, Alex, in Queensland.'

She nodded. 'And are you and your brother close?'

There was a short silence. 'Yeah, closer than I've been to anyone. Alex is the only one who knows —' He stopped short, a look of pain on his face.

'Knows what, Nic?'

He placed his head in his hands for a few moments, and when he looked up again, she could see the torment in his eyes.

'What is it?'

Nic felt his throat tighten, and he faltered before answering. 'You said my past doesn't matter the other day, Elena. But it does. It fucking well does. I can't go on like this without revealing something to you.'

'Okay.'

'When I was young and hot-headed, I joined a gang and soon became entrenched in the underworld. There was big money to be made and a chance to see the world by becoming a sniper.'

He looked at her, beads of sweat forming on his forehead. 'And I took them up on it. It cost me my marriage and self-worth, but what hurt most was the lies I lived my life around.'

'But the thing is, you owned up to your mistakes, learned from them and found a way to move on.' She shrugged. 'So, you turned the wrong fork in the road. Just as I did when I agreed to the job with Ava. We'll probably regret what we've done for the rest of our lives. But does that mean we don't deserve happiness?'

Tears welled in Nic's eyes, and he brushed them away hurriedly.

'I think you've punished yourself enough, Nic.' She reached out and gently stroked his cheek. 'It's time to put things behind you and find contentment in this beautiful place. You've got Talita to think of now.'

He nodded and slipped a hand around her shoulder, drawing her to him.

They sat silently for a long time, her head resting against his, eyes transfixed by the moonlight's milky rays through the open doorway over the lights below and across the Aegean. The only sound was distant voices and the faint beat of music.

'And by the way, I'm coming with you to Spain,' she murmured.

This time there was no objection. And with the ensuing silence between them came a desire he didn't know he could control. 'Come on, sleepy head.' He gently removed his arm, tussled her hair and rose. 'Let's get you to bed. You've got work tomorrow, remember.'

'I s'pose,' she mumbled, taking his outstretched hand.

'I'll see you in the morning, then. You've got everything you need?' Nic brushed her lips with his at the doorway to her room, causing her body to tremble.

'Yes. Thanks.' Elena closed the door and reached for the oversized T-shirt, burying her face in it for a moment and taking in his nearness before stepping out of her clothes and slipping it over her head.

All was quiet except for the occasional sound of a passer-by's feet on the cobblestones below and the persistent whistle of wind that had got up over the past hour. She lay in bed, mellowed by the wine but unable to drift off to sleep, acutely aware of how near Nic was. So close. Wanting him.

At 3 a.m., she swung her legs over the bed and tiptoed across the room, every creak making her jump, her mouth dry and hands clammy. The curtains were apart in Nic's room, and moonlight bathed the bed in a milky luminosity, outlining the dark face as he lay under the sheet, one arm flung carelessly across the bed like a garment removed. She smiled. He bore the innocence of a sleeping child. For a moment, she stood still in the doorway, filled with uncertainty, considering turning back, but a wave of longing engulfed her, so intense that she knew she couldn't. As she crept across the room, Elena's breath caught in her throat. She quietly slipped beneath the covers beside him and snuggled against his back, a hand reaching tentatively around to cover his.

Disoriented and wondering if it was a dream, he swung around in a daze. 'Elena, what the …'

'I just wanted to lie beside you for a while, Nic. I hope you don't mind.' Her voice was soft.

'No, I'm glad you're here. Very glad.' He rolled over, scarcely able to believe what was happening and encircled her in his arms, his chin resting on her soft hair. Saying nothing for some time, they were immersed in each other's nearness. Yet, every part of Nic's being ached with desire, his heart surging out of control.

After a while, she turned to him and murmured, 'Kiss me.'

He cupped her face with gentle hands, lips parting against hers with a lingering embrace, but he found himself unable to hold back. Reaching down, he caressed the soft skin of her thighs, breasts, and across her body. She moaned, trembling at his touch.

'Are you sure about this?' his voice was hoarse.

'Yeah, quite sure,' came the soft response.

Their lovemaking was slow and sensual. The antithesis of the urgent fierceness of Angelina, to whom Nic had always felt the need to prove himself just to keep her in his life. There'd always been a vulnerability about Elena, despite her grit and determination. He'd almost lost her the first time. There wasn't about to be a second. Nic would wait as long as necessary to form a relationship. He took her with a gentleness yet undisguised desire that Elena reciprocated, and as he lay beside her afterwards, waiting for his breathing to slow, she snuggled in the crook of his arm and smiled, one hand draped across his chest. Never before had she felt wanted like this, so safe.

And as Nic held her close and drowned in her scent, he couldn't remember the last time he'd felt so much at peace, his cares and worries dissipating. But this was just the calm before the storm, Nic soon reminded himself. He was prepared to lay his life on the line to get his daughter back and keep Elena free from harm.

37

'Elena tells me you have something to tell us, Nic,' Athena placed their coffees before them and sat expectantly beside Speros.

'Yeah.' Nic rubbed the back of his neck momentarily and looked from one to the other. 'Remember when I told you I had no kids?'

They nodded.

'Well, that wasn't exactly true. I had a little girl who I didn't know existed until I'd got word that she'd died. It was too painful to talk about. I just wanted to put it behind me.'

'I'm so sorry.' Athena reached for his hand across the table.

'The thing is though, three days ago, out of the blue I got word that Talita is still alive. Her mother has … has cleared out, and she won't be coming back.' He paused. 'I've found out where Talita is, and Elena's going with me to bring her back.'

Athena clasped her hands in delight. 'Why, that's wonderful news, Nic. I'm so happy for you. How old is she?'

'Almost three.'

Athena nodded. 'So, when are you leaving?'

'As soon as things can be arranged.'

'Yes, yes, of course. There must be a lot to organise. Australia's a long way.'

'Talita's not in Australia,' Nic remarked. 'She's in Spain.'

'Spain?' Athena looked at him incredulously. 'What's she doing there?'

Nic stiffened. 'I don't want to go into it if that's okay. The past's the past.'

Athena's response was cut off with a wave of Speros' hand. 'And your wishes will be respected,' he said firmly. 'Meanwhile, leave me to take care of the boatshed, and we'll find a replacement for Elena.'

Nic let out a sigh of relief. 'That's one thing less to think about. Thanks.'

Speros glanced up at the clock. 'Well, best you head down and open up. I'll drop by later to see what needs to be done.'

ᶜ

Elena's phone buzzed in the late afternoon. She picked up and smiled at the number. 'Hi Nic.'

'Hi. Sorry I haven't been in touch. It's all been a bit hectic. I got word back from Joaquin and have been up half the night booking flights and accommodation.'

Elena's heart skipped a beat. 'When for?'

'The day after tomorrow. Does that give you enough time?'

'Yes, of course.'

'Can I have a word with Athena?'

'Hang on.' She walked into the kitchen and handed Athena the phone. 'It's Nic.'

Not sure if she should wait, she headed to the dishwasher and loaded a pile of dishes.

'Nic wants to see you about something,' Athena called out, placing down the phone. 'Leave those to me.'

Elena removed her apron, made two takeaway coffees and headed to the boatshed.

'Thanks.' Nic took a coffee, then pulled up a chair alongside his. 'I won't keep you long. Athena said you're not busy.'

'No. Is everything okay?'

'Yeah, all good. Remember I told you I had something to discuss with Speros?'

She nodded.

'Well, how would you feel about taking over the taverna.'

Elena's jaw dropped. 'What?'

'Speros confided some time back it was time he and Athena sold up and retired.'

'But the taverna's her life, Nic. She loves the place.'

'I know. But what if Athena stayed as a cook under her terms and left you to handle the rest?' He paused. 'The suggestion was made to her last night by Speros, that's all, and she agreed. From what he told me, it almost came as a relief not to have the worry about everything. She didn't mention anything, did she.'

'No, she didn't.'

'I told her not to. So, what do you think?'

Elena's hands went to her face. 'I can hardly think straight. So I would rent the business, is that what you're saying?'

'No, buy it outright.'

'But I don't have the money for that.'

'No, but I have. Speros will be sure to come up with a good price, and you can pay me back.'

'I don't want a good price. Those two worked damned hard for that place. There'd need to be an independent valuation, and if you were agreeable, the answer's yes.'

'You're on.'

She tilted her chin. 'And you'll get every cent of it back.'

'Now, where have I heard that before?'

She playfully kicked at his leg, then proceeded with an animated spiel, barely pausing to draw breath. 'So much can be done to make the place more lucrative, Nic. Like setting up an area for locally produced goods for the tourists, with products from Leonidis and Selene's olive grove, or honey, goat's cheese and yoghurt. Come to think of it …'

The words washed over Nic's head as he watched her, thinking only how beautiful she looked with the warm, late afternoon glow backlighting her dark hair like an African creature at sunset.

'Well, you'd better get back in case it gets busy.' He rose and pulled her to her feet, his lips lingering on hers. 'I'll be in touch. Okay?'

38

Elena's luggage was already stacked outside Speros and Athena's front door when Nic arrived. Athena had insisted they have a full breakfast before their departure.

'You'll be fed nothing but rubbish aboard,' she'd declared with a snort. 'At least this will stand you in good stead for the journey.'

An hour later, having consumed much more than was needed, Nic and Elena said their goodbyes, and Nic reached for the luggage.

'What's with the empty case?' He looked up at Elena.

'It's for Talita's belongings, of course,' Athena cut in. 'And no need to worry about cots and the rest. I have it all in hand.'

With a shake of his head, Nic reached across and kissed Athena on the forehead.

'Of course you have. How could I think otherwise?'

Outside, as they wheeled their luggage down the path towards the marina, Elena said, 'Have you mentioned your plans to your brother?'

Nic shook his head. 'As far as he's aware, Talita no longer exists, and I aim to keep things that way until I get her back. He'd only want to join me, and the risk is too great, given his young family.' He paused. 'And it's not too late for you to pull out, either.'

'Not a hope in hell!' she exclaimed.

'Then let me make one thing clear.' Nic stopped, eyes fixed on hers. 'I accept everything about working together to get Talita out, but when it comes to Antonio, I've got to handle that alone. I'm not going to put you at risk.'

'Okay. But I'm sure things won't get to that.'

You have no idea, do you? he thought, his throat too tight to respond.

They walked on, to the rumbling of their luggage over cobblestones. As Nic followed Elena up the steps to the top deck of the ferry, they were met by an invigorating sea wind. They'd not long sat down when they were joined by a group of Chinese tourists chattering noisily among themselves, wind jackets rustling and cameras at the ready. Nic remained silent, but it wasn't long before his leg was jiggling with impatience and his jaw tight. Sensing his need for a little solitude, Elena made an excuse to head down to the lounge for a while.

He was alone when she returned, elbows propped on the railing and hands clasped, staring into the distance. Stepping alongside, she nestled into his shoulder and asked, 'Are you okay?'

He nodded. For some time, they stood gazing out at the gently rolling, sun-tinged waves, neither feeling the need to speak. All the while, Nic's mind was in turmoil. He had known for some time that he would eventually have to open up to Elena and reveal his complicity in Jennifer Lorenzo's death. Only then would he know her true feelings. *Will I ever find the courage to do so? And would she be able to forgive me?*

Difficult as it was, he took a deep breath, turned to Elena and said, 'There's something I need to tell you. It's to do with the past. With Ava.'

'It can wait. Let's not spoil the moment.'

He went to speak, but she placed a finger against his lips. 'I've moved on. You've moved on. Why revisit the past. I've never been happier, Nic. I just want to be there for you and Talita. Let's put Ava behind us.'

ɡ

Antonio arrived home late from his trip into town and stopped by the caretaker's cottage to check on Talita, but she'd been put to bed. As he turned to go, he paused for a moment, his astute eyes observing Filipe. Something was different about his demeanour. Imperceptible, but there nonetheless. He stood for a moment and then left without a word.

Outside, he turned up his collar and headed towards his house, deep in thought. He suspected that there was something Filipe and Joaquin weren't telling him and that it concerned Talita. *Why was she in bed so early? And why had Filipe been quick to change the subject when I'd mentioned taking Talita into town the following day?*

As he stepped inside and removed his coat, his hand brushed against the worn holster that housed the gun he wore pretty much every waking hour. Filipe had it handmade all those years ago in Argentina after he'd taken him into his favela when he'd arrived with nothing but the clothes on his back. He'd no reason to doubt that this man was still amongst his most loyal. *Perhaps I'm wrong,* he thought, reaching for his brandy decanter. Yet he had noticed subtle changes of behaviour here and there from Filipe since Rosa's death. Perhaps her loss was eating away at him in ways that he, Antonio, had not envisaged.

You'd better be careful old man, he thought, downing a mouthful of neat brandy and gazing out the window at the leaden sky as the burning liquid slid down his throat like an elixir.

39

It was 1 p.m. when the plane from Madrid landed at A Coruña airport, and another hour before Elena and Nic stepped outside with their luggage to where their hire care was waiting. The air was colder than expected, as Elena predicted, and a layer of thick cloud concealed the few remaining rays of the late afternoon sun.

It was an hour-and-a-half drive to Viveiro and by the time they'd settled into their hotel room, showered and slipped into their bathrobes, neither felt like heading out for dinner. Instead, they decided on a meal from the room service menu and a bottle of wine.

Later, Nic held Elena's sleeping body in his arms, all chances of sleep thwarted by unremitting images of dark, disturbing scenarios, any of which could come about. He glanced at the clock. It was 5 a.m. He groaned and pushed it to face the other way. He just wanted to get going. Not for the first time, he felt his nerves jangle and his body tense. If Antonio was predictable, he'd have a well-thought-out plan. But he was heading in there, blind-sided like a gladiator

It was nearly 10 a.m. when they checked out of their hotel. With another four hours to fill before their arranged meeting with Filipe, Elena took Nic for a stroll around town, stopping for lunch in a small restaurant. Although Nic's stomach was a tight ball, and eating was the furthest thing from his mind, it could be some time before he got another chance, and he needed a deep reserve of energy to draw upon at short notice.

Elena watched with a frown as Nic abstractedly swirled his pasta around his fork. His silence that morning had been unsettling, and his grim expression disturbing. She'd considered reaching out and asking him to open up, but instinct warned her against it.

She shivered. *What in the hell were they letting themselves in for?*

The wind had picked up when they stepped outside, and thick clouds were accumulating overhead, obscuring what was left of the sun. The car was parked some distance away, and they only just made it before the heavens opened. Trees shook, people scrambled for cover, umbrellas were hastily assembled, and a torrent of water gushed down alleyways and along kerbs. Elena pointed out that this was not uncommon despite the rainy season still to come. 'Tomorrow might well be sunny,' she assured him.

As they drove through the outskirts of town and onto the main road leading to Antonio's hamlet, windscreen wipers working furiously, Nic was suddenly overcome by a deep sense of foreboding and more than once found himself glancing in the rear-vision mirror to check that they weren't being followed.

It wasn't until the GPS showed eight remaining minutes until the hamlet that he turned to Elena and said, 'I need you to promise me something. If anything goes wrong today and I don't make it out, you'll need to get the hell out of there. Don't worry about Talita. I'm sure she won't be harmed in any way. But one day, when she's old enough to understand, I hope you'd track her down; explain that I loved her and did everything I could to get her back.'

Elena's heart lurched. 'Of course,' she said, struggling to keep her voice from cracking. 'But it won't come to that. You haven't come this far for no reason, Nic. We'll get her back.'

Nic didn't respond.

An icy chill crept down her back.

¶

It was just before two in the afternoon when Nic pulled into the driveway of the hamlet and reached for his phone. 'We've just arrived,' he said.

'Okay,' came Joaquin's voice. 'When you head up the driveway, you'll see a double garage beside the first house. Park in there. It's out of view of Antonio's house.'

The hamlet was in the ideal position, Nic noted, as the first of the old farmhouses came into view, further enough from the main road to retain its privacy and encircled by a thick covering of trees. Although the rain had ceased, drips of water splashed constantly from the branches onto the driveway, forming gathering puddles. He pulled up in the tight space alongside the grey SUV, noting how every inch of available space had been utilised. Boxes were stacked neatly against the wall, and tools and equipment were fastened to walls by hooks and brackets. The air was crisp and smelt of pine needles as they stepped out of the car onto the gravel driveway, and they heard the distant bleat of goats. Nic was quick to note a security camera fastened to the eaves and an uneasy feeling settled over him.

Joaquin emerged soon afterwards from the nearby stone cottage and came to greet them. Nic estimated him to be around his age, tall and lean, with dark, intelligent eyes. He wore a thick flannelette shirt over well-worn jeans and work boots. Nic shook his hand and introduced Elena, noting Joaquin's appraising eyes as she stepped forward to take his outstretched hand. 'She's a friend of mine who's come along to translate,' Nic elaborated.

'Good.' Joaquin gestured towards the cottage. 'It'll free me up to tend to Talita should she wake. I managed to get her to sleep so you and Filipe can talk.' He paused for a moment. 'Of course, if you want to meet her first —'

'No, no, leave her sleep. There'll be time for that later. Thank you for thinking of it.'

'That's okay. Mind you, there are no guarantees she'll stay that way for long. Let's say Talita's not the easiest child to put down to rest.'

Nic nodded and looked up at the security camera. 'Is that in operation?'

'Not as far as I know.'

Filipe was seated by the fireplace in an armchair that had seen better days and rose to meet them. His weathered face bore traces of long hours in the sun, but his tired, troubled eyes and stooped shoulders exuded a man way beyond his sixty-seven years. Nic's brow furrowed – the same bone-weary look his father had when he passed away well before his time.

As Joaquin struck up a conversation with Filipe in Portuguese, all signs of tension in the latter's shoulders and face vanished, and the ease with which they spoke indicated to Nic that they shared a close bond. Filipe nodded about something, then turned to face them with a welcoming smile, 'Coffee, yes?'

Soon afterwards, the four of them settled around the kitchen table, with Nic wasting no time seeking answers to the questions that preyed on his mind like bad memories that spilled over into his dreams. With Angelina's half-truths exposed and the callous indifference towards her child validated, Antonio was first and foremost in his mind. How to wrest his child from the clutches of a man who valued family above all else.

From what Filipe said through Joaquin, it was nothing unusual for Antonio to arrive unannounced to check on Talita, but now that Rosa had passed, the visits had increased, as had the hours spent with her. And each time, Antonio showed signs of overriding Talita's routine that Rosa had carefully set up.

Nic ascertained from Filipe's expression that all was not well. His jaw hardened, and his hands clenched into tight balls at his side. It would be only a matter of time before she was whisked away altogether and indoctrinated into the ways of the gang. He bit down hard on his lip. Clearly, there was no time to waste. But Antonio remained an enigma – unpredictable and ruthless. Nic cursed inwardly. If only he knew enough about the man to have a decisive plan, an exit strategy at least.

The small, warm room felt suddenly claustrophobic, and Nic was overcome by a desire to step outside for a breath of fresh air. It was now after 4 p.m., and according to Filipe, it was Antonio's invariable practice when staying at the hamlet to work at his computer through the afternoon and join them at 6 p.m. for dinner, before spending time with Talita and tucking her into bed for the night. But who was to say he wouldn't vary that routine, perhaps on impulse. He could be on his way now. Nic's mouth went dry and he rose quickly.

'Okay, I'm heading in there now. I'm not sure how long this will take, but no one is to join me under any circumstances. Got that?'

Joaquin translated, and there were three nods.

'Good. If there's a need to, I'll call.'

As he turned to leave, he noted the palpable fear etched on Elena's face. He kept walking without looking back.

¶

Antonio's phone pinged just as he was about to send off an email. He quickly clicked on the app linked to a recently installed security camera that could pick up the slightest movement between his house and Filipe's. 'Fuck!' he exploded in disbelief as footage showed Nic heading down the driveway towards his home.

Panicking and heart pounding out of control, there was little time to think. Antonio was only too aware of how enraged Nic must have been to be told that his daughter had been killed, only to learn he'd been lied to. He should have known it was only a matter of time before the truth came out, and that Nic would come in search of her.

Just the image of the toned, lean presence quickly gaining ground made him feel his years. Any attempt at taking on his much younger adversary, renowned for his split-second decision-making and coolness under pressure, would be fatal. He had to get out and fast. Opening the sliding door to the back patio he hurried outside, closing it behind him and waiting, back pressed against the wall, eyes fixed on the camera footage on his phone.

The late afternoon loomed bleak and chilly. The adrenalin had already kicked in and Nic could feel the rapid acceleration of his pulse, his mouth as dry as sandpaper. But when he stepped onto the porch his mind was focused only on what lay ahead, body poised and braced for a fight. At least he had the element of surprise in his favour if, as Filipe said, the house was unlocked. He was in luck. With one ear pressed to the door, he listened for any hint of movement and stepped inside, senses on high alert. Still no sound, but a door was open at the far end of the living room. And silently he made his approach. Nothing.

¶

The moment the footage revealed Nic stepping inside his home, Antonio fled. He had to turn things to his advantage and be quick about it. Voices could be heard within the caretaker's cottage as he approached, one of which he noted was a female's voice. He stopped for a moment and scowled. This complicated matters. It hadn't occurred to him that Nic might not be alone. His mind was ticking over quickly. No matter. Just a slight change in plans, that was all. It could, in fact, prove advantageous.

As he stepped inside the room there was instant silence, his menacing aura like an icy blast.

Antonio was a more formidable presence than Elena had expected, and the piercing glare he sent in her direction caused her blood to run cold.

'I don't like unannounced guests,' he growled.

Filipe was chopping vegetables beside a large pot on a bench dividing the kitchen from the living room, his hand still on the knife handle. But it was Joaquin, standing alongside Elena, to whom Antonio turned.

'Is Talita awake?'

Joaquin shook his head quickly, not mentioning the shot of brandy he'd slipped in her juice earlier.

'Good. If she wakes up, you'll stay with her till I say so. I've things to be settle here first.'

And with the three of them within sight, Antonio wasted no time seizing the upper hand. Charging across the room with a lightning rush of speed that belied his age, he hurled Joaquin to one side and, hooking an arm across Elena's shoulder with a grip so tight that her eyes smarted, drew a gun from the concealed holster beneath his jacket and pressed it hard against her temple.

'All right, nobody moves or speaks.'

¶

Meanwhile next door, Nic slammed his fist into his palm with a barrage of expletives, realising he'd been outsmarted and knowing instantly where Antonio would be. Hoping against hope that no one had been harmed, he flung open the front door and sprinted towards the caretaker's cottage.

An ominous sense of foreboding swept over him as he rushed inside, and the instant he stepped into the room, he knew he was moments too late.

'Stop right there or your girlfriend dies,' Antonio bellowed.

Nic halted on the spot, his heart squeezing with anguish at the sight of Elena's stricken face, and cursing himself inwardly for allowing her to accompany him in the first place. But such sentiments would get him nowhere. It was time to click into gear. He held up his hands. 'All right, all right. Tell me what you want.'

'The weapon you've got stashed on you, for starters. Place it on the floor, slide it towards me, then step back to the table and don't move.'

Nic hesitated.

'Do it! Or I'll see to you first,' he yelled.

Nic's gut wrenched. He had no choice but to give in to Antonio's demands until he could gain leverage. There'd be no second chance. Barely able to look Elena in the eye, he reached into his coat pocket and produced his 9-ml Beretta handgun, which felt cold and now useless in his hand.

There was a click and Nic froze.

'Just in case you have other ideas,' Antonio growled. A visible pulse appeared in his temple. 'Now put the gun down. Slowly. Slowly.'

Nic bent down and did what was asked of him, and Antonio dragged it closer with a foot. 'I'll discuss my demands once I have some answers. Starting from you.' He sent Filipe one of his deadliest looks and switched to Portuguese, letting loose a furious barrage, causing Joaquin to shrink back. After a tense few exchanges, Antonio turned to face Joaquin. 'That was a load of bullshit,' he blazed. 'Filipe doesn't know enough English to make contact. It was you, wasn't it? You made the call!'

'Leave him out of it,' Nic demanded. 'I would have hunted Talita down regardless.'

'Shut up.' Antonio glowered at him.

Nic gritted his teeth, conscious of keeping his emotions in check and knowing with chilling certainty that it would take just one wrong move for Antonio to pull the trigger. But it wasn't only his and Elena's lives at stake here. There were two witnesses sure to be next; realisation echoing in Filipe's ashen face.

'So, what is it you want, Antonio,' Nic said evenly, stalling for time.

'I want your word that the pair of you leave this place immediately and never seek contact with Talita again,' he barked. 'Otherwise, your girlfriend dies.'

'All right. You have my word.'

Antonio felt a rush of triumph. All had gone to plan, even though things had gone down to the wire. He couldn't see Nic risking his girlfriend's life, but he knew with certainty that he'd be back, and by then, he and Talita would be long gone, with protocols in place to safeguard them. But in the interim, there'd be round-the-clock security guards dispatched from Viveiro, just in case Nic was brazen enough to show himself sooner. Once the pair had left, he'd waste no time eliminating Joaquin and Filipe. *No one went behind my back and got away with it.*

'So let her go.' The words interrupted his thoughts.

'Not yet.' Antonio stamped his authority. 'I have further demands.'

But with a momentary lapse in concentration, Antonio was blind-sided to the glint of silver that flashed in Nic's peripheral vision. So stealthy, so swift was Filipe's approach from behind that it left Nic blinking in disbelief and caught Antonio totally unaware. In a split second, the hand with the gun was flung aside, the weapon bouncing off the tiles with a sharp, metallic clatter. Strong fingers clasped his chin, reefing his head backwards before he had time to react, as Filipe's kitchen knife sliced his throat with the clinical precision with which he would slaughter a goat or a sheep.

Freed from her captor's grasp, Elena stumbled forward into Nic's arms just as Antonio's thickset bulk toppled behind her, dropping to his knees and then crashing face down onto the floor, sprawled in the rapidly accumulating pool of red from the severed carotid artery.

For a moment an eerie silence hung over the room. Gently extricating Elena from his arms, Nic stepped across to the body and knelt down beside it, fingers checking for a pulse. He looked up at Filipe. 'He's gone.'

Filipe nodded numbly, eyes fixed on the lifeless form at his feet, still in disbelief that the once invincible gang colossus had been felled by his hand.

Nic rose and gently took the blood-covered knife still tightly gripped in Filipe's fingers.

'Thank you for saving her life.' His voice was soft.

Filipe barely heard him as the enormity of the situation began to sink in. He'd been fiercely loyal to the man who'd given him so much, guarded Antonio's inner secrets, and been led to believe he'd spend his final days tending to the property he considered home. *Where to now?*

Joaquin's heart lurched as he looked across at the shaken figure who had become a father to him after his own perished in a fire. *It was me, not just her, that you did this to protect,* he thought.

Meanwhile, Nic stepped across and took control. 'The body must be disposed of immediately,' he said to Joaquin, nodding towards Filipe. 'Can you ask the best place?'

Joaquin gave a quick nod, followed by a brief discourse. 'He said the bottom of the orchard,' Joaquin responded. 'No one goes down there.'

'But what about his gang? Won't they be wanting to know where he is?'

Another few words. 'He would tell them Antonio left for Rio five days ago, and he assumed he was back already.'

Nic thought; *not ideal, but who knew the gang's inner circle's sentiments regarding Antonio? Maybe they cared little whether he came back or not.* He nodded. 'All right, Filipe and I will see to the body while you clean up here. And be quick about it, would you? I don't want Talita waking up to this.'

Elena felt a sudden stab of panic as scenes from the night she was forced to mop up the blood of Angelina's victim came to mind, wincing at the memory of the sticky, flabby skin beneath her fingers. Pushing the thoughts aside, she squared her shoulders and met Joaquin's eyes. 'Tell me what's to be done.'

With help from Filipe, Nic rolled Antonio's body inside a timeworn rug and instructed Joaquin to bring the pick-up truck to the front door. The pair hauled the carpet outside, grabbed one end each, hoisted it over the side into the back of the truck, and climbed inside. The interior smelt of body odour, damp soil and diesel.

But they were not out of the woods yet. A sentiment shared by Filipe, who strained his ears, listening for any unexpected arrival. Nic glanced sidelong at Filipe's taut face and felt a pang of guilt for not taking Filipe and Joaquin's protection into account in the first place. The truth was, he'd been so hell-bent on exacting his revenge and getting Talita out of there it hadn't crossed his mind. The only positives were that they'd all made it out alive, and Filipe was free at last of Antonio's clutches. Hopefully, the old man would find some peace.

Nic found himself wishing he had a handle on Spanish, enough at least to hear what Filipe had to say about his wife; and the first precious months he'd missed of Talita's life. But upon reflection, he thought this discussion would have been too raw. 'You okay?' he asked, watching Filipe's blunt fingers switch on the ignition and shift the pick-up into gear.

'I'm okay.'

As they headed down the driveway towards the orchard, Nic was on high alert, eyes constantly checking the side mirror. Antonio's hamlet was nothing like he'd envisaged. Old stone outbuildings and farmhouses in various states of repair were set on the hillside overlooking ancient woodlands. Not a pothole, fallen fence or overhanging branch to be seen apart from the farmhouse furthest away that was beyond salvaging, its grounds littered with slabs of stone, tangled undergrowth and bits of wire. It was like going back in time.

Set quite some distance from the caretaker's cottage, the

orchard offered anonymity. Not far away was the relic of a rusted-out, weed-entangled tractor, and nearby were a large pile of branches, weeds and brambles awaiting burn-off. The silence was interrupted only by the occasional bird call from above as they dragged the body from the back of the pick-up and lugged it to a secluded spot amidst the trees. The air surrounding them was heavy, with the smell of damp earth and rotting leaves.

Filipe's lungs heaved as he dug deep into the heavy soil, shovelling mounds to one side and barely pausing for breath. Nic soon took hold of the shovel and resumed the digging, indicating to Filipe to keep watch. Overhead, as if befitting the occasion, dark rainclouds threatened to pour down at any moment and Nic increased the pace, his shirt drenched in perspiration and his throat parched.

It had turned six-thirty p.m. as the last of the dirt was shovelled into the grave. Nic tossed the shovel aside, straightened and stretched, hands on hips. Grit stung his eyes, and he wiped it away with his fingers. Physically and emotionally drained, he closed his eyes for a moment and gestured towards the vehicle. 'You go on ahead. I'll be with you soon.'

Filipe nodded and shuffled off. Nic took a deep breath and glanced with grim satisfaction at the crudely constructed grave befitting the ruthless, cold-hearted man he'd known Antonio to be. No other outcome bore contemplation. Not only would Antonio have dispensed with Filipe and Joaquin in cold blood, Nic was convinced that he and Elena would have been next on his list. No way would the gang boss have allowed them to slip quietly into anonymity. Their idyllic lifestyle would have been compromised for as long as Antonio was alive. Nic looked across to Filipe, sitting exhausted in the pickup, and realised what a debt he owed this man.

Filipe sighed deeply and leaned against the unyielding vinyl seat, gingerly rubbing his burning fingers, every joint in his body aching. He had lied to Nic. He could no longer remain here. The moment Nic took Talita and departed, he and Joaquin would have to disappear. Usually, members of Antonio's close-knit inner circle did not visit the hamlet while Antonio was in residence, but once they found they could not make contact with their boss, alarm bells would ring. It wouldn't take long before they arrived on his doorstep and started asking questions. They'd scour the property and the moment they set eyes on the pile of freshly dug dirt and discovered its grisly content, he and Joaquin would be subsequently eliminated. Only too familiar with the methods they used – he shuddered.

Despite his exhaustion, Filipe tried to estimate how much time they had. At least twenty-four hours, he surmised, knowing that only in an emergency would any gang member dare to contact Antonio in the evening or early morning – times they knew he devoted to his grand-niece. Nevertheless, to be on the safe side, they should all be gone by midday.

Filipe reminded himself that he held one trump card. Antonio kept funds stashed in a hidden recess in his cellar; money he didn't want the gang to know about. He let this slip one evening when he'd had far too much to drink. It was never mentioned again and Filipe was sure the indiscretion had been lost in Antinio's befuddled mind. Filipe never discussed the incident with Joaquin, but he made a careful examination of the cellar and was sure he had located the secret stash. He didn't know how much it contained, as he was careful to ensure there was no indication that anyone had ever been in the cellar, but he was confident that the amount would be sufficient for he and Joaquin to disappear without a trace.

§

Talita was sitting enfolded in Joaquin's arms on the old sofa, eyes transfixed on the small cotton reel that she repeatedly rotated in her fingers while he conversed with Elena. The moment Nic entered the room and set sight on the exquisite child with the same glossy dark hair and olive skin as her mother's, his breath caught in his throat and he stopped, overcome with emotion and at a loss of words.

Elena was quick to rise and, stepping across to him, reached for his hand and said softly, 'Come and meet Talita, Nic.'

Joaquin bent over and whispered a few words in Spanish, causing Talita to glance up at Nic. She then averted her eyes, nestling into Joaquim's chest with her thumb in her mouth. Elena felt Nic stiffen. 'It's okay Nic, she's a bit shy.' Her voice was soft. 'We'll need to take things slowly for a while, that's all.'

Nic felt a pang of panic. Never had he felt so grateful

for Elena's dignified strength to help see him through the uncertain times ahead together with Athena's child-raising expertise. The only young children he'd had much to deal with had been his boisterous twin nephews.

Sensing his hesitancy, Joaquin said, 'Why don't you both sit alongside Filipe later when he reads Talita a bedtime story. There'll be time to get to know her more tomorrow. I told her she was about to go off on a big adventure. It's probably enough for her to think about right now.'

'I've cancelled our hotel at A Coruña,' Elena elaborated. 'Filipe and Joaquin kindly offered to put us up for the night.'

Nic thanked both in turn, inwardly sighing with relief. Shivering in his dirty, sodden clothes, his face and hands still numb from the chill wind, all he wanted right now was a piping hot shower and change of clothes. Barely able to think straight after the day's events, the last thing he needed was a last-minute pack of Talita's belongings, then a late-night drive. Joaquim was right. Talita needed time to adjust to what lay ahead. And with the threat of Antonio no longer looming, there was no immediate urgency. Their flight to Madrid wasn't until 5 p.m. the next day. Sufficient time to pack and spend a morning getting to know Talita.

Nic watched as Filipe headed across to Talita and said a few words in Spanish, to which she responded with a nod and soft reply, then climbed down and followed him into the kitchen.

'Does she speak any English?' he asked Joaquin.

'Yes, Rosa was insistent on her speaking both Spanish and

English. But I'm afraid her English has lapsed since my aunt's passing. I do my best to keep up her skills though, when I'm around.'

'Don't worry,' Elena told him. 'I'll take care of things.'

40

Nic and Elena stood alongside Filipe and Joaquin in the living room, which was bathed in a brilliant pool of late morning sunshine. For Nic, it brought a sense of renewal and hope after the previous day's gloomy, inclement conditions. The room looked out onto a worn stone terrace and enclosed sheltered garden where Talita sat with her back towards them on a low wooden stool, absorbed in something before her. Nic found his mind drifting, with Elena's discussion with Filipe in Spanish fading into the background. All at once a surge of contentment washed over him that he never thought would be his.

After a while, there was silence. Elena turned to Nic, linked an arm through his, and rested her head on his shoulder. His heart skipped. 'You good?' she murmured.

'Yeah, I'm good.' Nuzzling his cheek against her freshly washed hair, he paused for a few moments, enjoying the pleasant fusion of essential oils and hibiscus. 'Well, I suppose it's time we got going, then,' he said. 'I don't want to leave things too late. Is everything packed?'

'Yes,' Elena replied. 'But I'll just take a last-minute check.' She withdrew from his arms and headed towards the door.

'I'll carry your luggage out if you like,' Joaquin offered.

'Thanks,' Nic said, adding, 'Could you ask Filipe if you're in need of money because I can help.'

Joaquin said a few words to Filipe and a smile came over his face as he responded.

Joaquin turned to Nic. 'He said we're going to be all right. But thanks.'

Nic nodded and said, 'Could you ask him to keep an eye on Talita while I go and get the car, then?'

'Sure.' Joaquin did so, then left.

Nic took one last glance out the window, turned to Filipe and remarked, 'She's so beautiful.'

Filipe gave him a strange look and said nothing.

There was a brief, uncomfortable silence, and Nic said quickly, 'Well, I'll be back soon with the car then.'

Filipe nodded and watched him leave with uneasiness.

¶

Outside, Talita lifted the lid of her plastic container and pulled out another butterfly, studying it intently then watching it squirm between her fingers. Pulling off each wing, she tossed it amongst the pile of others, still flailing, scattered on the grass before her. Then she reached for the next one.